Cassie shook her head and pulled away. "Don't lie to me."

Cal tugged her back. "This is not a lie."

"But everything else is. Something isn't right here and no one will tell me the truth."

He pushed his hand through her hair, tugged her even closer. "I only know that I came back here for you. And that is the one truth you need to remember."

Then he kissed her, his touch tentative and tender until Cassie sighed and returned the kiss, her arms grasping him and holding him close. Cal wrapped her in his embrace, his touch demanding and deepening until she felt herself falling into a blinding mist of longing.

Dear Reader,

I have always loved a good Southern gothic saga. So I was thrilled to be able to finally write the one that has been in my head for many years. This was a complex story, and I admit I struggled with it a bit. But I'm pleased with the final product. I hope you will be, too.

When ready-to-wear designer Cassandra Brennan returns to Camellia Plantation in South Georgia, she finds several surprises waiting for her—the main one being the man who broke her heart years ago. Her estranged father is dying, and Cal Collins seems to be taking over her beloved home. But as revelations keep coming, Cassie finds things are not always what they seem, and she also discovers that even though she still loves Cal, he might be involved in an elaborate plot to keep her from finding out what really happened the day her beautiful socialite mother died.

I grew up in a big Southern family, so I know a thing or two about secrets and scandals. But in the South, we tend to bring out our eccentric family members and show them off! In Cassie's case, however, she was embarrassed and ashamed that her own father had scorned her. The truth turned out to be a test of her love for Cal.

I hope you enjoy *A Southern Reunion*. I'd love to hear from you. Please visit my website at www.lenoraworth.com and send me a message. I'd appreciate your feedback.

Lenora Worth

A Southern Reunion
Lenora Worth

TORONTO NEW YORK LONDON
AMSTERDAM PARIS SYDNEY HAMBURG
STOCKHOLM ATHENS TOKYO MILAN MADRID
PRAGUE WARSAW BUDAPEST AUCKLAND

Recycling programs
for this product may
not exist in your area.

ISBN-13: 978-0-373-71750-7

A SOUTHERN REUNION

Copyright © 2011 by Lenora H. Nazworth

www.Harlequin.com

Printed in U.S.A.

ABOUT THE AUTHOR

New York Times bestselling author Lenora Worth has written more than forty books for three different publishers. Her career with Love Inspired Books spans close to fourteen years. Her very first Love Inspired, *The Wedding Quilt,* won Affaire de Coeur's Best Inspirational for 1997, and *Logan's Child* won Best Love Inspired for 1998 from *RT Book Reviews.* With millions of books in print, Lenora continues to write for Love Inspired and Love Inspired Suspense. Lenora also wrote a weekly opinion column for the local paper and worked freelance for years with a local magazine. She has now turned to full-time fiction writing and enjoying adventures with her retired husband, Don. Married for thirty-five years, they have two grown children. Lenora enjoys writing, reading and shopping...especially shoe shopping.

To my darling Big Daddy, my husband Don.
You were the first person to ever read the original
version of this story. Thanks for sticking with me
for all these years.
We've come full circle.

CHAPTER ONE

THREE THINGS HAPPENED the same week ready-to-wear designer Cassandra Brennan announced she'd be opening two more Cassie's Closet boutiques in the metro Atlanta area.

She broke up with her fiancé, Ned Patterson.

Her estranged father sent word that he was dying and he wanted her to come home.

And once she arrived home, the man who had been her first love in high school walked out onto the front porch of Camellia Plantation with his arms around the woman who'd come between them. And he still looked good doing it, too.

The house hadn't changed all that much in the past twelve years. But everything else certainly had.

Why was Cal Collins back at Camellia? And what was he doing with Marsha Reynolds? Last she'd heard, after Cassie had caught them together and broken up with Cal, things hadn't worked out for Cal and Marsha after all. Too bad. And too bad they'd decided to take right back up on the very day she'd driven the four hours from Atlanta to get here.

Anxious to get inside and see her father, Cassie swallowed and inhaled a deep breath. She could do this. She had to do this.

Memories danced into her head, taunting her, some beautiful, some tragic. Cassie tried deep breathing, her breath stopping near her rib cage. The old camellia bushes, from which the plantation had gotten its name, grew with a lush abandonment all over the side yards and in front of the pool, their velvet pink blooms popping and exploding in the sun like clusters of chiffon.

She and Cal used to meet each other in the shadows of those tall, rich green bushes. Usually they'd sneak out at midnight after her parents had gone to bed. Cassie would leave by the French doors in her room that opened onto the upstairs porch and make her way down the outside staircase.

But everything had changed. In the blink of an eye, she lost her mother to a tragic horseback-riding accident, lost the man she loved to another woman and lost the father she'd always adored because of something she'd done or said during that horrible week.

Bracing herself, Cassie got out of her late model convertible and slammed the door hard enough to get the attention of the couple on the porch. She wanted to tell them to get a room. She wanted to scratch Marsha's green eyes right out of her head. And she wanted to grab Cal by the collar and ask him why he'd hurt her so badly.

But she didn't do any of those things.

A Brennan didn't act like a redneck.

A Brennan held everything inside and was always, always civilized and polite. And she wouldn't make a scene when her father lay dying just beyond that front door.

Cal turned then, his eyes meeting hers as he held a hand on Marsha's bare arm. "Cassie."

Cassie's heart pumped against her ribs, trying to beat a path out of her body. Just hearing him say her name in that low drawl caused a hot chill to run over her.

She thought about turning around and heading back to Atlanta. But she'd been running for way too long now. Her father needed her, even if he hated to admit that.

And she needed him. She'd been waiting far too long. She wouldn't let anything or anyone stand in the way of this homecoming. Not even Cal Collins. So she stiffened her spine and held her head up high.

"Hello, Cal. Marsha—long time, no see. Looks like nothing much has changed around here."

Cal didn't say anything. He just stared at her long enough to make her sweat. But then, it was late spring in south Georgia. It was hot all the way around.

She stared right back at him, hoping her hurt and fear and confusion didn't show in her eyes.

His dark hair hung in thick chocolate-colored chunks around his ears and neck. He looked the same but different, his cotton work shirt stretched across a broad back, his worn jeans low-slung and not too tight. When they'd parted they'd both still been in their teens.

Now she was looking at a full-grown man.

Would he see her as a woman?

"Well, if it isn't the long-lost Cassie Brennan," Marsha said on a smirk. "And looking like she stepped right out of some fancy fashion magazine."

Marsha looked ready to explode, her red hair falling around her shoulders with the same vibrancy as the blooming camellias, her angry frown for Cal and only Cal. She'd gained a few pounds, but then Marsha had always had a healthy figure. The kind boys loved. Just like in high school. Just like the day Marsha had explained it all to Cassie, shattering what was left of her heart, after Cassie had caught the two of them together.

She was going to be sick, Cassie thought, her pulse sputtering out of control, her blood pressure rising. She might actually throw up. Sweat pooled down her back and across her chest, her white linen sundress wilting against her skin like bruised magnolia blossoms.

Had her father invited them here to remind Cassie of her one great sin? Well, she wouldn't give them the satisfaction of seeing her sweat. So she continued on, one hand clutching her white leather purse, her stomach knotting and twisting in pain. But she couldn't take her eyes away from the dark-haired man and the curvy red-headed woman. Memories of seeing them in just such a way long ago invaded her head.

This was certainly not the homecoming welcome she'd expected. Her life had changed forever. But Cal Collins was still the same. And he still got to her.

"I TOLD YOU, YOU NEED to leave."

Cal stared down at Marsha, hoping she'd take the hint. He'd been trying to get her out of the house before Cassie showed up, but now it was too late. He wasn't in the mood for a catfight. But both of these women, one cool and blonde and so in control and one ticked-off and redheaded and about to lose control, looked ready to go at each other.

This was a long-standing feud.

And obviously, he was still in the middle of it.

"I came to visit with Teresa, thank you," Marsha said, hurt in her eyes. "I like to give her some of the fresh produce from my garden."

Cal let go of her and put his hat on, adjusting it over his brow. "You still need to go. Hear me, Marsha?"

"I hear you. Don't get all hot under the collar."

Cal looked at the woman who tried to push his buttons and then he stared down at the woman he couldn't have—the one who went beyond button pushing to full-throttle. Then he lifted his head and sniffed, the scent of magnolias hitting his nostrils. The huge magnolia trees in the backyard weren't blooming yet and Marsha didn't wear magnolia-scented perfume.

But Cassandra Brennan always had.

He didn't show it, but he took his dear sweet time watching Cassie standing on the bottom step, her blond hair curled around her chin in a thick sleek bob, her bare shoulders tanned and buff, her legs still long and curved in the right places. She held a pair of black sunglasses in one hand and wore a white dress with thick straps and a flared skirt. Her sandals glistened just as white as the crisp dress, a line of silver medallionlike studs marching up her foot in gladiator fashion. And the heels were killer high.

He couldn't help it. His gaze slid down her body and back up to her red-lipped mouth. "I'm glad you're home, Cassie."

She lifted her fancy sunglasses and placed them on her head and flipped that cool bob. "Thanks." Then she shot a questioning glance at Marsha, her expression caught between polite and haughty. "What's going on?"

Marsha's face sweated with a soft sheen that turned to a beet-red blush. "Not what you think."

Cal glared at Marsha. She'd pushed her way into the back door earlier, probably to purposely cause a ruckus right here on the porch. "Marsha, you need to go."

She eyed him. "I was just on my way."

The redhead whirled like a tornado and stomped down the porch steps, her tight cut-off jeans barely meeting the hem of her pink T-shirt. She gave Cassie a thunderous look as she passed, then said over her shoulder, "Just a warning, Cassie. Some things around here *aren't* the way they used to be. And I should know that better than anybody."

Cal watched her traipse around the side of the house then heard a motor revving.

When Marsha's battered red pickup peeled down the long driveway, leaving a trail of mad dust, Cassie took her shades off her head and turned her face up, her eyes glistening as blue as the sky behind her.

"You don't let her park up front?" she asked as she swept up onto the porch.

He didn't know how to answer that. He wasn't even sure he should answer that. Cassie had left behind this little town and this South Georgia plantation and she'd never looked back.

And he couldn't ever look forward. Otherwise, he wouldn't have come back here to work for her father and torture himself with memories at every turn.

He let out grunt of a breath. "Marsha still thinks—"

"It's obvious what she thinks. I don't know why y'all didn't go ahead and get married all those years ago."

He gritted his teeth then inhaled a breath. "There was no baby. So there was no reason for me to marry her."

Because he didn't love Marsha.

Cassie touched a hand to her hair, but she appeared flabbergasted. "Okay, enough about old times. I'm a bit confused. What are you doing here?"

"You really are behind on the family news, aren't you?" he asked, wondering how he was going to be able to stay here now that she'd come home. When Marcus had first come up with this plan, Cal's gut had told him this was a very bad idea. Now his stomach burned with the proof of that. No use trying to hide the facts. "I work here."

And that's all he needed to say to set things straight. So he turned and walked in the direction of the small foreman's cottage where he lived.

No, he wasn't married to Marsha. He'd never been married to anybody. But he wouldn't tell Cassie the whole ugly story. She didn't care and it didn't really matter. He'd only come back here as a favor to her sick father.

As a favor to the man who'd once told Cal he'd kill him if he ever set foot on this land again.

Sometimes Cal wished Marcus Brennan had made good on that threat.

CAL WORKED HERE. AGAIN? How? Why? None of this made any sense to Cassie. That little welcome-home scene on the front porch had left her shaking, but she got herself together enough to go through the double oak doors of the house she'd grown up in. Camellia Plantation had been in her family for over a hundred and thirty years. Her ancestors had bought it in 1880 and restored it after the ravages of the Civil War had caused the previous owner to take his own life—out under that infamous oak tree that hung over the drive-way, as the legend went.

The same oak tree where her mother had died.

The same oak tree where Cal had kissed Cassie and promised her he'd always love her.

The oak tree had been here over three hundred years, its trunk and branches scarred and twisted. No wonder it was cursed. The big square house with the massive columns and wide wraparound porches on both floors had been in her family for a long time, passed down from generation to generation with a legacy that told many tales, her own parents being part of that. Her father was the last of the Brennans. If she didn't marry and produce offspring, she would be the last once he was gone.

Since she wasn't very good in the relationship department, there was little chance of Cassie ever becoming a wife and mother.

Maybe that was the reason she'd decided to come home. Because in spite of everything, this was her home. Lately, living in Atlanta had become unpleasant in spite of her growing fame as an up-and-coming fashion designer and the success of her downtown boutique aptly named Cassie's Closet, in spite of the spiffy midtown loft she'd redecorated and spruced up herself. And in spite of her much-touted love life with lawyer and hotshot Atlanta businessman Ned Patterson.

Or maybe because of her love life, or lack thereof. She'd broken things off with her fiancé. But Ned hadn't taken it very well. Cassie couldn't blame Ned. She hadn't loved him very well.

Then she remembered Cal's eyes when he'd turned to look down at her there on the porch. Blue, a rich navy blue that bordered on velvet. Once a beautiful, loving blue that wrapped her in warmth. Now a hard cold blue that raked her with what looked like scorn and disdain.

Did he hate her that much?

Looking up the curving staircase, Cassie had to wonder if she'd gone from the frying pan to the fire, coming back here. Had she run away from one bad situation only to rush headlong into another one?

Hearing pots and pans being shuffled in the kitchen, she walked up the wide central hallway past the staircase, her heels clicking against the aged heart-of-pine floors, the smell of wisteria mixed with lavender wafting by and bringing memories that assaulted her with such clarity, she felt sixteen again.

"Hello?" she called, praying Cal would be long gone by now. Praying he wouldn't make this any more difficult than it already was.

"Cassie, is that you?"

"Teresa, yes, it's me." She hurried into the kitchen to the left of the hallway, rounding the corner in time to see Teresa Jordan wiping her hands on a fluffy towel. "Hi."

"Hi, honey." Teresa opened her arms wide. "C'mon and give me a hug."

Teresa had been with Cassie's family since Cassie was a little girl. Her mother, Eugenia, and Teresa had been like sisters. Eugenia had introduced Teresa to Walt and had been matron of honor at their wedding here on the grounds. They'd never had children, but Cassie didn't understand why Teresa had stayed after Eugenia, and later Walt, had died. Teresa was loyal to Marcus Brennan and even though they hadn't communicated too much during recent years, Cassie sure was glad to see the woman now.

Cassie rushed into her arms, taking in the scent of Jergens lotion mixed with the smell of bacon grease and cornbread. Tears pricked at her eyes. This was what it felt like to be welcomed home. This was what she'd missed all of these years. These things and…being here with Cal, of course.

But she put that thought out of her head.

Teresa finally let her go then stood back, her brown eyes wide, her smile genuine. Pushing a hand through her short grayish-brown hair, she said, "Look at you. As pretty as ever. I saw your picture in *People,* you know. One of the up-and-coming designers of last year.

Cassie's Closet seems to be the thing these days. They carry your ready-to-wear in Belk's and Dillard's. I have two of your dresses that I wear to church. Lordy mercy, ain't that something now."

Cassie's smile was shaky and shy. "Something, all right."

She had last-minute promos to do for the fall line and paperwork for the production of next spring's collection, not to mention finishing up the actual designs for the next season. The fashion industry dictated that she stay a couple of years ahead. Taking a breath, she willed her nerves to calm down. "I'll have plenty to keep me busy while I'm here. But…I'm hanging in there."

"And you're good at it from what I see and hear." Teresa pushed at Cassie's hair. "How you doing, honey?"

"I'm not sure," Cassie said, wondering how many more surprises she could handle. "How is he today?"

"Not good." Teresa shook her head, tears springing up in her eyes. "I'm so glad he let me call you."

"Me, too. But does he really want me here or did you force him into letting you call?"

"No, he wants to see you. He sure does. I think he's decided it's time to mend his ways and…let go of the past."

"Can we do that, really?"

"We have to," Teresa said. "Want to see him now, or would you rather freshen up and have some lunch first?"

"Now," Cassie said, the thought of food turning her stomach. "Is he upstairs?"

"No, darlin'." Teresa motioned to what used to be a big office-and-den combination at the back of the house. "We had to move his bed down here. He can't make it up the stairs anymore."

Cassie nodded, put down her purse and straightened her dress. When they got to the closed door of the den, she pivoted around, wishing she could bolt out of the house and hide in the stables the way she used to do when she was young and afraid.

That was how she'd met Cal face-to-face, after first seeing him from a distance…and keeping her own distance. He'd found her hiding in the stables late one fall afternoon. And after that, she hadn't been nearly as afraid or lonely as before.

A lot had happened since then.

But she wouldn't be scared anymore. She had a lot of questions.

Beginning with one.

"Teresa, after I visit with Daddy, I want you to explain to me what Cal Collins is doing back at Camellia."

And why no one had bothered to warn her about that.

CHAPTER TWO

CASSIE ENTERED THE darkened room, her heart whispering a silent warning. The ceiling-to-floor windows across one wall of the big square room usually showed a panoramic view of the sloping backyard and the pool area. But today, the heavy beige drapes were drawn shut, causing patches of desperate sunshine to break through like lurking spotlights onto the high ceiling.

It took her a while to focus and get her bearings. The hospital bed had been set up in the corner where her father's big oak desk used to be. The desk was gone but the sitting area remained the same, centered around the brick fireplace across from the bed. The row of bookshelves surrounding the fireplace remained full of volumes of various sizes and types, reminding Cassie of what a bookworm she'd always been in school.

Until that summer when Cal had brought her out of hiding and brought the world to her with all his talk of traveling and buying up land and…so many other dreams.

It felt surreal, being here in this room, hiding in darkness, shaking away in this atmosphere of sickness and death.

She didn't want to advance toward the bed in the corner, toward the still, skeletal man lying in that bed. He didn't look like the father she remembered.

Marcus Brennan had been larger than life—a

rancher, a cowboy, a hunter and sportsman, a businessman and a gentleman with impeccable manners when
around ladies and a brawling disregard when he went
hunting or fishing with his cronies. He ruled this part
of the state of Georgia and people either feared him or
respected him.

At times, Cassie had felt both. Right now, she wasn't
sure what to feel, or what to say. So she just stood, her
prayers centered on the next step. Then she heard her
father's voice for the first time in twelve years.

"Cassie?"

Cassie gulped back a silent sob. She wouldn't cry
now, not when she'd cried so many tears she'd probably be able to fill the Chattahoochee River. Not now,
after she'd had to endure seeing Cal with her nemesis,
Marsha, the woman who'd managed to break them apart
even after Cassie's powerful father had tried and failed.

Not now. Not now.

"Cassie, come over here and let me look at you."

She advanced a step, then another, until she was at
the foot of his bed. "Hello, Daddy."

Marcus was propped up with pillows, his frail hand
reaching toward her then falling away, back to the folds
of the dark comforter covering his lower body.

"You came home."

He said it in a way that ripped at her heart, his voice
soft with yearning and awe. Had he expected her to
ignore him?

"Yes, I'm here. How are you feeling?"

The cliché was the only thing that came to her mind,
emerging through the unspoken, unasked questions that
held her in a tight spasm of pain and fear.

His chuckle sounded like jagged rocks hitting

against each other. "You see how I look. I feel about twice as bad as that. I guess I'm done for, girl."

Cassie gripped the cold steel of the bed. "Teresa didn't explain exactly what...what kind of illness you have. I've talked to several of your doctors since she called me regarding your health, but they didn't want to discuss your medical condition with me."

Another rumbling, hacking chuckle. "I'm dying. What does the rest matter?" He let out a rasping sigh. "I've drank too much, smoked too much, and seen and done too much. I have cancer and several other maladies with names longer than my seventy-nine vintage Cadillac."

Cassie let that declaration take hold, willing herself to remain quiet and still. He appeared so fragile, so deathly, she was afraid to move, afraid her touch on his arm might shatter him. "I understand you have nurses?"

"Day and night. Draining me dry, too."

Her father was a very rich man, so she doubted that. "Where is your nurse right now?"

"Told her to come later this afternoon. Wanted some time alone with you. They hover over me, drives me nuts."

Cassie could only imagine that and pity the nurses who had to deal with Marcus Brennan. "Do you need anything?"

"I need to go back about fifteen years, is all."

Don't we all, Cassie thought, one single tear escaping down her face. Grabbing at courage, she moved around to the side of the bed. "Why am I here, Daddy? Why did you wait so long to call me home?"

"Why did you wait so long to come home?" he countered, his expression creased with frustration and too much time alone.

Cassie didn't know how to answer that question. She'd called home time after time, especially during that first rough year of college. Teresa would take her messages but she'd never hear back from her father. After the first awkward, awful Thanksgiving and Christmas here when her father didn't even bother to eat meals with her or exchange gifts, either, she'd swallowed back the pain of holidays spent alone or with friends, with long nights of worrying and praying for things she couldn't have. After a few months, she'd given up, her heart breaking into brittle little pieces each time her messages were not returned.

"I'm here now," she said, blinking back the stubborn tears. "I'm here, Daddy."

Marcus gazed up at her, his shrewd brown eyes hollow and hard-edged, his mouth open in a rasping for each breath. "As pretty as ever." He swallowed, closed his eyes for a moment. "You are the image of your mother."

And that was why he'd hated her so much, Cassie realized.

CAL STOMPED INTO THE kitchen, searching, the scent of Cassie's perfume lingering in the air like a low-hanging flower, teasing him while he searched for her.

"Where is she?"

The housekeeper who also served as his sometime-therapist and wise counselor said, "In with her daddy."

"How is she?"

Teresa automatically filled a glass with ice and poured him some sweet tea. "Shaky. Confused. Wanting to know why you're back here and why her daddy called her home."

Cal lowered his head, his hand absorbing the condensation on the crystal glass. "Did you tell her anything?"

"Not yet. She went straight in. Poor girl. She looked so lost. It didn't help one bit that Marsha decided to come calling today of all days. Did she know Cassie was coming home?"

"No. At least she didn't hear it from me." Cal took a long sip of his tea, the syrupy sweetness of it hitting the dry spot in his throat with a soothing rush. Then he put down the glass and stared at the melting ice. "This is hard for all of us."

Teresa went back to wiping and putting things away. "Yep, I reckon it is. I should have warned her. I don't like keeping things from her."

"She wouldn't have come if she'd known I was here."

"And that's why I didn't tell her."

That reality made Cal wince with a soul-deep pain but he fought it. He'd been fighting against it for so long now.

"Guess I'd better get back to work. I'll check back in later."

"You want to come for supper?"

He and Teresa had taken to eating their meals together, just in case Marcus took a turn for the worse. "No. I think it'd be better if I keep to myself for a while. Jack's waiting for me in the east field. Soybeans need my attention today."

Teresa didn't say anything and her expression held no judgment. Maybe that was why Cal liked her and trusted her.

That and the fact that she was more like a mother to him than his own had ever been.

"Be careful out there," Teresa said, as always. "Tell Jack to drink plenty of water."

Teresa had a crush on the burly old field hand. As always, Cal saluted her. "It's just tractors and dirt, Teresa. I think Jack and I can handle it."

But they both knew managing a big plantation was about a lot more than tractors and dirt.

He turned toward the kitchen door that led out onto the back porch and came face-to-face with Cassie as she rounded the corner from the hallway. One look at her and his protective instincts picked right back up where they'd left off so long ago. "Are you all right?"

She reached toward the counter, her face pale and drawn, her eyes glazed into an icy blue. "No."

The one word, whispered on a rushed breath, caused Cal to step forward and tug her close. "Here, sit down."

She tried to push him away but he'd always been bigger and stronger. And she used to lean on him when she was afraid or tired.

She looked around, her eyes now wild. "I'm fine. I'll be okay."

"You're not fine," he said, guiding her to a high-backed chair by the window. "Teresa, can you bring her some water."

He heard the faucet turning on, heard Teresa hurrying across the room. "Here, honey."

Cassie looked up, her eyes turning the innocent blue of a confused hurt child. She took the water, sipped it for a minute, then handed it back to Teresa. "He's really dying."

Teresa shot a stern look toward Cal. "Yes, he is."

Cassie glanced down at her hands. "I thought maybe it was just some kind of ploy, a trick to get me to come back. But he looks so sick. So small."

Cal bent down in front of Cassie, forcing her to look at him. "He wanted you here but it took him a long time to admit it." He shoved the glass of water back toward her. "He didn't want to…go…with things the way they were between you two."

She sipped the water then stared down at the glass. "Why didn't he want me here while he was still alive enough to really spend time mending things between us? I would have come. I tried coming home, then when that didn't work, I wrote to him, sent him cards, left messages. Then I gave up and got on with my life. But I would have been here if he'd only asked."

Cal couldn't explain that one. He'd often wondered the same thing. He knew why he wasn't wanted here before now, but how could a man turn on his only daughter like that? Since returning, Cal had thought many times about calling her, but Marcus Brennan was a stubborn man. And Cal had to be honest. He'd been too bitter and hurt himself to ask Cassie to come back, especially when he knew she wouldn't like being around him. And that she would hate him all over again when the truth came out.

"I don't know," he finally said. "All I know is that he asked us to get you home and you're here now." He looked up at Teresa. "We're all here. We have to do our best for him."

She stared at him as if she didn't know him at all. "And how long have you been back?"

He didn't dare lie about that. "A few months. Since last fall."

"What else are you two keeping from me?"

Teresa busied herself with cleaning off the counter and moving a bowl of fresh fruit into place. Not bothering to address Cassie's last question, she said, "I thought it best you didn't know about Cal. You didn't call that much anymore and when you did, I just didn't know what to tell you. Your daddy made demands and I abided by those demands." Her shrug said it all. But Cal knew there was much more to all of this.

Cassie got up then, pushing past Cal, her hands tightening against the wide butcher-block island. "And *I* didn't abide by his rules and his demands. So I got banished until…the bitter end. Until it was almost too late."

Cal hadn't planned on explaining his presence to her, but she deserved to know. "C'mon," he said, grabbing her by the arm. "Let's go have a talk."

Her frown held disbelief and distrust. "What's there to talk about?"

"Lots." He practically dragged her toward the back door.

Teresa called after them. "She needs to eat something. She didn't have a bite of lunch."

"I'm not hungry," Cassie said on a grumbling breath, her eyes on Cal. "And I'd not ready for this."

"Oh, yes, you are." Cal held her elbow, urging her toward his cottage. "We're going to get this over with here and now, Cassie."

"Why? Whatever you have to say won't change a thing."

"It'll explain a lot, though. I thought you wanted answers and explanations."

"You don't have to explain anything to me. This is between my daddy and me."

He didn't blame her for that. He'd lied to her once before and it had destroyed both of them. "I don't care what you think about me, but you need to understand how things are around here now."

She hurried toward the farmhouse cottage, pushing at camellia bushes as she went. "Yes, I guess it would be nice if someone would enlighten me about the status quo. I've had quite enough surprises for one day."

Her silky, cultured Southern voice poured over him. Even spitting mad, she still had class. Which was only one more reason he should have stayed away from this place. Or left as soon as Marcus told him the real reason he wanted Cassie to come home.

But he'd stayed, of course. To see her again. To finish what he'd started. And to honor a dying man's wishes.

Or so he told himself.

Taking her up onto the back porch, he pointed to a white rocking chair. "Have a seat. I'll get you something to eat."

"I told you I'm not hungry."

He ignored her and went inside to search for something that would fill her up without making her sick. She'd always been a picky eater. Then he remembered she used to like yogurt. He didn't have any of that, but he did have some ice cream. He grabbed the container out of the freezer then found a spoon and took it out to her.

Cassie stared up at the container, an amused look clearing away some of her disdain. "Butter-pecan ice cream? Are you serious?"

Glad to see her diva attitude kicking back in, he nodded. "Just take a couple of bites."

"I rarely eat ice cream."

"Well, maybe it's time you try. I love it on a summer night."

She glared at him then took the open container and the spoon. With a defiant dig, she scooped up a mound and shoved it into her mouth.

"See, not so bad, is it?"

She took another bite. "No. It slides down rather smoothly, unlike some of the preconceived notions I have about you."

Ouch. He deserved that. "I know you don't want me here, Cassie. But I'm not leaving. I've put too much into this place to leave now."

She put down the ice cream and tossed the spoon onto the table by the chair. "And why exactly *are* you here, Cal?"

Cal took the ice cream back inside to the freezer then came out to sit on the porch rail in front of her. "Sometimes, I ask myself that same question."

"I never expected to see you again," she finally said, her tone so soft now he barely heard her words. "I'd forgotten how much you love ice cream."

He stared down at her frowning, pouting face, remembering how he used to be able to kiss that pout right off her pretty lips. "Will you listen to me?"

"Do I have a choice?"

"Not if you want to understand."

She sat back in the rocking chair. "Okay, but I need to get back, so talk fast."

Cal let out a long sigh. "After I left, I moved around a lot, working on farm after farm, doing whatever work I could find. Then I saw this little bit of land up north of here and bought it with borrowed money, thinking I'd settle down and farm for myself since I'd learned everything there was to know about growing food and producing livestock."

She shot him a wry smile. "Does that include the load of manure you're about to give me?"

"You said you'd listen."

She started rocking again, her modern outfit a sharp contrast to the old-fashioned high-backed chair.

"After a couple of years, I made a profit so I bought the neighboring farm and added it to mine. And one thing led to another. I wound up owning a lot of land about fifty miles north of here. Well, actually the bank owns it but I'm making the payments."

"Why didn't you stay on your own place?"

He put a finger to his lips. "Listen."

She rocked back and forth. "All right."

His gaze hit hers and she looked away. "I was at a land-management seminar in Tifton last fall when I ran into your daddy." He paused and let out a breath. "He looked like he didn't feel good and I noticed he'd lost a lot of weight."

She lowered her eyes then nodded. "Go on."

"At first, we were kind of standoffish with each other but he finally approached me and told me he'd heard good things about my farm-management experience and how I'd acquired a lot of acreage. He was impressed. He told me the foreman he'd hired after Walt died wasn't doing a good job and he'd been looking for someone he could trust to take over. Then he offered me the job of foreman for Camellia, right there on the spot. But I had my own land and I didn't want to work for anyone else, especially him. A few weeks later, he called me and made another offer and told me he was sick. Since I wanted to pay off my land, I took him up on it. I rent out my land now and I work here. I get back up there once or twice a month, just to check on my workers."

She stopped rocking. "So you're telling me you turned your own land over to someone else so you could come back here and work for my father?"

"Yes. I know it sounds crazy, but that's the truth. The

rent money helps to pay down my mortgage and the money I'm making here helps me to fix up the place."

"I don't believe you."

He stood up and leaned over her, holding his hands on both arms of the rocking chair. "I don't really care whether you believe me or not. It's the truth."

She lifted her gaze to his, her eyes full of accusation and doubt. "That doesn't make a bit of sense, Cal. My father is dying."

"Yes, and he had just recovered from a heart attack when he offered me the job. He needed my help, Cassie."

She went still again. "He had a heart attack?"

"Yes, but he made me swear not to call you. And since I didn't think you'd talk to me anyway, I stayed out of it."

"But you dropped everything and gave up your dreams to help my father?"

He got so close, he could see the light blue of her irises. "Yes, I did."

"Why? What's the real reason? I know you always had this dream of owning your own place and now you say you do. But why come back here, after the way my father treated you?" She stopped, took in a breath. "After what happened between us? Why would you even want to come back here?"

He hadn't planned to tell her that but maybe she needed to know. "You, of course. I did it for you, Cassie."

She inhaled a deep breath but she didn't speak.

Then he stood up, his eyes centered on her. "That's the truth. I did it because your daddy needed someone he could trust and because…you couldn't be here. I did it to help a bitter old man, but mostly I came back *for you*."

CHAPTER THREE

CASSIE STARTED LAUGHING.

Then she gulped in a deep breath, mortified that she'd let him get to her so quickly. She was laughing because this was so unbelievable. But she wanted to have a good long cry. Or maybe a good, long hissy fit. But a Brennan didn't behave that way. She would show some backbone. Her pride wouldn't allow anything less.

"Don't tell me you're doing this for me, Cal. How can you even think I'd fall for that? I didn't know my father was ill or that you'd come back to work for him. And you're not even married to Marsha. You don't have a child with her. But you were with her again today, of all days. Do you know how many times I've thought about that over the years?" She stopped, shaking her head. "I imagined what your son or daughter would look like. Wondered why you didn't marry Marsha." And why he didn't bother to come and find *her*. She leaned back in the chair. "Forgive me if I sound doubtful. I'll need time to let this soak in."

Cal touched a hand to the rocking chair. "Contrary to what you saw today, Marsha and I are history."

"History?" Cassie felt sick to her stomach, the few bites of ice cream she'd managed to swallow churning through her insides like sour milk. "That scene out on the front porch looked pretty current to me."

He jabbed a hand through his hair, his expression

etched in anger and frustration. "She and Teresa keep in touch so she still comes around sometimes...thinking—"

"Thinking she's the one, the way she told me a long time ago that she would always be the one you loved? That she would always be the one you turned to? Thinking maybe since you're back here, and you and I *are* history that she'll be able to take up with you again? Whether you were married or not, there's a lot of history still brewing between you and Marsha, I think."

And the one jarring realization of that was that he hadn't even cared enough to find Cassie and tell her the truth. He hadn't even tried to fight for what they'd had together. Or what she'd *thought* they'd had. But then, neither had she.

"You never bothered to find out what happened," he said, slinging the words at her as if he'd read every thought in her head. "You just left, Cassie. You never looked back and you never tried to find me. So don't go accusing me."

Hurt and feeling as if she were seventeen again, Cassie moved off the porch. She wouldn't acknowledge the hurt she'd seen in his eyes. It couldn't be real. "I don't have to accuse you, Cal. I caught the two of you together, remember?"

He looked down at her then shook his head. "You still don't get it, do you?"

"No, I don't." She started walking away, her heart so heavy it was hard to breathe. Then she turned back. "I came home because my father asked me. But while I'm here, maybe you and I need to keep our distance. And maybe Marsha should stop personally delivering produce. Especially since we have a garden of our own."

With that, she whirled and stomped back toward the

main house, all the while remembering the nights long ago when she'd run barefoot at midnight out here amid the camellias and roses to find Cal waiting underneath an old live oak draped in Spanish moss. Remembering how he'd take her into his arms and kiss her over and over until she thought she'd die from loving him and wanting him.

I didn't die, she told herself as she hurried toward the mansion. *I survived and I left.*

But her heart had certainly died. She'd gone on to college, burying her hurt in her studies, working at any job she could get, hoping to find a way to get past her mother's death and her father's cold, uncaring attitude.

And Cal. She'd been trying for years to get past the hurt of Cal's betrayal.

Now that she was back and had seen him in action again, maybe she'd be able to finally accomplish that. Somehow.

CAL WATCHED HER GO, wishing he could call her back and take her into his arms. Wishing he could make her see that he'd never stopped loving her and that he'd never wanted to hurt her. But how could he convince Cassie that he had not and did not love Marsha? It was way too late to make excuses for that now. Now, he had to keep this place intact and solid so she'd inherit more than a bankruptcy notice. He'd made a promise to her dying father and he aimed to keep that promise. For Cassie's sake.

Even if he'd never be able to explain that to her.

Cassie had made a name for herself and was rumored to be one of the most successful women under thirty in Georgia now that her design business had taken off. But the mounting debts on Camellia Plantation could wipe her clean if he didn't finish what he'd started. He wouldn't tell her the truth. Marcus had to be the one to do that. Marcus had made both Cal and Teresa promise not to discuss his situation with anyone unless he gave them permission. Teresa had agreed because after her husband's death, her job here was the only thing she had left.

And Cal had agreed because he couldn't walk away from a dying man's last request. And he couldn't walk away from Cassie a second time, even if she'd walked away from him. He wanted Marcus and his daughter to reconcile before it was too late. He wanted Cassie to be able to return to the home she'd always loved, knowing that her father had finally forgiven both of them—and himself.

Cal would work day and night to make sure this plantation didn't get auctioned off to the highest bidder. Marcus wanted this place to stay in Cassie's hands. That much was evident.

And Cal was here to make sure that happened. Somehow.

Cassie's manners had shielded him from the worst of her pent-up anger. He didn't care as long as she was here and safe. Before Cal had agreed to take this job, he'd forced Marcus to promise that he'd reconcile with Cassie. That was all Cal really wanted and the main reason he'd agreed to come back here in the first place. It had taken several months of weeding through the financial mess and the depths of Marcus's sickness to convince Marcus he needed to honor that promise before it was too late.

And then, Marcus had come back at Cal with an ultimatum. One that had left Cal reeling. One that would only work if Cassie agreed to it. Which she most certainly wouldn't.

But she was here now, good or bad. It was a start.

Cal would settle for that, at least. And he'd do his best to save this plantation.

Because he knew what he really wanted couldn't happen.

He'd never have Cassie back in his arms again.

CASSIE STEPPED OUT OF THE shower and draped a big, fluffy white towel around her body. Her room had been redecorated to look updated and fresh but the memories remained, dark and misty and edged in a lacy haze of pain. But somebody had remembered how much she loved the color green. Probably Teresa.

The cherry-wood four-poster bed had been in her family for generations and was as solid as the day it had been hand-built. A bright green-and-peach floral comforter matched the dainty green brocade chaise lounge sitting near the French doors that opened out onto the upstairs gallery. Bright red, green and peach cushions lay against the chaise and across the shams on the bed. A mint-green chenille throw also lay across the chaise.

The matching mahogany dresser and vanity were also antique, but polished to a high sheen. The sweet fresh scents of lemon oil and vanilla merged with Cassie's magnolia-blossom shower gel to make the big square room smell like a summer garden.

She walked barefoot across the plush cream carpet, her toes digging into the heavy threads. When she reached the big double windows that looked out onto the backyard, she remembered the first time she'd seen Cal. She'd been standing right out there on the porch, but her room had been done up in deep pinks, bright greens and crisp white back then, with a rose-and-camellia motif mixed in with rock-star posters and cheerleading memorabilia.

But on that summer day, she'd forgotten all of her teenage dreams as she stood watching Cal strolling up the dirt lane from the stables, guiding a beautiful chestnut gelding. He'd been dressed in the standard jeans and T-shirt that he always wore when working. His dark hair had been longer and curling around his face and forehead. When he'd stopped and looked right up at her, Cassie had felt like the princess in the tower waiting for her forbidden prince. After that, their relationship had taken on a dreamy fairy-tale kind of intensity.

But her fairy tale had not ended happily ever after.

And she'd learned that Cal Collins was no prince, even if the gelding he was escorting had become her own prized horse—aptly named Heathcliff, after the character in one of her favorite classic books, *Wuthering Heights.*

Cassie closed her eyes now, swallowing back the sweet desire she remembered from that day. It wasn't so much a physical desire, even though Cal certainly won out over all of the bad-boy rock stars she had plastered on the wall. It was more of a desire to find out who this man was, to ask him how he'd found his way to Camellia Plantation. Sheltered and pampered, she longed to get to know the mysterious older boy who had not come from any of the neighboring plantations and farms, a boy who hadn't gone to prep school with her or driven some fancy sports car bought with his daddy's old money. She wouldn't find Cal Collins at the cotillion or any of the debutante balls.

In other words, Cal represented everything she'd

been sheltered from and protected from—the real world.

And Cassie so wanted to break away and find that real world. But reality wasn't so exciting after the way their summer had ended.

And now, her reality was centered on watching her estranged father die and finding out why Cal was really back here. She wasn't buying that he'd returned for her sake. They'd both moved on with their lives after that long-ago summer. And there was no going back. Ever.

Her cell phone rang, causing her to whirl and patter over to the rolltop desk on the far wall, where she'd left her big leather tote bag and her sketch pads.

Looking down at the number on the phone, Cassie grimaced. Ned Patterson. When would her ex figure out that they were finished? Why couldn't she love him the way he deserved to be loved? Pushing thoughts of Cal away, she ignored the incoming call. Ned was dreamy and debonair, everything a woman could ask for. But theirs had been a chaotic kind of relationship. Cassie had finally ended things, which she'd needed to do a long time ago. Because she didn't want to marry Ned.

Was her love life destined for self-destruction with every man she met?

Cassie threw down the phone, determined to put Ned—and Cal…for now—out of her mind. She hurried back into the big bathroom with the claw-foot tub and the old marble vanity, combed out her hair and threw on the barest of makeup. After drying her hair, she put on a white button-up shirt and skinny jeans with a pair of black flats then gathered her courage to return downstairs.

But what would she do while here? She stopped to stare down at her phone, thinking it looked out of place on the century-old desk. Did she dare sit with her father and try to talk to him? She had plenty of work to keep her busy and a whole slew of phone messages to wade through, some regarding business, some from concerned friends and...that one from Ned.

She deleted Ned's message right away. She didn't need to listen to his pleas or his promises anymore. Next, she called her assistant, Rae.

"Cassie, how are you?"

Rae's deep rich voice always soothed Cassie. They'd met in college at the University of Georgia in their freshmen year. Rae, a soulful expression on her cocoa-colored face, had taken one look at Cassie and become her mentor and soul mate.

"Girl, you look like you are as lost as a little kitty cat," Rae had said at the time.

"I am," Cassie had responded. Then she'd burst into tears.

Over coffee in a nearby coffeehouse, she'd blurted out all of her woes, including her mother's horrid death and her father's silent treatment and finding the man she loved in the arms of another woman. And Rae Randolph had listened and advised and suggested and... become a fast friend. On those days when Cassie wanted to give up, especially the holidays, Rae had been her rock. Following those awkward attempts to go home during her freshman year, she'd spent most of her holidays and summers with Rae's family in Atlanta.

Rae's mother, Louise, had helped Cassie get a summer job in a fashionable Buckhead department store. And since Rae's mother sewed most of their clothes, Cassie was allowed to use them for models for her own designs. She learned how to be an expert seamstress under Louise Randolph's keen eye. That experience had helped her become a better designer.

After college, they remained friends, both seeking work within the fashion industry. Rae had been there when Cassie sold her first designs in trade shows and obscure boutiques. So it was only natural that Rae would become her head assistant and confidante and advisor when Cassie finally branched out on her own three years ago with Cassie's Closet.

"I'm okay, Rae Rae," Cassie said now, wishing she could have brought Rae with her. "It's been so hard, coming back, facing my father. He's sick—much worse than I realized."

"I think you're in the right place," Rae responded, her signature hoop earrings jingling through the airwaves. "You can't let him pass on without making amends and forgiving, girl."

Rae had a way of stating the truth in soft, flowing euphemisms. She'd never tell Cassie her father was dying. No, he was just passing on. Passing on to somewhere with no pain and no regrets, according to Rae's reassuring words when Cassie had first received the call regarding his illness.

"Rae, Cal is here, too."

"Huh?"

"Yes, exactly. Cal Collins is back here, working for my father. He's the plantation foreman, which means he's pretty much running the whole show."

"Get outta here."

"I wish I could. He's here and he's single. He never married Marsha. They never had a child together. Can you believe that?"

"I mean," Rae said, louder this time, "get outta here and tell me that so ain't happening."

"It's happening, all right. We've already had a fight of sorts. I was a bit mean to him, but seeing him here again had me so flustered I don't remember what I said."

"Oh, now, Cassie, you need to just stay away from that man. Don't provoke him. It won't work."

"Don't I know it," Cassie said. She paced across the bedroom and sank down on the chaise, memories of all the great books she'd read while sitting here merging with all the memories of Cal she'd tried to bury forever. "I just can't figure out why he'd come back here after everything that happened."

"Yeah, like your daddy telling him to get lost and like you seeing him with that redheaded floozy right after he promised to stick by you and love you no matter what?"

"I can't believe he's here," Cassie said. "I can't believe *I'm* here."

"*I* can't believe y'all are there together," Rae added. "You know Mama Louise is going to freak, right? So what're you gonna do now?"

Cassie could just see Rae's mother rolling her eyes and shaking her head. "I'm going to work on making sure my inventory is updated and my fall and spring lines go into production and then I'll focus on my future collections, all the while staying near my father. I'm going to meet with his doctors and get the real story and I'm going to do a thorough review of everything that's going on around here, starting with my father's holdings and assets and ending with a long talk with him regarding the future of this place. And while I'm at it, I'm going to forget that the man who broke my heart is now back in my life."

"It's like déjà vu all over again."

"Yes, it is. I'm not so sure I can go through this again," Cassie said, tears springing to her eyes. "It was horrible when my mother died but Cal was there to help me through that." Even if he had betrayed her a few days later.

"And now he's there to help you through this, maybe?" Rae asked.

Cassie sat straight up, her mind whirling like a tilling blade. "He did tell me he came back here for me, but I didn't believe him."

"You think maybe he's trying to make amends?"

"No. He was with Marsha when I arrived. Right there on the front porch, at that."

"What? And you let him stay on after that?"

"He claims things are over between them, but he never explained how that whole marriage-and-a-baby thing never happened. I still don't know what to believe."

"Oh, this is getting better and better." Rae let out a huff of breath. "Maybe he came back because he knew you'd come home, what with your daddy's condition and all. He must want to see you again in a bad way."

"Well, he had to agree to this for some reason. He claims he's here to help my father and he is good at his job. He was always good at dealing with the land and the livestock and the million things that can go wrong on a working farm. But he had to leave his own farm to come back here. I just don't get it. Why would he choose this place over the one he's obviously worked so hard to acquire for himself?"

"But he told you he'd come back for *you?*"

"Yes, but maybe that's just an excuse, a cover. I don't know why he's here and I don't care. Let's change the subject. Anything urgent I need to handle?"

"No, nothing. Everything is going smoothly here. We got the mock-ups for the ads we placed in the spring issues of *Vogue* and *Marie Claire* and we're all set for the fall show at the Atlanta Trade Center. Well, as all set as we can be, barring the models show up and the designs work. You just need to create some great, gorgeous pieces for the next few seasons' collections, okay?"

"I'm afraid with the mood I'm in, my collection might be more Gothic than gorgeous."

"How about gorgeous Gothic then? Use all that angst to create your designs. Go with the *Wuthering Heights* factor."

Cassie thought of flowing linen top coats and wispy dresses and skirts, maybe with cashmere sweaters and draping wraps. Rae knew all about Cassie's fascination with the Brontë sisters.

"Good idea," she told Rae. "Maybe with a little steam-punk thrown in. I'll get back to you. Right now, let's go over some of the things I have on my urgent list."

After a half hour of work details, Cassie finished the call. "I think that's it for now. I'll set up a video conference with the whole team once I get my bearings. And remember, no one else needs to know where I am, especially Ned."

"Got it," Rae said. "Take care of yourself, okay?"

Cassie smiled into the phone. "I will. You, too. Call me and keep me posted."

"Same here, darlin'. And hey, you know I can send Mama down there in a flash."

"I appreciate that, but I have to handle this myself."

Cassie disconnected, determination overcoming her fears now that she'd had a heart-to-heart with Rae.

Work and her daddy, those were her goals for now. Those and trying not to think of Cal living down in that two-bedroom foreman's cottage right out past the garden proper.

He'd always been just out of her reach. Nothing about that would change now.

She got up and opened the French doors then walked onto the broad wraparound gallery to look out over the sloping garden and the fields and pastures beyond. Camellia Plantation covered close to a thousand acres, some of that in cash crops such as corn, soybeans and peanuts, some in pastureland and pecan trees and the rest in forests and woods that hunters paid to lease so they could roam around during hunting season. Her home was vast and all-encompassing and worth millions.

As she made her way downstairs, that thought hung over Cassie's head like a dark cloud. Millions. Millions of dollars and thousands of acres. Prime real estate in fertile, lush southwest Georgia, made for cash crops and hunting leases and fishing lakes and pastures for livestock and horses.

And it would all be hers after her father died.

Unless, of course, he'd decided to cut her out of his will.

She stopped at the bottom of the stairs, her mind whirling. She didn't want to lose the land or this house, but she didn't care about the money. Maybe somebody else here did.

Then instead of going into the kitchen to find Teresa, or turning toward her father's sick room, Cassie headed out the back door, searching for the white Chevy pickup she'd seen parked by Cal's house. But she didn't need to find the truck.

She saw the man himself down by the stables. He didn't notice her as he entered the big open barn. Cassie wanted to finish their earlier conversation.

Hurrying down the dusty lane, Cassie almost trotted toward the big red barn where her father kept several workhorses. As she entered the stable, she blocked out the memories of her clandestine meetings here with Cal and the memory of her father shooting her beloved horse, Heathcliff, after the nervous gelding had spooked and thrown her mother to her death out underneath that old oak near the driveway.

But she couldn't block out the rush of warring feelings crashing throughout her system. "Cal?" she called, the smell of horses and hay assaulting her. "Cal, where are you?"

"In here," he called from the tack room, his head sticking out, his expression full of surprise and wariness. "What is it? Is Marcus okay?"

Cassie shook her head, her earlier anger boiled down to simmering. "It's not that. He was sleeping last time I checked. I need to ask you something." She pivoted toward the door of the small office. "And I need an honest answer."

"Sure." Cal came to lean a shoulder on the doorjamb, his eyes sweeping over her before his gaze settled on her face. "What is it?"

She met him face-to-face, her dry throat giving her time to compose herself. "Did you come back here for *me,* or did you come back here for this plantation?"

He lifted off the jamb, his wariness changing to disbelief. "Excuse me?"

"You know what I mean." She pushed against a stall, leaning back. "My father is dying. There's a lot at stake here. You always wanted a place like Camellia and you two were close before…before everything fell apart. So close that he often talked about letting you take over one day. So tell me the truth, Cal. Did you come back to take over this plantation and make it your own?"

CHAPTER FOUR

"YOU JUST DON'T GIVE up, do you?"

Cal waited for Cassie to answer the question, hoping it would deflect the one she'd just thrown at him. He couldn't be the one to explain things to her. She'd take the information and turn on him. And how could he blame her? He'd vowed to never come back, so he did look suspicious. Wishing he'd defied Marcus and at least warned her, he figured even that might have backfired. If she'd known he'd be waiting for her, she wouldn't have come home. He had no doubt of that. And she needed to be with her father, if for nothing else then to hear the truth from Marcus. Even Marcus deserved to die with everything off his chest. So now Cal stood and felt the force of her suspicions sizzling over his system.

"Give up?" She pushed off the stall and stood close, her blue eyes shooting fire. "I had to give up. I *had* to leave and start over on my own. I had nothing, Cal. Nothing and no one. So I reinvented myself, or rather, I found myself. I worked hard and I didn't come begging to anybody back at Camellia Plantation. My father paid for my education, but I paid for my sins. Over and over."

Her hand fisted against her chest. "Me, Cal. By myself. I did give up for a long time, but I'm back and I need to know the truth. I have a right to ask questions now, don't I? So do me a favor and answer me. Don't you think you owe me that at least?"

She stopped, heaving a great breath, her cheeks high with color, her expression still consumed with shock and confusion.

"I need some answers, Cal. I've held things inside for a long time now. I'm trying to understand. I need to understand."

Cal dropped the papers he'd been planning to go over. He couldn't give her the answers she needed. But the guilt of letting her go without a fight long ago festered in his soul like a disease. Why had he allowed Marcus to do this to her? To do this to their love? Why hadn't he fought harder for her?

But his hands were tied. He'd promised Marcus. And he'd protected Cassie. He was still protecting her. "You need to talk to your father. He's the one who hired me and he's the one who summoned you home."

"Summoned? That's a good word for it." She paced and then looked around as if she'd just realized where she was, the fire in her eyes changing to a smoldering awareness. "Summoned back to my own home and only because it's the end and he doesn't want to die with our nonexistent relationship on his conscience. You know, I almost didn't come home. But I couldn't live with myself, thinking of him being so sick, so alone. I had to come on the hope that he'd forgive me for whatever I did, not so much to give him any kind of peace, but to make me feel better. That sounds selfish and horrible, but it's the truth. I don't understand my father, but I need him to forgive me. Does he still hold it against me, this thing that happened with you and me? Or is there more that I don't know? Does he ever talk to you about any of this?"

Cal didn't know what to say since Marcus had never truly confided in him. But he'd pretty much figured the rest out. What could he say? He'd come back here for so many reasons, but only she mattered. He could deny that all day, but the truth shadowed him the same way the scent of magnolias haunted him.

"He talks to me about the plantation. Business-type things that he's worried about. He's never once mentioned us or anything else that happened before you left." Well, that wasn't exactly true. Marcus had talked to Cal a lot about the past and the future. But he wasn't ready to go there with her. One more topic Marcus would have to bring up, because Cal sure wasn't.

Marcus had talked about a lot of things, including Cassie and Cal. At least when he was coherent. Cal couldn't tell her about the confused rants and unknowingly blurted confessions. Or the grand idea her sick daddy had presented.

"You mean my mother's death," she said, taking up the conversation when Cal had sputtered to silence. "That's when everything changed. I thought he was angry because he'd found us together but there was something else. That's when he turned against me. He found her dead and then he shot my horse and after that day he caught you with me, he'd hardly even look at me. What did I do?"

He wanted to take her in his arms and tell her she didn't do anything. Marcus Brennan was a miserable old man who'd treated everyone around him with disdain and demands. He wanted to tell her that he hated what he'd done to her. But he didn't have all the answers even if he'd pieced things together enough to understand. But if he'd guessed right, it would destroy her.

"I don't have the answers, Cassie. I swear to you, I don't know why he treats people the way he does, especially you. I try to steer away from anything that upsets him."

She whirled, her hand going to her mouth. "In other words, he never talks about me? Because I upset him, right? Maybe I should have stayed in Atlanta."

Cal came around the desk then, his hands fisted at his side so he wouldn't touch her. "No, you need to be here. That much I can tell you. He made sure of that, Cassie. You want answers, well, then, go talk to Marcus. Make him explain things to you. That's the only way you'll ever understand."

She looked at him, her eyes widening. "You do know something but you're not going to tell me, are you?"

"It's not my place."

She put her arms across her chest. "I think you've already answered me. I remember enough about you to consider that you'd find this place extremely lucrative. Add this property to what you've acquired over the years and it all makes sense. You could finally establish yourself as one of the most powerful landowners in southwest Georgia. I want to believe you came back here to help me, but you'd certainly have a good reason to want revenge, too. I just have to decide which. And I'm gonna need some time to make up my mind."

With that, she turned and pranced out of the stable, her silhouette darkened by the late afternoon sunshine.

The light from that brightness, pitched against the shadows of dusk, hurt Cal's eyes. She had a point. He'd thought of a lot of reasons for accepting Marcus Brennan's offer. And revenge had crossed his mind a time or two. But so had the possibility of finally making amends for breaking Cassie's heart.

CASSIE OPENED THE DOOR to the dark study. The nurse sitting with her father nodded to her then got up to meet her.

"He's sleeping, Miss Cassie. But it's almost time for his dinner if you'd like to stay and talk while I feed him."

"I'll feed him," Cassie said, the words sounding strange on her tongue.

Having to spoon-feed her once-proud father caused a giant lump to form in her throat. How had she let it come to this? She should have forced her way back into his good graces years ago. But she'd been too hurt to think beyond getting away from this place and the condemnation and hatred she'd seen in his eyes.

"Are you sure?" the nurse asked, her eyes full of sympathy and understanding. "My shift's over at five-thirty so I can do it."

Cassie glanced at the clock on the bookshelf. "That's another hour. Why don't you go on home? I'll stay with him until your relief comes."

"I'm not supposed to leave him without permission. Usually Teresa or Mr. Collins makes that call."

Cassie's anger resurfaced but she couldn't blame the aide for doing her job. "I'm his next of kin and I say it's okay. You can go and I'll stay with him until the shift changes. Don't worry, I'll take full responsibility."

Her father stirred at the whispered voices. "Gennie?"

The aide gave Cassie an apologetic shake of the head. "He's always asking for her. Your mother?"

Cassie nodded, her silence holding back the dam on her emotions. Glancing at her father's struggle with the covers, she whispered, "Go ahead and tell Teresa to prepare his dinner. I promise I'll stay with him. I need to get used to doing this. I'll go over his medication with the night-shift aide."

"Yes, ma'am." The woman gathered her things and went out the door, quietly closing it behind her.

"Who's there?" Marcus tried to sit but fell back against the pillows.

"It's me, Daddy." Cassie hurried to the bed and stopped him from pulling the breathing tube out of his nose. "It's Cassie. Just calm down."

"Where's your mother? I saw her. I saw her right over there."

Shock jolted Cassie into action. "Daddy, it's okay. No one's here but me. I told your aide to go home. Teresa is bringing your dinner. Are you hungry?"

He seemed to realize he was in this room at this time. His eyes went from a vacant stare to a more lucid clarity. "I must have been dreaming. I thought you were your mother." He shrank back into the pillows, his disappointment heavy in the air. "I forgot that she's dead."

Cassie couldn't speak. The depth of his grief ate at her with a stinging that felt like fire ants biting into her skin. She'd allowed this to happen. She'd stayed away, hating herself, and hating the man he'd become. She'd let this estrangement rip them apart and now it had made her bitter and distrustful and her father so ill and grief-stricken he was dying a slow, horrible death.

He opened his eyes to stare up at her. "Cassie-girl, you came home. I'm so glad."

Cassie inhaled a gulping breath. "Are you, Daddy?"

"Of course I am, girl. I told 'em to call you home. I have a lot to discuss with you. Not much time."

She wondered if Cal already knew what her father wanted to talk to her about. She'd just have to keep digging until she found out. "What do you want to tell me?"

He let out a shuddering cackle. "So much. Too much."

Cassie found a chair and pulled it up to the bed. "I'm here now, Daddy. You can tell me whatever you want."

But did she want to hear everything he had to tell?

CAL CAME IN THE BACK DOOR and turned toward the long, sunny kitchen on the right. Teresa was in her usual spot in the little sitting room by the breakfast nook, watching the evening news. Her apartment was next to the sitting room. "Hey," she said, never taking her eyes off the television. "Looks like rain tomorrow."

"Yep." Right now he didn't really care about the peanuts and corn. "Time for his tray?"

She got up. "It's on the stove." She went over and pulled the foil off the mashed potatoes and tiny chunks of beef stew and gravy. "Cal, Cassie's in there with him. She sent the day nurse home."

Cal braced his hands on the long butcher-block counter. "She came to see me in the stables, wanting to know what's going on. I can't tell her so I hope he explains things."

Teresa glanced across the wide central hall. "But he doesn't realize—"

"I know that." He lowered his head. "If I tell her the truth, she'll go ballistic and think I cooked up this whole scheme. I'm hanging on by a thread here, Teresa."

Teresa put the tray in front of him. "We don't have a whole lot of time left. Before that man dies, the truth has to come out, and I mean all of the truth. That's why you're here. You can help her. You can make her understand."

"Like I did last time when she needed me and...I wound up hurting her?"

Teresa leaned over the counter, her whisper carrying through the high-ceilinged house. "No, this time you won't hurt her. You had your reasons back then. This time, you'll stay and show her the man you've become."

Cal hoped he could do that. "But what if she doesn't stay? What if *she* leaves again?"

Teresa wiped her hands down her apron. "Then you'll go after her, Cal. This has to end, one way or another."

The door across the way opened and closed and Cassie came into the kitchen. She looked at Cal then turned to Teresa. "Is that my father's dinner tray?"

Teresa nodded. "I was about to let Cal bring it in to you, honey."

Cal reached for the food tray, but Cassie tugged it away. "I've got it."

"I'll sit with you, if you want," Cal offered, hoping to find some common ground.

"No, thanks."

With that, she lifted the tray and walked back across the hall.

Cal glanced over and realized the door was shut so he rushed to open it for her. Their eyes met but her expression never yielded. She went into the room, leaving him to close the door.

Teresa lifted her chin toward the stove. "Your dinner is ready if you want to eat now."

"I'm not hungry," Cal said. "I'll come back later."

He walked out onto the back porch, the crisp gloaming hitting him with a refreshing burst. He wasn't sure he could do this. How was he supposed to stay here and run this place knowing Cassie was around day in and day out?

I've made a deal with the devil, he thought. Marcus Brennan always had some sort of deal up his sleeve. And this one was a real kicker.

But he'd made the deal, taking a big risk, so he could see her again and hopefully make up for the past. Well, that day had come and now he wished he'd just stayed up the road on his own place. He'd been content there, happy to work his land in solitude. He could leave now and go back to that solitude.

But then, he'd be leaving Cassie with a mess on her hands and a dying father on her conscience. He couldn't do that even if she did think the worst of him.

So he stood and watched the sunset settling over the pines and pastures, his memories as golden and glistening as the rays falling across the distant corn fields. He remembered the first time he'd seen Cassie standing up on the second-floor porch, her long blond hair tumbling around her face, her expression haughty and full of dare. He'd pegged her for the spoiled princess, a rich girl who had a powerful father.

Forbidden and out of his reach.

He'd fallen for her right then and there.

Then he remembered finding her later in the stables, tears running down her face, her vulnerable angst over hearing her parents fight making her even more desirable because she needed him.

Their first kiss out underneath that old oak tree had been magical, like a soothing balm. It had brought him home to a place he'd been searching for all of his life.

He wanted to be back at that place. But he didn't know how to find it again. Cassie had grown up in the

years she'd been away. It was obvious she was a so-
phisticated woman who'd done things her own way.
Maybe she'd outgrown those intense feelings they'd
shared back then.

While he'd been standing in the same spot, waiting
to rekindle something that could never be.

The back door banged open. "Cal, we need to talk."

He turned to find her standing there, her eyes dark
with a boiling rage. "What is it this time?"

"My father told me that I need to talk to you about
the future of this plantation. What did he mean by
that?"

Cal let out a long sigh. "What else did he tell you?"

She stalked to the porch railing. "Not much. I tried
to get him to eat but he kept pushing me away." Her
shoulders slumped. "He seemed desperate to explain
things, but maybe not sure what to do or say. He got
upset and told me to leave. He told me to find you and
come back in there."

Cal rubbed a hand down one of the massive columns
supporting the house. "Welcome to my world, darlin'.
Some days he makes perfect sense. Other times he ram-
bles and gets so agitated, we have to give him a pill to
settle him down. It took me months to figure out the
records and books."

Cassie placed her arms across her chest. "Is that
what he's talking about?"

"Part of it." He glanced back inside. "If you'll come
to the cottage with me, I can show you everything. All
the files are in my office and on my laptop."

She shook her head. "I have to wait for the night
nurse. Let me go back in with him for a few minutes,
okay? Maybe he'll forget that he wanted to see both
of us."

"Okay. I'll wait in the kitchen. Teresa has dinner ready. Did you eat?"

"I'm not hungry."

"Cassie, you have to eat."

"I'll grab something later."

She opened the door, waiting for him. "Are you coming?"

He followed her. "It's not like he and I haven't gone over and over this. Sometimes, he comprehends things and sometimes he's just not listening."

"I noticed that," she said, her head down, her expression grim. "He thought I was my mother when I first went in. Go ahead and eat and then come in. Maybe he'll talk with both of us there and tell us what's bothering him."

He took her by the arm. "I have a better idea. Let Teresa sit with him a few minutes and you try to eat something, too."

Teresa came out of the kitchen. "It's on the stove and still warm. The sooner y'all eat, the sooner I can go to my room and rest."

Cassie was too polite to make Teresa wait around to clean the kitchen. "Go ahead now. I'll clean up."

Teresa glanced toward the study door. "I'll sit with him until the night nurse shows up. You need to eat your dinner."

Cal watched Cassie's face. She wanted answers right now. How could he explain all the workings of this place and make her see he was busting his tail to save it? Maybe it was time to just lay all the cards on the table and be honest. About the plantation, at least. But not about Marcus Brennan's other ridiculous death-bed wish.

The exhaustion etching her face stopped him.

"Listen, you're tired and it's been a long day. Try to eat then we'll go in and see him. After that you need to go upstairs and rest. We'll start over fresh tomorrow. And I'll be as honest as I can, about everything."

He wouldn't tell her about his own part in this, about all the things she didn't know about her parents and what had happened on that fateful day so long ago.

What else could he do? He'd made the decision to go along with Marcus Brennan last desperate attempt to get his daughter back. Cal couldn't stop it now. But he could tell her the truth regarding her heritage.

She would hate him even more, but he had to take that chance.

"Cassie, will you eat and then rest?"

She finally nodded. "I'll rest after we visit him again, just to make sure he's okay."

"We'll do that," Cal replied, hating the defeat in her voice.

A few minutes later, they both sat staring at their half-eaten meals. Cal had talked to her about mundane things—the crops, the weather, a new foal that had just been delivered two days ago. She asked him about his mother—a subject he didn't like to talk about.

Teresa came out of Marcus's room. "I can't get him to eat."

"I'll try," Cal said, getting up.

"No." Cassie pushed ahead of him. "Let me."

Cal followed her into the room. "How 'bout we work together on it?"

She shrugged. "We can try." Then she moved ahead of him into the room. "But the only way we can work together is to be honest with each other."

Did she see it in his eyes? That he was holding back?

Of course she did. But Cal wasn't ready to give up all the secrets buried on this old plantation.

CHAPTER FIVE

CASSIE TRIED TO COAX her father to take another bite of the beef stew. Marcus glanced at the spoon then back up at her. "I'm finished. Didn't you hear me?"

Cal took the spoon from Cassie. "C'mon now, old man, eat something so I can give the night nurse a good report. You don't want to have to resort to taking your meals through a tube, do you?"

Marcus turned from Cassie to send Cal a heavy scowl, his wizened face expanding until he almost looked young again. "You like being the boss around here, don't you?"

"I'm not the boss," Cal said, a spoonful of tender meat and thick gravy moving toward Marcus. "You're still the man around here, so eat up and keep your strength."

Cassie resented the way he'd taken over, but was glad to see her father listening to Cal. Marcus took two bites of the stew then fell back against the pillows. "I'm full."

Cal gave him some water through a bent straw then glanced over at Cassie, the sympathy in his eyes raking her like talons. She didn't want his pity. She wanted his honesty. But then, he'd been dishonest with her before. Why change now?

Marcus glanced at Cassie then turned to Cal, his gaze now hooded and shuttered. "You two speaking?"

"Yes," Cassie said on a rush of breath. She refused to elaborate.

"We're being civil," Cal said. He shot Cassie a look that dared her to disagree.

"That's not good enough," Marcus retorted through a grumbling cough. "I need more than civil. I need you two to work together."

"What did you expect, Daddy?" Cassie's eyes locked onto Cal. "I found a lot of surprises here since I arrived this morning." Had she only been here one day? It seemed as if she'd aged in those few short hours. She was bone-tired and weary and still in shock from all the revelations nipping at her like mosquitoes.

Marcus coughed again, prompting Cal to give him another sip of water. He looked up at Cal, another dark scowl on his face. But the expression in his eyes held trust and what seemed like a grudging respect. Cassie glanced at Cal and saw that same respect in his gaze, too. Something passed between the two men, something secret and sacred and scary.

Cassie's resentment crashed in an ugly wave of green envy. Did Cal really care about her father? Or was this part of his plan? He'd never confirmed or denied her accusations. Cal had never been one for confirming or denying. He wasn't great at conversations or confrontations.

Deciding to cut to the chase, she touched her father's arm. "Cal says we need to talk. Are you up to that, Daddy?"

Marcus heaved a deep breath. "Of course I'm up to it. I've been waiting for this conversation a long time, Cassie-girl."

She couldn't take any more. Her nerves were twisted like fence wire and her head pounded like a herd of stampeding cattle. "Then tell me, please. Somebody tell me what's going on, beside you being so sick. Besides Cal being back here. What is it?"

"We're busted," Marcus finally said, his once-blue eyes watery and piercing. "Camellia Plantation ain't what it used to be."

Confusion crashed with exhaustion inside Cassie's head. "But it's still here. Our home is still intact."

She saw the lifting of Cal's head and the widening of her father's wrinkled brow. "Cal?"

Cal stood with his feet planted apart, his broad shoulders slung back as if ready to do battle. Until she looked into his eyes. The uncertainty of his gaze shattered her.

"Cal?"

"I brought Cal back to save the place," Marcus said, his voice weak now. "He can give you the details."

Cassie stepped back to stare over at Cal. "Is that true?"

Cal nodded. "Your daddy got in trouble in some areas and I've been fighting fires since I came back. That's why I wanted to show you the records and files."

"And?"

"And we're leveling off but it's gonna be a long haul."

She pushed a hand through her hair. "Is this what you've been keeping from me?"

"Partly," Cal said, glancing down at Marcus. "It's hard to explain all of it."

Marcus nodded. "He's right, honey. I won't be here much longer, Cassandra. That's the truth. We don't have much time. And I need you—"

"Daddy, don't talk like that. I'm meeting with your doctors. I'll bring in a specialist—"

"Don't need a specialist. Just need to rest."

"You can't just give up!"

But her father was already drifting off again.

Cassie touched a gentle hand to his bony shoulder. "Daddy, how bad is it?"

Marcus opened his eyes, but the vacant darkness she saw in them caused Cassie to step back. He looked as if he'd seen a ghost.

"Gennie, I'm so sorry. I tried to forgive her. I really did, darlin'." He coughed, his eyes wild now. "But she looks too much like you."

He dropped back to sleep.

Cassie gasped and turned away, the tears she'd held at bay all day long pricking at her eyes. Was her father talking about her? Everyone told her she looked just like her mother and she'd always believed that was part of why he found it so unbearable to be around her.

Just the thought of it made her feel sick to her stomach.

When she felt Cal's hand on her arm, she recoiled from the heat of it. "I'm okay. Just go."

"No," he said, dragging her toward the door. "No. You're coming with me so we can discuss this. I should have explained first thing this morning when you got here."

She couldn't speak so she allowed him to get her out of that suffocating room. Once out in the hallway, she pulled loose of his grasp. "I was right. You're going to take over Camellia Plantation, aren't you? You somehow managed to get back in with my father and now you're like a vulture waiting to pick his carcass. And you greet me at the door with…that woman. Is Marsha in on this with you, Cal? Is she?"

CAL COULDN'T BELIEVE the things coming out of her mouth. He'd done Cassie wrong all those years ago, but did she actually think he'd somehow managed to maneuver into position over her father's deathbed? Chalking it up to shock and grief, he cut her some slack but he couldn't get past his own frustrations and anger.

"You must really hate me," he said, seeing what looked like hatred in her cold blue eyes. "You can't honestly believe I'd be so cruel."

"I don't know what to believe," she said, her eyes misty, her tone low and unsure. "I'm sorry, but I just wish—"

The sound of a car door slamming caused her to stop. "I'm going upstairs to my room."

"Cassie, you need to go over the books with me. So I can show you that you're wrong."

Teresa stepped into the hallway. "That's the night nurse. Cal, let Cassie get some rest. Tomorrow is soon enough to get down to business."

"You knew about this, too?" Cassie asked the housekeeper, her voice rising.

"Honey, I know about a lot of things," Teresa replied, lowering her voice as the back door swung open. "But until you're ready to listen, it won't matter what we tell you."

Cal watched as Cassie went into debutante mode, her back going straight, her cool resolve slipping back into place while she closed her eyes to shut down the tears. "You're right, of course. I'm exhausted and I'm not thinking rationally. I shouldn't be lashing out at Cal. But tomorrow, I want the truth. From both of you. I mean it, Cal. If I don't get some answers, I'll have to figure it out for myself. But I'm hoping you won't force me to do that."

She nodded to the shocked woman standing at the door. "I'm Cassandra Brennan, Marcus Brennan's daughter."

The hefty red-haired woman stepped forward, apparently undaunted by Cassie's cold demeanor. "I'm Sharon Clark. Your daddy mentions you all the time."

Cassie's manners kicked in to cover her discomfort and pain. She shook the woman's hand. "It's good to meet you. Can I go over his medication schedule with you before I go upstairs?"

"Of course," the woman replied, clearly confused. "I'll get his chart."

Cassie nodded and followed the woman into the kitchen.

Cal shook his head at Teresa's warning look then went out the back door, slamming it behind him.

Now he could put her out of her mind, the way he'd done so many times before. But he'd never be able to forget the indignant expression on her face when she'd accused him.

The woman would never trust him again. And he needed her trust now more than ever.

CASSIE WOKE WITH A START, shadows of dusk washing her bedroom in a golden-hued sheen.

Then she remembered how she and Cal had eaten an early dinner before she'd gone back in with her father. The night nurse had come in and they'd discussed his medications. Marcus had finally settled down for the night, so she'd come upstairs to rest and she'd fallen asleep. It was only eight o'clock.

She'd been dreaming about the day her mother died. She'd had this dream many times over the last few years. Two therapists and lots of long discussions hadn't kept the dream away. Always inside the dream she was running from something she didn't want to face.

Well, she didn't want to face her father's death and she didn't want to face Cal ever again. He'd become a coconspirator with her powerful father and she wasn't sure she could forgive and forget on that front. Just being back here a day had set her back years in emotional security. No wonder she was having nightmares.

She sat up, staring at the digital clock. Out of habit, she got up and went to the ceiling-to-floor window and stared out into the coming night. Not surprised to find a light on in Cal's house, she thought back over their conversation earlier today. She knew Cal. Or she had once known Cal. The old Cal had probably been honest with her up until that horrible time when her world had fallen apart. He'd told her about his life before he'd come to Camellia, endearing Cassie to him even more. But his betrayal with Marsha had cut too deeply for her to think about that or to trust him now. Cassie had never understood why he'd turned to Marsha right after her mother's death. She'd needed him then, but she didn't need him now. Just knowing the other woman had been hanging around made her sick to her stomach.

Back then, she'd never given him a chance to explain. Now she needed explanations and suddenly, he'd become even more noncommunicative.

"I still know you, Cal," she whispered now. "I know your heart. You always were a decent person." Feeling mortified about the way she'd treated him, Cassie decided she couldn't put all the blame on Cal. He'd at least stepped in to help her father when she wasn't around.

Cal wasn't one to lie and keep secrets even if she had accused him of those things, but his refusal to tell her

everything right up front grated at her raw nerve end-
ings like barbed wire. He'd betrayed her with Marsha
all those years ago, but she'd never once asked him why.
She'd been too hurt, too confused, to bother asking. So
she'd just left.

But now, she'd come back and demanded answers
to questions she'd long ago tried not to ask. No wonder
Cal didn't want to be honest with her. She hadn't exactly been a model daughter. And she certainly hadn't
tried to fight for Cal's love.

Maybe she still didn't want to know the answers
to those questions. But it did make her think about
her part in all of this. Cal had never had a real home
but he felt at home here. She couldn't deny him that.
And somehow, in spite of his horrible upbringing, he'd
turned out to be a decent, hardworking man. Maybe he
was trying to help and nothing more.

But what about her? Now that the dreams were
coming back, she had to wonder if she'd held some deep
dark secret locked away in her heart. Did she know
something, something so horrible she'd buried it be-
neath her guilt and her pain?

"Impossible," she whispered to the night. Grabbing
her robe, she decided to head down to the kitchen to
make a cup of chamomile tea. It was the only way she'd
ever get back to sleep. She'd check on her father and
see if the nurse needed a break.

She hurried past the two upstairs guest rooms at the
center of the big square-framed house, then moved past
the master bedroom—the room her parents had always
shared. It was an enormous suite located on the oppo-
site side of the house from her room. It took up that
whole side of the house and mirrored her room since it

also included a setting room, a dressing room and large closet and a bathroom.

Cassie smiled, remembering how she used to sit at her mother's vanity and powder her face with Eugenia's scented makeup puff. Eugenia would allow Cassie to put on a spot of lipstick, very sheer and pink, then go into her closet and pull out pumps and pearls and a pretty floral scarf. Cassie so wanted to be like her beautiful mother. She wanted to dress in the billowy, flaring dresses her mother adored or wear cute capris and cashmere sweaters with black flats. She wanted to wear her hair curled into a fashionable bob like Eugenia's. Her mother had always dressed like a 1960s movie star, regardless of the fads or fashions. She'd been so young when she died—not quite forty years old. Marcus Brennan had married a woman fifteen years younger than him. A beautiful Southern belle who captured his heart and ruled over his domain with polite dignity. Cassie had tried all of her life to live up to her mother's image.

"But I'm not you, am I, Mother?" Cassie asked the face staring back at her from the formal portrait of Eugenia, dressed in creamy silk and satin, that hung on the staircase wall. "I'll never be you."

Cassie's designs reflected her mother's grace and classic sense of style but she wasn't sure she could ever capture the true essence of Eugenia Brennan. No one ever had.

Was that why her parents fought so much and yet loved each other so deeply? They'd both always held something back, something that no other human could discover or figure. But in the end, they'd always held fast to each other. Maybe in their most intimate moments, they'd all let their guards down.

Their saving grace.

Perhaps she should try that. Even with Cal all that time ago, Cassie had held back. She'd loved him but she'd never been completely sure of him. When they'd first met, he'd accused her of being a spoiled snob. And he'd been right in some ways.

But so wrong in others.

Her parents had loved each other in a way Cassie always envied. Until that horrible day so long ago.

She shivered then hurried past her mother's brilliant blue eyes staring down at her, the light from a hall lamp illuminating the huge portrait like a shrine. Making her way to the stove, she switched on the muted overhead light, hoping not to disturb Teresa. She'd make her cup of tea, check on her father and go back upstairs to play with the designs she'd tried to sketch that afternoon. At least she might be able to get some serious work done. Maybe she'd take a look at the website and see how the current spring line was doing. With Easter just a couple of weeks ago, Cassie's Closet should have a good retail month and a solid first quarter earnings. Not that she was a millionaire by any means, but she was making an honest living.

She'd need to keep doing that if she intended to help Cal and her father salvage this house and this land. But that would mean putting her plans on hold. No second boutique in Buckhead or Roswell and certainly no long-term plans to open one in New York, either. She'd have to put a tight rein on everything. And pray her anchor store held on and continued to thrive.

She grabbed the teakettle off the stove just as it started gurgling then poured the hot water over the tea bag in her cup. She'd always hated a whistling teakettle and she didn't want to disturb anyone else. Settling onto a stool near the long counter, Cassie let the memories pour through her with each sip of the soothing tea.

They'd had elaborate parties at this house. Christmas parties complete with a buffet full of ham, duck and turkey and all kinds of side dishes and luscious desserts. Barbecues held after great hunting trips, the grills rich with smoking meat served with fresh vegetables and cold sweet tea. Pool parties with martinis for the adults and fresh lemonade for the children. Birthday parties and clowns, balloons and ponies.

The perfect childhood.

She listened, the soft sounds of the ghostly gatherings drifting through her mind with all the sweetness of an old song. She'd missed this. Missed the parties and her friends and the life she loved here. Where had it all gone? How had things gone so wrong?

She thought of Cal, standing out on the edge of the property, watching her at her high-school graduation party but refusing to be a part of things because he didn't think he measured up. He'd always been a loner. And what they had was a secret even though most of Cassie's friends knew about Cal.

But later, after the party, she'd rushed to find Cal and he'd held her and told her how pretty she looked and they'd made those solid promises amid stolen kisses in the middle of the night.

"I don't care about your rich friends. One day, I'll have my own place and I'll take care of you. As long as we have each other, Cassie, we can make it work."

She'd believed that with all her heart. Then. But not now. Not anymore. Yesterday was gone, but oh, how she longed for that promise of tomorrow.

Cassie got up to go back upstairs, the creaks and

moans of the old house making her shiver. And that's when she heard her father screaming into the night.

"Gennie, no! No!"

CHAPTER SIX

CASSIE DROPPED HER TEACUP to the floor. The cup crashed to pieces, hot liquid and shards of porcelain hitting her bare feet. She rushed across the hallway and opened the door to her father's room.

Sharon Clark stood over her father, trying to hold him down. "It's all right, Mr. Marcus. You're having a bad dream."

"No," he said, his arms thrashing out, his eyes wild in the muted light from the nearby bathroom. "I have to get to her. I have to save her. Please, don't let her die."

Cassie ran to his side. "Daddy, it's me, Cassie. Daddy, I'm here. It's okay. Everything will be okay."

Marcus reared up, trying to sit. His eyes went wild again as he stared at her, his frown cutting like a gash through his leathery skin. "I don't want you here. I want her. I've always wanted her. I told him that, too. Told him…"

Then he sank back down on the bed and fell into a fidgety sleep.

Cassie sucked in a hot breath, the despair she'd felt so long ago hitting her with a renewed vengeance. She turned away, the shock of seeing the rage and hatred in her father's eyes breaking her heart into shattered pieces.

Teresa came into the room. "What happened?"

"He had a nightmare," Sharon said. She touched

Cassie's arm. "Honey, he didn't know what he was saying."

Cassie whirled to stare at her father. "He knew exactly what he was saying. My father hates me." And he must have told someone that. Cal, maybe?

She rushed past Teresa and out the door. She didn't stop until she was deep into the garden, the white blossoms of a moon vine glistening like a beckoning light in front of her. Cassie grasped at the wrought-iron trellis, holding on while she gulped in air. The night was full of a melody of nocturnal noises. Crickets sang. Frogs croaked. The buzz of mosquitoes teased at her ears. The pool's pump gurgled a steady roar.

And the sound of footsteps rushing toward her caused her to turn and stare out into the night.

"Cassie?"

Cal? What was he doing out here? She almost didn't answer but her heart was pumping so fast she couldn't run away. And she knew he'd follow her anyway.

"I'm over here," she called, her voice sounding hoarse and raw in the crisp night air.

He came around a giant oak tree, his shirt billowing open over jeans. He was barefoot, too.

Cassie started shivering in her thin robe and gown. "I...I couldn't breathe in there. I'm all right. I'm all right."

Cal grabbed her into his arms. "You don't look all right. Teresa called me. Said your dad had a bad spell."

She nodded against the tangy scent of his shoulder. "A dream about my mother." She raised her head to stare up at Cal. "I was dreaming about her earlier, too." She looked back at the house. "He told me he didn't want me here, Cal. He still hates me."

"He doesn't, honey. He's just a sick man. He's dying

and he gets confused. He loves you. When I'm with him, sometimes he calls out for you." He held her head between his hands, his gaze focused on her. "You, Cassie. He loves you. He doesn't know how to tell you that."

Cassie shook her head and pulled away. "Don't lie to me."

But he tugged her back. "This is not a lie."

"But everything else is. Something isn't right here and no one will tell me the truth."

He pushed his hand through her hair, tugged her even closer. "I only know that I came back here for you. And that is the one truth you need to remember."

Then he kissed her, his touch tentative and tender until Cassie sighed and returned the kiss, her arms grasping him and holding him close. Cal wrapped her in his embrace, his touch demanding and deepening until she felt herself falling into a blinding mist of longing.

I shouldn't be doing this. I shouldn't—

"Cassie?"

Teresa's voice calling out into the night brought them apart and brought Cassie out of her trance. She stood staring up at Cal, her breath heaving, her mind swirling. "That can't happen again."

He stood back, his eyes as dark as the night sky. "Probably not a good idea." Then he yanked her back for another round.

"I have to go," she said, twisting away, her heart begging for more.

"We're not done," he said, the whisper of that statement sending shivers down her neck. "Not nearly."

"I'm coming, Teresa," she called, her voice wobbling.

Cal hurried to button his shirt. "I'll come with you."

"I don't think—"

"I said I'm coming with you."

Cassie didn't argue with him. She couldn't. She was freezing hot, cold shivers of icy heat racing through her body. The dew tickled at her bare feet while Cal's brand still burned on her lips.

She shouldn't have let him kiss her.

It was wrong. He was just as forbidden now as he'd been over twelve years ago. Even more so.

They met Teresa on the porch.

"Are you all right?" the housekeeper asked Cassie.

"I'm fine," Cassie said, her spine straightening. "I just needed some air. You didn't have to call in reinforcements. I'm not as fragile as I used to be." She turned to Cal. "Go home. No need for you to hold my hand."

"He can't go yet," Teresa said, her gaze moving between them. "Your daddy is awake and he wants to see both of you."

"Right now?" Cassie asked, frowning. "It's getting late."

"Yes, right now," Teresa replied. "He seems lucid and he said it's time to have the talk."

"The talk?" Cassie glanced at Cal. "What talk?"

Cal shrugged, his expression going blank. "He has a lot he needs to say but half the time I have no idea what he's talking about." He sent Teresa a cryptic glance. "Are you sure he's not just on a rant?"

Teresa waved a hand in the air. "Yes, I'm sure. He's making sense for once and he told me to bring you both to him. But if you don't hurry, he could slip away again."

Cal let out a sigh then took Cassie by the hand.

"She's right. These moments of clarity are rare these days. If the man wants to spill things, we'd better head inside. I'm ready to get this over with so I can get on with my job."

Cassie felt as if she'd slipped down the rabbit hole. "You can't be serious. He just told me he didn't want to see me. He's still mourning my mother. He's delusional."

Teresa shook her head. "He's in his right mind this time. He told me to find you and bring you to him, Cassie. He called you by name."

"Let's go," Cal said. "I'll be there with you, just to make sure."

But he didn't look too sure. In fact, Cassie noticed he seemed downright full of dread.

"Let's get on with it then," she retorted, wondering if she'd finally get some answers.

Teresa turned toward the open door. "I'll make a pot of coffee. I think it's gonna be a long night."

Cal dreaded each step they took toward that sick room. He knew what was coming. He'd known for weeks now why Marcus had insisted Cal come to work here. Cal had almost left the first time Marcus brought up his plan. But the old man had a way of guilting a person into a reluctant agreement. And he'd waited until he was close to death to announce his grand scheme. Which meant Cal was in so deep he couldn't get out.

Classic Marcus Brennan mode of operation.

At times, Cal prayed Marcus would forget what he'd suggested, or that it would turn out to be one of his irrational illusions. At other times, Cal thought about things and wondered if this could actually happen.

Now he wished he'd stayed on his own farm.

He guided Cassie into the room. It smelled of antiseptic and warmed-over soup. A single light from a shaded lamp sent twisted shadows out over the dark square room. Moonlight tried to slip through the drawn plantation shutters, little slivers of light piercing the darkness with scattered shards. The whole scene appeared eerie and dreamlike.

Maybe he was the one having a bad dream.

Cassie stared at her father then sent Cal a confused glance. He touched a hand to her elbow, a singe of awareness coursing through his system. Kissing her had been a dumb thing to do. And yet, he wanted to do it again. Over and over.

"I see everyone is accounted for," Marcus said on a rasping voice. "Cassandra, forgive my earlier outburst. The dreams sometimes merge with reality."

As always, Cal was amazed at how commanding Marcus could be when he had all his wits about him. He could also be at his most dangerous then, too. Cal steeled himself for what might come next. That one kiss might be the only time he'd ever have Cassie back in his arms.

Teresa came in and stood at the foot of the bed.

"I'm glad you're home," Marcus said to Cassie, a genuine smile on his withered face. "I didn't tell you that, did I?"

Cassie's joy transcended her confusion. "It's all right, Daddy. Are you feeling better now?"

"Just peachy," he said, his smile making him look young and carefree before his expression sank back into a wrinkled frown. "I told Sharon to take a break." He glanced at Teresa. "Why don't you go and keep her company?"

Teresa's eyebrows shot up but she nodded. "I'll be in the kitchen. Coffee should be ready in a few minutes."

Marcus cleared his throat and closed his eyes for a minute. "Coffee. I do miss my coffee. But then, I miss my Scotch and my whiskey, too." His laughter was as brittle as the whiskers springing up around his jawline.

"Would you like some juice or water?" Cassie asked, her voice calm—too calm. Cal saw the way her fingers shook while she straightened the blanket.

"No, sweetheart. I need to talk to you and Cal."

Her eyes caught Cal, the blue depths spilling over like a flowing waterfall. "We're here," she said, her voice small and quiet now. "What do you want to talk about? If you're worried about this place going under, I promise you I won't let that happen."

Marcus glanced over at Cal. "Have you said anything?"

Cal shook his head. "No. I told you I don't like this idea."

"No, of course you don't. But you'll do it for her, right?"

Cal shot Cassie a glance. The questioning doubt in her eyes made him wince. He didn't think he could go through with this. Then he thought about kissing her earlier, about how having her back in his arms felt like home. "Yes, I'll do it. If she agrees."

"What are y'all talking about?" Cassie asked. "I've had enough of guessing games. Daddy, what do you want to tell us?"

Marcus let a chuckle rattle through his chest. It turned to a cough, but he waved Cassie away until he could grasp a breath again. "I have a request, Cassandra. And before you say no, just hear me out."

CASSIE'S CHEST HURT WITH the weight of the oppression pushing down on her. The very air in this room seemed to cloak her and choke her like a kudzu vine, cutting off what little breath she could muster. She wanted to run again but she realized she'd always run away when life got scary.

She'd run right into Cal's arms when she was a teen-ager, pouring all of her angst and loneliness out on him. And then when things had gone bad with her family and with Cal, she'd run away from Camellia, using college as her excuse for hiding from her worst fears. Then she'd poured herself into work, content for a few years at least. But when her relationship with Ned started to sour, she'd pushed him away, too.

Now, she'd come home, but she saw that she'd used her father's summons and sickness as a means of getting away from Ned because she couldn't make him happy. She'd believed Ned's way of loving was the only kind of love she was entitled to. But now, she had to wonder—after that kiss she'd shared with Cal—if she'd been wrong on that account.

Cassie tried to find a breath, tried to take in some air, but her throat was dry and her eyes burned. Her father finally wanted to talk to her, and pathetic and needy, she wanted desperately to hear what he had to say.

"Go ahead, Daddy," she said. "I'm listening."

Marcus reached out his hand.

Shocked, Cassie put her hand over his, her fingers bending around his bones. His hand was cold, his sagging skin rough-hewn and dry to the touch. But that touch warmed Cassie's heart and brought tears to her eyes. "Talk to me, please."

Cal cleared his throat and nodded at her. But he still had that evasive dread in his eyes. Was this talk going to turn out good or bad?

Marcus gave her a thorough look, his eyes watery and red-rimmed. "You've grown up."

"Yes. I've been this way for years now."

"But you've lost something. Your smile used to be so sure and sweet."

"I had a sure and sweet life back then, Daddy."

"You have your mother's sharp wit."

"It gets me into trouble."

"I'm sure it does."

He shifted but held tightly to her hand. "She was so special, your mother. You know I loved her, right?"

Cassie knew that more than anyone. Yes, he loved Eugenia to distraction, to the point of ignoring everyone else. Even his own daughter. "Yes, Daddy. I know that. I always knew that."

He nodded, the lifting of his chin an effort. "Good. It's important that you understand. Never wanted to hurt her. Or you."

Cassie couldn't speak. Had her father finally seen what he'd done to her? Did he regret his words, his actions? Or was this just a deathbed confession to ease his conscience?

"It's all right," she said, wishing it were so.

"It will never be all right," Marcus said on a winded hiss of air. "Never the same. Too late for me."

Wanting to give him some sort of reassurance, Cassie leaned close. "We'll go to Emory, Daddy. You need doctors and a hospital. We'll find the best specialist—"

"Stop, girl." He held up a weak finger. "Too late for me. I don't want to live anymore."

"How can you say that?" she asked, tears streaming down her face. "How, after all this time, when I'm here now and we both can find a way to forgive each other?"

"No need," Marcus said, glancing over at Cal. "I'm done for, honey. But you have Cal now."

Cassie looked from her father to the man standing across from her. "Yes, Cal is here. But he's here to help you."

Marcus tilted his head to stare over at Cal. "He's been a big help. But I bribed him to come back."

Thinking he was joking, she nodded. "Yes and he's doing a good job. Things might seem bad, but Cal's trying to fix all of that and I'm ready to do my part. I'm here for as long as you need me."

She realized that was true. She could work from here all summer if she needed to, somehow. It would be impossible to leave knowing this place was in trouble. Knowing that Cal had given up so much to keep Camellia intact. Now, if her father was willing to forgive her for whatever she'd done, she might be able to find some peace, even with his death looming. It wasn't about the property or money. It was about holding on to her home and the things she'd lost.

"We can bring things back around, Daddy."

"I won't be here," Marcus said. "But Cal will need you."

Cassie's heart did a little flip-flop of confusion. Did her father think Cal would be here for a long, long time? Maybe he needed that as a reassurance.

"Daddy, Cal has his own place. Once we get Camellia back into shape, we'll…" She stopped, the future murky and muted in her mind. If both she and Cal left, what *would* become of Camellia?

"Can't go back," Marcus said. He sounded tired. His eyes drooped. "Can't go back." Was he talking about her staying here or was he referring to the past?

She looked at Cal, grasping for help. "Cal, tell him.

Make him understand that we won't abandon this plantation." She looked at her father again. "Even after Cal leaves, I'll make sure our land is secure. Don't worry about that."

Marcus jolted back awake. "No, let me finish." He grasped Cassie's hand. "Have to stay here, *together*. Should be the way. Always should have been you and Cal."

"Say something," she whispered to Cal. The man stood there like a block of stone. Why didn't he speak up, try to make her father see that the future wasn't so sure for any of them?

"Cal has responsibilities, his own farm to run. And you understand I have people depending on me, employees and commitments. But I'll do whatever I need to do. I don't want you to worry."

"I understand more than you think, girl," Marcus retorted, some of his once-commanding demeanor resurfacing. "And I say you need to stay here, with Cal."

Cal shook his head. "Marcus, I told you this was a bad idea. Why don't you try to rest? Cassie and I will figure out what to do next."

"I'm telling *you*," Marcus said, his eyes wide with determination. "Cassie, I only want one thing from you before I die. I want you both to have Camellia Plantation. Together. I want you to marry Cal and...then I can die in peace."

CHAPTER SEVEN

SHE COULDN'T SPEAK. The air hissed like a hot branding iron against her skin. The room seemed to drift into darkness, the echo of her father's words swirling in the shadows.

"This has to be a bad dream," she whispered, looking over at Cal. "Tell me this isn't real."

But his silence revealed that he'd known all along. "Cal?" She let go of her father's hand. "Cal?"

Marcus tried to reach for her, but she moved away. "I can't believe you reeled me in like this. Daddy, you're dying, for goodness' sake. You can't actually expect me to go through with this."

"Yes, I'm dying," Marcus said, his tone remarkably clear. "And that's why you have to agree." His chin jutted with a stubborn twist. "I had it put in the will, girl. No marriage, no Camellia. This place will be auctioned off if you two can't save it."

"What?" Cassie locked her gaze on Cal. "Did you know about this? Did you help plan this?"

Cal didn't speak. He stood there with his lips parted, as if he couldn't say what he wanted to say. His expression held a hint of embarrassment and dread.

And then, Cassie understood everything.

He didn't want *her*. He wanted her home. Maybe that had been his goal when they'd first met, too. When he'd lost Cassie, he'd also lost his chance at having Camellia Plantation. But if he married her...

Cassie gazed down at her father. "I can't do what you're asking. I won't do it."

"I'm asking it for you, girl."

She backed away, her hands out, pushing at air. "No. Everyone keeps telling me all of this is for my sake. But you've both had your own agendas the whole time." She shook her head. "I won't be a part of this. I won't."

She turned to leave, rushed to the door and almost collided with Sharon. The nurse looked worried. "Everything all right?"

"Just fine," Cassie said, nodding toward her father. "Although I don't think he's as lucid as we believed."

"I'll check on him then," Sharon said, heading toward the other side of the room.

Cassie hurried toward the stairs, intent on getting to her room so she could lock herself inside. Or maybe pack her bags and leave.

Teresa called after her. "I have coffee and toast."

Cassie kept walking. "Not hungry."

She made it to the entryway, one foot on the first step, before a strong hand pulled her back around. "Not so fast, Cassie."

She glared at Cal, wondering how her heart could hurt any more, wondering why the newly opened wounds seemed to ache much more than the old, scarred memories. "How could you be a part of this? Oh, let me guess—if you marry me, you get it all, right? The land, the house and the girl. Wow, you really did set out for revenge, didn't you?"

He held her arm, his gaze sweeping over her, a hint of pain flashing underneath the anger in his dark blue eyes. "You can't seriously think I set this up."

She huffed a breath, felt his fingers scalding her arm. "You had to know what he had planned for us. He said he bribed you to come back. You let me walk into that room thinking he only wanted to offer me forgiveness and love, but that's not what he did. And you let me play right into this...trap."

"It's not a trap," he replied, his hand going loose on her skin. "It's not a trap and it certainly wasn't my idea. He's talked about this for the past few weeks, Cassie. I tried to stop him, told him it was a crazy idea."

Cassie slumped down on the stairs, too tired to move. She wanted to believe Cal, but she'd held her anger and bitterness too close, for too long, to let the past go. "So you knew? Why didn't you at least warn me?"

Cal wondered for the hundredth time why he'd let Marcus talk him into going along with this ridiculous plan. Hadn't he known all along that Cassie would never agree to marry him?

Yes, but fool that he was, he'd held out hope that maybe they could pick right up where they'd left off, with Marcus's blessing this time. He'd been the one who'd gotten caught up in the persuasive tactics of a manipulating old man. And why? Because he still wanted that man's daughter.

"You have no idea what's been going on here, Cassie."

"I think I have a pretty good idea, now that I know the truth. And I hope that's the last of it. And the end of this ridiculous charade. I'm so sorry he forced you into this."

Cal put a hand on the stair rail. "It's not the way you think. I told you the truth about meeting up with him and about how he coaxed me to take this job."

"So you did this out of the goodness of your heart?" Needing to lash out at someone, she frowned up at him. "You had no other motives than just helping us?"

How could he explain something he didn't even understand? "I told you, I did this for your sake."

"Yes, but Cal, you have to see things the way I see them. You'll inherit everything right along with me if I agree to this farce of a marriage. You're working so hard to turn this place around because you have a vested interest in the well-being of Camellia Plantation. Did you actually think I'd fall for this request?"

"I know how it looks, but I figured you'd never agree to marry me," he said, his voice lifting to the high ceilings. "And I would never have come to work for him if I'd known he had this in mind. He didn't bother telling me about this request until about six weeks ago. I talked to the man until I was blue in the face. Sometimes, I thought I was getting through to him. Other times, it was like arguing with a mule."

She let out a groan, the disbelief in her expression making her blush. "For weeks? He's been senile and sick for months now and you just went along with him when he asked you to do this?"

Cal pushed at his hair, his head throbbing with tension. "No, I told you he came up with this a few weeks ago. Told me he'd hoped to bring us back together. But what he called his 'death sentence' made him speed things up. He had planned to call you, ask you to come home for a visit and see where things would go between us. But once he heard the doctor's last report, he became determined to get you and me together. That's when he called in the lawyers and changed the will. I promise you, I've tried to talk him out of this. I don't care what the will says. Camellia belongs to you."

Cassie couldn't take any more. She got up, determined to find a quiet spot to think this through. "We can't get married. We both know that." She moved up a step then whirled around. "I don't expect you to honor his request. And I'm hoping he'll forget all about it. I don't want to have to contest the will, but it might come to that."

"I don't think he'll forget," Cal said, aggravation putting an edge on his words. "But we don't have to worry about that right now. Marcus helped me out once. And in return, I was trying to help you because I believed you loved this place. I debated walking away and letting him die alone, or calling you in and letting him make his peace with you. I chose the second option. Maybe I was wrong on that." He hitched a breath. "I can walk away now, knowing I at least tried. *I* came back."

She put a hand to her throat. "Oh, and I didn't? You're going to throw that in my face, too?"

"If it makes you wake up and see what's going on, yes, I will."

His words halted her. She turned to stare at him. "Maybe you're right. I didn't come back and now it's almost too late. But you don't need to be a part of this, Cal. I'll figure out something."

"You want me gone?"

"Yes," she said, her hands gripping the banister. Then, "No." She crossed her arms. "I don't know. I have to get the big picture, see where we need to go from here."

Cal didn't know how to respond to that. His heart crashed in his chest while his world crumbled around him. The woman he'd always loved didn't trust him enough to let him help her.

Even worse, once again he'd made a deal with her

father. A deal he hadn't been able to talk about. Only this time, it was twice as hard to walk away.

"Maybe I was wrong to come here," he told her, the pain of that admission coloring his world. "But I need you to trust me, Cassie."

She stood at the top of the stairs, looking like the princess she was. "I need some time. It's a lot to digest on my first day home. I'll talk to you in the morning."

She turned and walked away. Cal heard her bedroom door slamming, the sound hitting like a nail against his heart.

JUST AS THE MOON CRESTED over the pasture, Cal turned off his cell phone and got in his truck and drove toward town. He didn't want to be bothered tonight. The next thing he knew, he was pulling into the gravelly parking lot of the local watering hole. The Pig and Plow Bar was hopping, as always. Even though it was getting late, the all-night bar stayed busy. Some of the customers would be leaving for home and some would be arriving to party.

Marsha served everything from beer to breakfast. She didn't care what they ordered as long as the doors stayed open and she raked in some serious revenue. Which she did. Even in hard times, men tended to cluster at this old bar for food and commiseration, no matter the time of day.

Cal could use a little of both right now.

Mud-splattered pickups and late model cars were parked like a pile-up all around the grassy yard of the log cabin building. The big front porch served as part of the restaurant and bar, its rickety railings wide enough to hold a longneck and an order of Buffalo wings or a ready-to-go ham biscuit. Battered bar stools holding equally battered farmers and field hands sat around the planked porch.

Cal wasn't all that hungry, but he sure could use a drink. But it was either too late or too early for that, depending on how you looked at it. He went inside, the strong aroma of cigarettes and cooking oil assaulting his senses. Several of the local farmers tipped their John Deere and International embossed caps to Cal. He nodded and headed straight to the bar.

And came face-to-face with Marsha Reynolds.

"I thought it was your night off," he said, wishing he'd gone to another bar.

"I had a waitress call in sick." She stared at him with raised eyebrows. "She kicked you out, didn't she?"

"No. I just needed a break."

"Already?" Marsha uncapped a longneck beer and sent it sliding across the old walnut counter toward Cal.

Cal took a swig of the cold dark liquid then stared at Marsha, wondering with all his might why he couldn't love her the way he loved Cassie. Why had he come in here? Had he purposely come to find Marsha? He put down the beer. "I *want* coffee and I *don't* want to talk about it."

"No, you never do. But drink the beer anyway. On the house." She turned and went back to helping her waitresses serve the other, more friendly customers.

Marsha had taken over this old place years ago. She loved the wild lively atmosphere and she'd at least cleaned up the menu. The food was pretty good—old-fashioned greasy-spoon-type meals and lots of liquid refreshments. Cal didn't drink the way he used to. But every now and then, he'd stop by for a cold beer. Marsha worked a rotation of the crazy shifts, same as her waitresses, and hung around even when her other manager came to take over. She and Cal talked about everything from the weather to the crops to why they'd managed to stay friends and nothing more. Even when Marsha pushed the issue, she always backed off at just the right time. Maybe because she knew more about Cal's secrets than he did himself.

Cal sat with his beer while he tried to decide if he wanted to go back to his own life.

For good.

Forever.

He couldn't wait to get back to his place. He'd left it in good hands, but he'd neglected it, too. Whatever possessed him to take on Camellia Plantation and Marcus Brennan in the first place? He had a lot of capable hands who could take over on the plantation. He'd already told Jack Howard he'd be the acting foreman once Cal left. The men could do the work. And Cassie would be the boss. She was the rightful heir to the land anyway. Let her figure it out from here.

And what about the will?

He took another long swig and hit his empty beer bottle on the counter with a jarring frustration. The will would have to be changed because he sure wasn't going to honor it. Had he actually believed he could win Cassie back by forcing her into an arranged marriage?

Marsha sauntered up to the bar. "Want a refill?"

"No, I've had enough."

"Of her, I hope?"

"Not going there, Marsha."

She leaned over just enough for him to notice her low-cut blouse. "Are you sure? You always come in here when you need cheering up. I've been here all night. I can take an early break."

Her eyes were seductive and steady. Cal had refrained from giving in to Marsha's obvious appeals. But tonight, she looked serious—and ready to take the next step. He didn't want to give her the wrong impression and he'd never been one to play with a woman's feelings. He wasn't about to start now, even though it was mighty tempting. He refused to think about how he'd been playing along with Marcus Brennan without considering Cassie's feelings.

Marsha seemed determined to fix his foul mood. She came around the bar and positioned herself right by him, her arm going around his neck. "C'mon, Cal. For old time's sake. No harm in hanging out, right?"

Cal looked over at her, wishing he could wipe the image of Cassie's hurt out of his mind. "We've had this conversation before," he told Marsha, whispering so only she would hear. "I don't want to hurt you."

"Don't worry about me," Marsha said, moving in for the kill. "I'm a big girl, you know."

Cal took her hands away, holding her wrists in the air. "I can't do this, Marsha. I need you to understand."

Her sweetness turned to a chilly petulance. "She's gonna walk right over you, all over again, Cal. Are you too stupid to see that?"

"No, I can see things just fine," he said, getting up, his hands still on Marsha's arms. "And that's why I'm not going to call it quits. Not yet, anyway."

He turned just as the front door banged open.

And saw a tall blonde woman standing there.

Cassie.

CHAPTER EIGHT

WHAT HAD SHE BEEN THINKING, coming to this place to look for Cal during the late night honky-tonk's busiest time? It was crowded with workers lingering after a long day, along with the late night drunks who'd go home and sleep off their hangovers.

But *she'd* known instinctively that she'd find him here. The half-dozen calls she'd made to his phone had gone to voice mail. He'd turned off his phone because he was probably fed up with her temper tantrums and mood swings. And that might be the reason he'd decided to seek comfort with his old friend Marsha.

Cassie had second thoughts after her father had called out for Cal over the last hour. Marcus had told her she and Cal deserved a second chance, that he was sorry he had come between them. After finally calming him down with a promise to go and find Cal, she'd decided having Cal around might be best for now, for her father's sake, at least. If Marcus wanted to think he could bring them back together, she couldn't stop him.

But she'd have to steer clear of Cal.

And she'd have to dig a little deeper into what had happened since she'd been gone.

What else was her father sorry for? Because she was pretty sure there was still a lot she wasn't aware of, things that had happened right under her nose.

Should she ask Cal if he knew the whole story?

Or should she let him do his job and leave it at that?

Marcus seemed to rely on Cal more than he'd ever relied on her. He wanted Cal back so he could manipulate both of them. That thought rankled her all over again, especially after seeing Cal with Marsha for the second time that day. So instead of asking Cal to come back to the house, she was once again trying to run away.

Cassie was halfway to her car when she heard Cal calling her name.

"Cassie, hey, wait a minute."

She ignored him, wishing she'd stayed at home. But the memory of the nurse's words forced her to stay calm.

"He's asking for Cal, Miss Cassie," she'd said. "And Cal's not answering his page. I don't know what to do. He's pretty agitated. I can give him a sedative, but I just wanted you to know."

Cassie tried calming her father. But to no avail.

"No, Cassie. You have to go after him. You have to go talk to him, make him stay. You and that man need to get married. It's the only way."

Could she possibly run Camellia Plantation without Cal's help? Could she keep things going after her father was gone and Cal had retreated to his own land? She wasn't so sure she could, but she knew she'd give it everything in her power.

But coward that she was, she'd promised Marcus she'd find Cal. Because she was angry with both of them and she was torn between duty and that anger—and the deep need to please her father? And maybe because she was still itching for a fight with Cal, to clear the air between them once and for all. Seeing him with

Marsha made her want to lash out against all the old hurts and pains.

Having proved that theory, she could now leave. Her daddy couldn't play with their lives anymore, no matter how it would hurt her to see hatred in his eyes again.

She'd started her own business and she'd worked hard to build her name and her fashion line. Surely, she could learn how to run a vast plantation.

"Cassie!"

Okay, Cal sounded angry, too. Good.

She opened the door of the convertible and got in.

But he was right there, his hand on the passenger door. And since the top was down, she couldn't escape.

"What?"

"Did you follow me?"

"Of course not. But I did come looking for you because your phone is off and my father is asking for you again. How's Marsha?"

He hurried around the car and got in. "Drive," he said, his tone commanding.

"We can talk back at the house," she retorted to counteract that tone.

"We need to clear the air," he replied, fastening his seat belt. "Let's do it away from the house."

"I don't know about that." She waited. When he didn't listen, she said, "I told him I'd find you. Now I have. I wanted us to start over since I've had time to cool off. I'm just having a hard time with all of this. You and Marsha and my daddy…and of course, the wedding request." Shrugging, she said, "Daddy's probably asleep now though. Sharon gave him something to settle him down."

"But you came to find me anyway?"

"Yeah. I thought the night air would clear my head. Another dumb assumption."

"Well, you're here now and I'm glad. I'm not getting out so you might as well crank this fancy machine and clear this parking lot before Marsha comes out and tries to get in the mix."

"Well, she's always been in love with you. So…"

"So you had to come here to make sure of that? Your timing is lousy."

She shot him a frown. "Did I not just see you with Marsha yet again?"

He leaned across the bucket seats, his eyes shimmering like smoking coals on a slow burning fire. "Drive the car, Cassie. I'll come back and get my truck later. It'll give us a chance to get this all out in the open."

Cassie debated her options. She really didn't want to get into a catfight with Marsha Reynolds. And even though she was spoiling for a fight, she really couldn't bear any more lame explanations from Cal. But she did need some fresh air. "What about my father?"

Cal pulled out his cell. "Sharon, it's Cal. Cassie's with me. How's the old man?" He waited, his glance skimming over Cassie. "Okay. I'll tell her."

He hung up. "He's asleep. We've got some time, so drive."

"Better fasten your seat belt," she said, daring Cal to ignore that suggestion.

He did, his eyes on her, his long legs almost touching the dashboard.

She cranked the car and spewed rocks all the way out of the parking lot and she didn't let up on the gas, even when they were out on a long winding country road that would take them to nowhere.

CAL LET HER BLOW OFF a little steam but pitied this sweet little convertible. She just might burn up the engine. After she'd taken a curve with a bit too much gusto, he reached out a hand. "Pull over near the river bridge."

"What?" She shrugged then shifted gears.

"Stop up ahead," he shouted, his mouth near her ear.

She shot him another frown then slowed the car near the little roadside park by the Flint River. But she slid the car off the road and got a little too up-close and personal with the cement picnic table.

Cal held to his seat. "Are you trying to kill me?"

"The thought did cross my mind."

He got out of the still steaming car and walked around to help her. But she was already out, her jeans tight and crisp against her long legs, her button-up blue blouse tidy and stitched to perfection. Her hair, usually sleek and tamed, was wild and windblown. And so was the expression in her eyes.

They stood there for a few seconds, the river gurgling nearby while the hot car ticked and clicked in exhaustion. The night air was crisp and chilly but the full moon hovering in the sky heaved a beam of warmth.

He looked down at the wire grass growing into the trees that lined the high riverbank. Longleaf pines towered over needle palms, giving this area a lushness that only reminded Cal of her. The wind hissed and moaned, causing the pines to sway and shimmer.

Cal let the memories merge with the heated discussions they'd had over the last few hours. His gut ached with longing but his heart hurt with bitterness. "I wanted to leave," he finally said. "I should have kept going when I left the house. I stopped at the Pig and Plow Bar to—"

"Tell Marsha goodbye?"

She pushed at her luscious hair then stalked toward the dark water that flowed beyond the hilly bluff.

Telling himself not to follow her, he stomped after her.

"Cassie, Marsha and I, we aren't...anything. How many times do I need to say that? We're friends."

She turned to give him a direct stare. "Have you been stringing her along all these years?"

"No." Sweat pooled between his aching shoulder blades. "No. I didn't see her again after I left the first time, and when I came back, I tried to avoid her. But that's kind of hard to do in a small town. Me and some of the guys wound up in the bar one night and there she was. She owns it now."

"I see she's moved up in the world."

Cal grunted. He'd never understand women and their feuding ways. "What's the deal with you two anyway? Y'all hated each other long before I came along."

Cassie dropped her gaze to her fancy sandals. "It's a long story." She shrugged, the scent of sultry magnolia blossoms all around her. "Marsha resented me for being the daughter of a planter...and I envied her for being courageous and full of attitude."

He laughed at that. "Oh, I think you have a whole lot of attitude yourself, sweetheart." Then he swallowed a mouthful of need. "Marsha would take things to the next level if I indicated I wanted that, but I don't."

"Are you sure?" She headed back to the cement table and sat down on top. "Isn't that what happened to us, Cal? Marsha was all the things I wasn't—sexy, steamy, willing to try anything."

"No, it wasn't like that."

He couldn't deny she was close to the truth. He'd been in love with Cassie, but he'd also been terrified of a future with her. What did he have to give her, anyway? Marsha was more on his level, at least. With Cassie, he'd always been way out of his league. And after her formidable father had voiced all of Cal's flaws and blamed Cal for his own woes, Cal had believed the worst. He'd never be good enough to have Cassandra Brennan.

She shook her head. "I think maybe you only wanted me because I was some sort of trophy, but I know I was hard to understand. Marsha loved you and she was available. Maybe y'all should have married and had a real baby."

"I didn't want to marry Marsha."

The heavy words, slung low and with a soft rage, caught her attention. She shifted and glanced away, confusion shattering her pretty face. "But now, you think you want to marry me. Or rather be forced to marry me so you can take over Camellia. Ridiculous."

"Yes, it is ridiculous," he said, bobbing his head. "Your daddy got this in his head and he won't let go of it."

"And why is it so important that we marry each other?"

Cal wished he could explain, wished Marcus had explained. "He thinks… He believes I'll take care of you…after he's gone. He wants me to always be here with you. And he wants to keep his legacy intact, I think."

"I don't know if I can live on that plantation anymore," she said, her breath hissing through the words. "I will fight to save it, but I have to go back to Atlanta one day. We're not the same, Cal. I'm not the same. I won't be forced into this because of guilt."

"I tried to tell him that."

"I'll just reckon you did."

"Look, you can believe whatever you want to believe. I don't care anymore. But you came to that bar looking for a fight. I'm not going to fight with you. I've told you the truth. Your daddy told you what he wanted from both of us. I don't like the idea any more than you do. And we don't have to honor his request."

She frowned at him again, the moonlight highlighting the golden-white glints in her hair. "No, we don't, no matter what the will says. But if I don't agree, this'll be one more mark against me when my father dies. How am I supposed to live with that?"

How am I supposed to live without you? he wanted to shout.

"I can't answer that." He sat down beside her. "There's a lot I don't know. Your father is a mysterious man." Deciding he might as well go the distance, he said, "I think he's holding back a lot. And I don't know if we can ever figure out the truth." But he wouldn't dare open that can of worms by speculating with her about what he now knew.

"I remind him of that time, all that pain. He can't even look at me."

Cal got up and stood in front of her. "You do look a lot like your mother. I think he was just heartbroken and didn't know how to reach out to you."

"So he's trying now, by forcing us into this archaic arranged marriage?"

"He's trying to show you in the only way he knows how that he cares about you. The man does have this old-fashioned notion that someone needs to look after you."

She stood just inches from him. "But you and I both know that's not true. I've been taking care of myself for a long time now." She held her hands together. "And I'll take care of Camellia Plantation, too."

"Yep." He let his gaze take its time going over her face. "Anyone can see that you're capable."

She stepped around him. "It's late and I've got a lot to do tomorrow. We should get back. I just… I wanted to tell you I'm sorry for overreacting to everything. I've behaved badly."

Cal should have let it go at that but he didn't. Instead, he tugged her close. Too close. "Can we call a truce, Cassie? The past is over but for now your daddy needs us, for whatever reason. He has his own reasons, but my only agenda is to keep the land going so you won't lose your home. You have to remember that about me. I'm a farmer. I can't watch that place go on the auction block."

She looked surprised and then hopeful. "You're willing to stay, after all that's happened?"

"Yes." He held her there, forcing her to face him. "If I leave you with this and it all goes bad, I'll blame myself even more."

Shock echoed through her expression. "Will it come to that?"

"I hope not. But if I walk away now, it could." He touched a hand to her chin. "And make no mistake, I was thinking about doing just that when I left earlier."

"What changed your mind?"

"What else, sweetheart? You."

He leaned in and tugged her into his arms. Then he kissed her, a soft grazing that left him wanting more. But his words were a lie all the same. "I want a truce, Cassie. Nothing more. No more fighting, no more accusing. No more talk of Marsha or marriage. Let me help you."

She drew back, her lips swollen and parted. "What if he insists?"

"We'll figure something out." Cal let her go, his hands dropping as he forced himself to take a step back. "If I ever marry you, it'll be on my terms, not his."

"And what are those terms, Cal?"

He lifted a finger to her hair, touched a sleek curl. "I want you to come to me willingly. I'll marry you the day *you* tell *me* you want to marry me."

Then he walked back to the car, the slamming of the door jarring his soul like a gavel hitting wood.

Marcus Brennan wasn't the only one dying here.

CHAPTER NINE

CAL'S CELL PHONE BUZZED at eight-fifteen the next morning. He'd been up since five, doing a check on the delicate budding peanut crop, and worried since—according to the local weather report—a storm was coming. This field had been planted in late April, after the last of the winter frost. A month later now, what had once been seed kernels planted from last year's crop had become rows and rows of plants that would soon flower and produce the legumes.

Cal nodded to the team of men who worked the crops each day. They were all walking the long rows, doing their own survey. Because they knew this year's peanut crop needed to be a moneymaker. Jack Howard, his right-hand man, scowled. Jack always scowled. He resented Cal being the boss and questioned everything Cal tried to do around here. He sure wasn't happy to see that Cal had decided to stay on as foreman, thus making him a right-hand man again.

Ignoring Jack, Cal spoke into his phone. "Hello."

"I want to meet with you as soon as possible. Where are you now?"

Cassie. Her voice dripped culture and self-assurance.

"And good morning to you, too, Princess."

"Don't call me that. I'll be waiting at your house, in your office."

"You can't get in. The door's locked."

"Not anymore."

Apparently she was feeling better this morning. And back in full diva mode after their talk last night. Or rather their *truce*. And what a truce. After he'd kissed her again last night, Cal wondered if he'd truly lost his mind. He wasn't sure yet how he was supposed to maintain his cool and keep his job when all he wanted was to be with Cassie Brennan.

Maybe he should have kept right on going when he'd had the chance.

Tossing his phone in the truck seat, Cal motioned to one of the workers. "Looking good." He again went over the instructions on what to expect with strip-tillage, a method he was implementing that would help prevent erosion and conserve moisture.

"Ain't gonna work," Jack said, spitting into the dirt. "Just wasting our time."

"We're not wasting anything," Cal said, impatient to get on with things. "Just hang in there with me and you'll see."

"Right." Jack turned and headed for his truck. "If you'd just make up your mind if you're staying or going, we'd all get along a lot better."

Old farmers didn't like new ideas. Cal instructed the rest of them on taking care of a few odd jobs for now. Later, he'd ride the cotton patch and check on the soybeans and corn. And have another talk with Jack Howard. Maybe remind Jack that things had been pretty bad before Marcus had brought Cal in.

Everything about farming depended on the weather first and a good yield second. He wanted good weather and a healthy yield. But he also needed people he could trust to do their jobs.

The workers nodded and went about their chores.

They couldn't afford to stand around doing nothing. And they all knew it. He'd already had to let three people go.

Cal really didn't have time to explain the ins and outs of running a plantation to Cassie. But he didn't own the place. Her daddy did. But it was up to Cal to be the middleman, to show Cassie what she needed to know in order to convince her that this place could be salvaged. Even if their relationship couldn't be.

He revved up the big white Chevy and gunned it, spinning dirt as he headed up the clay land between the rows and rows of flowering peanuts. The yellow flowers would fall off while the tender pegs shooting out into the earth would grow and turn into peanuts by the end of the summer.

Cal passed the big pond where he and Cassie had often gone fishing and swimming. Memories of her were everywhere on this plantation. That had been tough at first, coming back to work here. Falling back into the daily routine had been hard physically, but re-membering Cassie had been even worse, mentally.

And each time he thought about Marcus wanting him to marry her, and how she'd reacted to that, his heart did a little roll and tumble. They'd have to find a way to work around that request.

But how did he get past the memories? It looked like those memories wouldn't let up now. He had the real thing right here, and she obviously hadn't forgiven him. Last night, he'd wanted to tell her everything, but thankfully common sense had stopped him. Then later, he'd seen her standing out there on the upstairs porch, looking down on the moonlit garden.

And he'd wanted so badly to go to her.

Stupid. He'd have to avoid the garden at night.

And the house during the day.

He pulled up to the little side yard behind the stark white cottage, wondering if she'd found a key or just kicked in the door with her stilettos. Since the door looked intact and the screen was still on, he braced himself for her high heels.

Cassie had always looked good in high heels.

But he was a bit disappointed and appreciative when he saw she'd dressed sensibly today. Jeans and a T-shirt with a cute pair of flat sandals. Well, she still looked great. Even if her blue eyes shot sparks of attitude toward him.

"That was quick," she said, her hands on her hips.

"You rang, madame?"

"Very funny."

Her hair was pulled back in a thick short ponytail, but her eyes, as vivid and blue as ever, looked tired. He had to wonder if she'd tossed and turned all night right along with him. And because he didn't need to be thinking such thoughts, he headed to the refrigerator and found a soda.

"Want anything?"

"No," she said, her gaze moving over the combination kitchen and den. "This place hasn't changed much."

Cal glanced around at the dark paneling and the old linoleum flooring. "You don't approve of my decorating skills?"

"I didn't say that. But some new curtains wouldn't hurt."

He saluted her with his drink. "I'll put that on the top of my to-do list."

She walked over to the sink and turned to stare at him. "I need to know how bad it is, Cal. Are we going to lose Camellia?"

Deciding the small talk was officially over, Cal drained his can of soda. "Not if I can help it."

"What exactly happened?"

He motioned to one of the other rooms. "I have an office in here. C'mon in."

She hesitated at first. "That used to be your bedroom."

"I have the master now, darlin'. You're welcome to give me decorating tips in there, too."

Her carefully controlled expression collapsed into a blush. "I suppose you do need some tips, but bedrooms aren't my thing."

Cal angled his head. "Cassie, I won't bite and I don't plan on making any moves on you. I just want to show you the records. I have a laptop and I have files in the desk drawer. I'll pull everything up and leave you to go over it."

"What if I have questions?"

"I'll try to answer them, but I got new crops coming in and men waiting to get on with their work."

She followed him into the tiny bedroom he'd turned into an office. It was cluttered with papers and old mail.

"No wonder no one knows what's going on around here."

"I've got it under control." He glanced around. "In spite of how this might look."

"Maybe I can straighten things as I go."

"No. Don't move any of my paperwork."

She shot him a frustrated look. "You must have forgotten I'm a neat-freak."

"I haven't forgotten anything."

Their gazes held for a ticking moment then Cassie turned toward the computer. "Let's get busy so you can get back to the crops."

Cal would rather be anywhere else than caught in this little room with Cassie and her magnolia-scented perfume and his own tormenting memories. But she needed to hear this, so she could understand firsthand that he'd been fighting an uphill battle. He pulled up two battered folding chairs. "Have a seat. I'll start at the beginning."

AN HOUR LATER, CASSIE sat back in her chair and pushed at her hair. "I can't believe this."

"You've seen the proof," Cal said. He rubbed his eyes then stretched his neck muscles. "Your daddy has been sick for a long time. But he started letting things go around here after your mother died and you went away. He's fired more people than he's hired. I had to do a lot of sweet-talking just to find qualified people to help me. I'm trying to do as much as I can, but we're running out of time and money. And some of the workers still want to do things the old-fashioned way. It's an uphill battle." He looked down at the desk then back at her, the hesitation evident on his face. "This year's crop is important. We need a positive yield. No room for mistakes."

"What are you not telling me?"

Would she ever trust him again?

"You know everything now. There are things that *he* needs to say to you, Cassie. Things that don't involve me anymore. I can't get in the middle of that. I'm here to keep the place going so you don't lose all of your inheritance."

"You mean, so *you* won't lose my inheritance, don't you? If you and I were to get married."

Cal leaned close, so close she sat back and waited for him to speak, her breath stabbing against her ribs.

"Listen to me and listen good. Your daddy came up with that scenario all by himself. I don't care about the inheritance."

"I don't care about the inheritance, either," she said, biting back tears of regret and frustration. "I care about him and…my home. I should have been here. Someone should have told me."

"He didn't want you to know. He didn't even realize he'd let things slide until it was almost too late. It took a lot of pride for him to come to me for help. But he did it for the same reason I agreed to help. He did it for you."

Cassie's heart hurt for her father and for her home. For the first time, she felt a deep appreciation for what Cal had been forced into. But she still didn't believe he'd come back to Camellia just for her sake.

Her feelings softening just a little bit, she asked, "So you don't care about this crazy arranged marriage and all that implies? I get that you love to farm and that maybe you truly wanted to help my father, but I don't understand how you could walk away from your own land to work for him again. Nobody is that noble."

His eyes widened in disbelief. "After seeing all of this, after what I just told you, you still have to question my motives?"

"Yes, I do." She got up to pace around the room so she could put some distance between them. "I can accept that I have some responsibility in allowing this to happen. Pride kept me away and I'm regretting that now. But you…you don't have anything at stake here. You're free to go."

"Are you firing me after all?"

"No."

She stopped to think about that. She could easily

dismiss him and send him packing, and make it stick this time. But he'd organized the various holdings and the extensive investment accounts and he'd shown her the bottom line on what few assets her father had left. This place was bleeding money and Cal was holding his finger on the wound. She needed him to finish the job he'd started. And maybe he realized that.

She voiced her thoughts. "I can't afford to let you go now. I need you to continue working here until I can figure out what to do. You seem to be doing the best you can."

"Thanks for that rousing endorsement." He got up and stalked to the kitchen. "If we're done, I really need to get back at it. I'm trying some new techniques and the natives are restless. I have to keep pushing them to give things a try. Farming has changed since you lived here. But the risks are the same."

Cassie followed him into the kitchen, thinking the risks still applied to her being here, too. Had Cal taken the same kind of risk? She noticed the dark lines of fatigue around his granite-blue eyes and the way he fidgeted and paced—the same as she was doing. Cal had always been the calm one while she'd been the needy wild child. Why did he seem nervous, almost apprehensive, around her now? In spite of being grateful for the way he'd stepped in to take charge, Cassie couldn't help but wonder about all the secrets. He'd kept her father's stipulations a secret. What else could he be hiding?

"We're done for now with the business side of this problem. But I still get the feeling that I'm not hearing everything from you. Why can't you just be up front with me?"

He hit a hand on the counter. "Because it's complicated. I didn't bring up the marriage thing because

I hoped your old man would forget about it. It didn't matter if you never knew—no harm done. I can't explain everything, because I don't even know everything. I've had to piece this together over months and months, Cassie. Your old man isn't the most forthcoming person in the world."

Cassie could agree to that, at least. Growing up, she'd seen her parents in fight after fight because her father refused to open up and communicate with her mother. Eugenia often times seemed lost and withdrawn after those arguments. Their last fight had been horrible. Shouting and glass-breaking, footsteps running down the stairs and then, her father calling after her mother to come back.

That day, Eugenia hadn't come back. She'd gone straight to the stables and grabbed Heathcliff's reins from Cal. Cal had run after her mother, trying to stop her. But no one could stop what happened next.

Cassie closed her eyes to the memory of her mother being thrown from Cassie's horse. Closed her mind to the sight of her daddy running down the stairs and out the front door to jump the pasture fence and grab his wife up in his arms, tears rolling down his face.

"Cassie?"

She turned to find Cal standing too close, his gaze full of questions. "What?"

"Are you all right?"

She shook her head. "Too many memories and now, too many demands. But you're right about my father. He's not easy to deal with. And he's so sick now, Cal. So sick. Half of what he says to me doesn't even make any sense. So I can understand why you dismissed his deathbed wish for us to be married."

"I hear that," Cal said, some of the tension draining

out of his expression. "He's made other demands, some of them just plain crazy."

"What kind of demands?"

He shook his head. "He thinks he has to convince you to stay here. He's desperate, Cassie."

"But you're not. Not desperate enough to marry me, right?"

She said it with a tight smile, but in her heart in that secret place where she kept her dreams, she couldn't help but wonder what it would be like to be married to Cal.

Only, she wouldn't force that on him, even if it meant saving her home.

His eyes went black-blue, his gaze moving over her face to settle on her lips. "I told you, if we were to ever get married, it would be on my terms, not his. Or maybe I should say, on our terms. The kind of terms that bind a man and a woman forever."

Cassie's heart lurched and shifted. "Is that what this is all about? Whether I'll stay or not? Are you both testing me? I should have been here sooner, but I was afraid and angry and I'm not proud of my actions. I don't have any idea how long I'll be here and I don't dare leave, but I can't deal with his death on my head, too."

"What do you mean, too?"

She didn't want to get into this, not with Cal. Not with anyone. But what did it matter now? "I always thought I had something to do with their fight that day. That my mother was defending me when she ran out of the house." She slumped toward the counter, her arms draped across her stomach. "I guess I'll never know the truth."

Cal was right there, his hands on her arms, a look of concern on his face. "I think you're wrong about that."

"And how would you know?" she asked, the heat from his touch reminding her that she might be playing with fire.

His expression became evasive and closed. "I don't know for sure. But he talks about things. Things that happened a long time ago. I don't know if he's dreaming or remembering or just imagining things."

A current hummed through Cassie's system. Would her father be able to tell her the truth? "What sort of things?"

Cal shrugged then let go, leaving a chill around her. "You know, you as a little girl. Your mother. Sometimes, he thinks she's still alive and you're still in high school." He looked out the window. "And sometimes he thinks she's young and he gets jealous about things. He gets kind of emotional when he's like that."

Cassie thought about her time with Marcus early this morning. He'd been sleeping so she hadn't dared bother him. Afraid he'd insist on the marriage again, she'd sat there, watching him, remembering him as a good father in many ways. But there had always been a part of Marcus Brennan that no one else could touch. Not even her mother. Certainly not his only daughter. She'd always assumed that he loved his family in his own brooding way. He'd showered them with gifts and material things. But none of that mattered now.

"He keeps thinking I'm my mother. It's heartbreaking."

"You look a lot like her. She was a beautiful woman. I can understand that kind of jealousy."

Cassie glanced up to find Cal's eyes on her. Stammering, the awareness of his words washing over her, she said, "Yes, she was beautiful. Kind and gracious and always so understanding. She was my champion."

She stopped, inhaled a breath for courage. "She always understood about things. About you and me."

The expression in his dark eyes shattered her. The longing, the need she'd felt for so long, was mirrored in there in the depths of his gaze. A new realization dawned. Cal was here because her family had become his family. He wasn't alone, working here. But this was too raw, too painful. She turned away.

He pulled her back.

"Cal—don't."

"What happened with us?" he asked, keeping her at arm's length while his eyes captivated her. "We had it all, Cassie. We loved each other. What happened?"

She pulled away, her emotions cresting on a shuddering wave. "You know what happened. My parents had that terrible fight and my mother died. Daddy was out of his mind with grief when he caught you and me together. He told you to leave." She stopped, closed her eyes. "But you came back for me. I'll never forget that. You held me and told me—"

"That I'd never leave you again," he finished, the words raw with emotion.

She opened her eyes, his nearness triggering both affection and rage. "But I saw you with Marsha. She had me believing the worst—that you loved her, that you took money from my father. That she was carrying your child." She shook her head. "It was the final blow, after losing my mother and somehow alienating my father."

"She lied," Cal said, the words grinding and bitter. "We all lied."

That was like cold water hitting her. It brought her back to the here and now. "And you're still lying."

He lowered his gaze, but his expression was once again guarded and mysterious. "I'm not, not anymore."

"Yes, you are. You're still keeping something from me. I can see it in your eyes, Cal." She started toward the door. "I'll do whatever I can to save my home, but I left here to get away from the lies and the secrets. Don't make me have to live through that again. I won't survive any more betrayals."

"Cassie—"

But she was out the door, hurrying across the yard, the need to get away from him and her memories pushing her until she was running. She'd deal with the unpaid bills and the outstanding bank loans, but she couldn't deal with Cal and how he made her feel. Not when the memory of him holding her in his arms again was still so fresh and raw. And not when her own feelings were brimming over like hot, boiling water.

She wouldn't be fooled twice. And certainly not by Cal Collins.

CHAPTER TEN

THE NEXT FEW DAYS BECAME routine for Cassie. Today, after sitting with her father and helping him eat his lunch, Cassie tried to reach the two doctors listed on his medical sheet but to no avail. She left messages for them to return her calls then again went over his medications with one of the nurses who kept a steady shift around him.

Sharon Clark was a few years older than Cassie and married to a trucker. They'd never had children so Sharon liked having something to keep her busy while her husband traveled. She seemed to care about her patients and she put Cassie at ease right away.

"Have you talked to his doctors before now?" Sharon asked while they sat in the kitchen sipping on tea. Teresa was in the laundry room down the hall washing sheets.

"I had a long discussion with his specialist in Macon before I came down from Atlanta," Cassie replied. "And I have calls in to the list of doctors the night nurse gave me. My father chose to go to a hospital in Macon, rather than come up to Emory in Atlanta and, probably per my father's request, the specialist didn't even tell me he'd suffered a recent heart attack. I wonder if I might have had better treatment at Emory."

Sharon shook her head. "Your daddy waited too late for better treatment, honey. Any kind of surgery or treatment doesn't do a bit of good if you don't listen to the doctors and take care of yourself."

"And he refused to let them call me," Cassie said, the depths of the tear in their relationship swallowing her up in pain. "You must think I'm the worst daughter in the world."

Sharon patted Cassie's hand. "You'd be surprised what I've seen and heard working as a private nurse all these years. Some people are too stubborn for their own good. Your daddy ranks right up there with the best of them. So don't fret. You tried to keep in touch. But the man seemed to want to be all alone."

"Yes, he did want to be alone. I'm surprised he didn't fire everyone on this plantation."

"I'm sure he's tried," Sharon said on a low chuckle. "Lord love him, he's a tough old bird."

"How long does he have, Sharon?"

The nurse glanced up, shock on her face. "Didn't the doctors tell you that?"

"Dr. Sherwood said months maybe."

Sharon looked down at the papers in front of them. "Make that weeks now, honey."

A great ripping pain crested in Cassie's chest and formed a hard lump in her throat. She couldn't believe it had come to this. What if her father died without ever telling her what she'd done to make him hate her so much? They had to reconcile everything, and soon. She couldn't bear to think about anything else.

"I need to talk to our family doctor, too. I'm surprised he hasn't been by to see Daddy since I've been home."

Sharon checked the records. "Dr. Hendricks?"

Confused, Cassie shook her head. "No. I don't know

him. Has my father changed doctors? We always went to Dr. John Anton. He was a family friend."

"Oh, I remember him." Sharon gave Cassie a bewildered stare. "He died about eight years ago, Cassie."

"Died? Dr. Anton?" Cassie put her head in her hands. Yet another surprise. Apparently, Teresa had not been thorough in trying to keep Cassie up-to-date on everything. Or had her father forbidden everyone to talk about this, too? "Oh, I'm so sorry to hear that. He was always so gentle and sweet when I'd go in to see him. He treated me for scrapes and bruises, bad colds, the measles, everything. He took care of my parents, too. He and his wife were like part of the family."

"Well, he was a good man. But he died a tragic death. I read about it in the *Albany Herald*. A fishing accident. Right here in that big pond on the back of the property."

"What?" Cassie's shock made her pulse echo inside her head. Remembering the tiny camp house near the water, she thought about how she and Cal had spent countless hours down at the pond. Hours of being together as much as possible. And the Antons had visited there many times to fish and hunt or attend cookouts and parties. "How did it happen?"

Teresa came hurrying toward them. "Sharon, maybe you'd better go check on Mr. Brennan."

Sharon got up then glanced back at Cassie. "You have any more questions, just let me know. And call Dr. Hendricks."

Cassie tried to comprehend that the doctor who'd delivered her and treated her up until the day she'd left had died on their property. Dr. Anton had been like a favorite uncle to her. He'd always made her laugh, no matter the circumstances. And he'd been just as upset by her mother's death as the rest of them.

"That's horrible, about Dr. Anton." She glanced up at Teresa. "What happened at our pond, Teresa?"

"Boating accident," Teresa said, turning to wash some fresh turnips so she could prepare them for dinner.

"Was he alone?"

Teresa ran water over the crisp greens from the garden.

"Teresa?"

The water shut off with a sharp hiss. Teresa turned and leaned back on the sink. "No, he wasn't alone, Cassie. Your daddy was with him."

"What?" She stared up at Teresa. "That's horrible. Daddy must have been devastated." Cassie thought about asking her father how Dr. Anton had died, but she didn't want to upset him. If Marcus had been there, he would have done everything in his power to save his friend. "I'm sure he tried to help Dr. Anton."

Teresa pressed her work-roughened hands down on the counter. "He said he tried to save him. It was another one of those awful times. Just awful." She shrugged. "His wife moved to Tallahassee. Last I heard, she'd remarried."

"Do you have a phone number or address for her?" Cassie asked. "I'd like to get in touch with her and give her my condolences. I hate that I didn't know."

"It happened so quickly," Teresa said, her head lowered. "I guess we were all in shock. I never thought to call you. She didn't leave any forwarding information. I think she wanted to get as far away from here as possible."

Teresa picked up a basket and went back into the laundry room.

Cassie sat there, surprise at this latest revelation numbing her. She'd seen the hesitation on Teresa's face. Had she deliberately kept this from Cassie for some reason? Why was everyone around here being so tight-lipped about everything?

Maybe because you never bothered to come home when all of this happened. You weren't a part of things anymore, so no one informed you on the everyday events around here.

Of course, her father's friend and family doctor drowning on their property wasn't an everyday event. It was a tragic accident. But maybe the people here thought it wouldn't matter to her.

Cassie didn't have a good excuse for turning her back on her father or her home. But she'd had a very good reason by her way of thinking. Her mother was dead and her father had stopped loving her. Cal had stopped loving her, too. Or so she believed.

Had she been wrong on both accounts?

Had she been wrong to stay away out of pride?

But it did matter to her now. Marcus was filled with guilt and Cal was just as bitter as her father. They'd both hidden things from her. And she'd hidden her heart from them.

Her phone buzzed, pulling her out of the fog swirling around her confused thoughts.

Ned again.

Cassie thought about not answering but maybe she needed to remind her ex-fiancé that they were through. She'd tried hiding away and staying silent. Those tactics hadn't worked with her father and they probably wouldn't work with Ned, either. Unlike her father, how-

ever, Ned would keep at it. He was known for his te-
nacity.

"Hello."

"Cassie, honey, why haven't you returned any of my
messages? I've been sick with worry."

Cassie sank back in her chair, her bones aching with
a soul-weary fatigue while she pictured Ned sitting at
his desk with his expensive loafers propped against the
desk pad. "Ned, I've been busy. And there's nothing
more to discuss. We can't go back to the way we were.
Neither of us was happy."

"But you know I still love you. We can figure this
out, I promise."

"You've promised that before. And I promised you
things I couldn't deliver." She closed her eyes, weary
from all the broken promises from people she cared
about. She'd thought she loved Ned, but now she could
see she just needed someone to cling to, someone to
offer her hope. Her feelings for Ned could never match
real love. The image of Cal pulling her into his arms
slipped through her mind. "We both know it was over
a long time ago."

"Look, we just hit a bump in the road. If you let me
come down there…"

Cassie stopped, her heart bouncing off beat. Only
Rae and a few trusted members of her staff knew where
she was. The last thing she needed was Ned here in the
already volatile mix. "You don't need to do anything,
Ned."

"I've always wanted to see the place where you grew
up."

"No, please, don't make a trip down here," she said,
a rush of breath leaving her body. "It's not a good time."

His voice went low. "I want us to be the way we used to be."

"We can't go back," she said. "I'm sorry but it's over."

"Did you ever really love me, Cassie?"

She didn't know how to answer that. "I tried. I thought I did. It's not fair to pretend."

"You and I had a good thing. Maybe after you return—"

"I can't," she said. "I have to go."

Cassie disconnected, a great sadness weighing at her heart. She wished she could have loved Ned the way he wanted her to, but it was over now. And she needed to remind herself of what she'd just told him. *You can't go back.*

She might be home again, but she couldn't go back to being the meek, quiet, good girl everyone had wanted her to be.

Those days were over.

Pulling up Rae's number, she waited for her assistant to answer. Rae immediately asked about her father. "No—no changes. He's still very sick. Yes, I'm okay. Listen, has Ned been around asking about me?"

"No," Rae said, her tone low. "I haven't seen him or heard from him since y'all broke up. And I haven't told a soul where you are. The whole staff understands it's on a need-to-know basis."

"Okay, good. He's been calling and I finally talked to him today. He hinted that he wanted to come down here."

"Cassie, I can assure you, he didn't get any information from me. As far as I know, he hasn't been by the office in weeks."

"Good. Maybe he's just trying to figure things out.

But I didn't tell him anything, either. Please warn the staff for me. I don't want anyone to know where I am. My father deserves his privacy."

"Of course. But Ned was a big part of your life until recently. I'm sure he's just worried."

Cassie pinched two fingers on her nose. "I can't deal with him right now. Besides, if Ned showed up here with Cal, it would probably make matters worse."

She turned to business and spent the next thirty minutes going over notes. "I've sketched a few things but it's hard to find inspiration right now. I have a bleak mindset."

"Use that angst the way you always have," Rae suggested. "You'll find the light inside there somewhere."

Her friend had always had more confidence in Cassie than she did in herself. "Thanks, Rae. You're right. It's spring and I do see colors everywhere. The magnolias are beginning to show their white buds. Think I'll go for a long walk after I sit with Daddy awhile. Maybe I'll head back to the pond."

She didn't tell Rae that she'd just found out a man had died there.

Cal drove up the dirt lane toward home. He made this trip each day, watching the crops for any signs of stress. The corn was over a foot high, but could use another good rain to bring it up. The peanuts were taking hold and looked to be a bumper crop. The soybeans glistened green in the late afternoon sunshine. And the pecan trees in the grove by the pond budded with fresh green tips that would provide hearty nuts for cooks as well as grocery stores and other food service industries.

He loved farming but he always waited for the next setback or disaster. These past few days had held a few.

Now he just had to worry about the weather. Looked like a big spring storm was headed this way.

But right now, he was glad it was the end of the day. Then he caught a glimpse of someone sitting on the old bench by the pond.

Cassie.

How many times had they sat there together…talking, kissing, loving. The memories swirled up into the light dust cloud his Chevy left behind. After all of their heated discussions, he should gun it and get on home. But he didn't. He stopped, pulling off the lane underneath the shade of a towering pecan tree.

Cassie glanced up from her sketch pad and waved to him. But even from a few feet away, Cal could see the apprehension and hesitation on her face. He was interrupting her work.

But then, she'd sure interrupted his.

"Hey," he said as he approached the bench. "You're sketching."

She gave him a wan smile. "I'm trying to get some work done."

"How's it going?"

She shut the big pad with a thud. "Could be better. I did some sketching on my electronic pad, but this scene seems to beg for an old-fashioned sketch pad."

Cal picked up a rock and sent it skipping over the water. "You always did doodle and draw. Teresa told me how you've created your own ready-to-wear designs. She had to explain to me exactly what that meant. I thought all clothes came ready-to-wear."

Cassie laughed. "I used to explain to you about haute couture and designer handbags."

"Yeah. Guess I'll stick to my Levi's and T-shirts."

Then he looked at her. "I'm glad your dream came true. You always knew what you wanted out of life."

"Yes, back then I wanted to be a famous New York fashion designer. You know, runways, shows in Paris and Milan, big spreads in *Vogue*—"

"I take it that's not ready-to-wear."

"No." She twisted her pencil in her hand. "I was bent toward high fashion, but one day a friend looked at one of my designs and said something that changed my way of thinking. She was a voluptuous woman, or as she would tell you, chunky. She said she wished someone would design clothes for real women. And put them in all the stores."

"So your mind started clicking and you got right on that?"

"Not exactly. It took a while to make it happen. It's not a new idea, but a hard one to implement in the right way. I struggled with the concept for a couple of years after I graduated, but I worked in several boutiques learning the whole process until I got it right."

"According to Teresa your designs were picked up by one of the major department stores and a lot of real women liked what you created. I guess your friend got her wish."

"Yes. She's one of my best models. And a great customer."

"And it all started right here. In spite of everything, you were able to follow your dreams. That's something, Cassie."

She didn't say anything but the look she gave him told him she was remembering their time together, same as him. "We both followed our dreams. You always wanted to be a farmer."

"Yep. Some days I wonder if that was wise."

Her smile was indulgent. "You look tired."

"I am." He gazed out over the blue water. "This is one of my favorite spots."

She moved over. "Have a seat."

"Are you sure?"

She shot him a sideways glance. "Yes. I know I've been a pain but I'm still adjusting to you being here."

Cal sank down, the scent of magnolias surrounding him. "Hey, *I'm* still adjusting to you being here, too. Some days, I wonder why I didn't stay on my own place. I was happy there."

"Tell me about your place."

He smiled, glad to be on a safe subject. "It's not as much acreage as Camellia, of course. I started out buying a little farmhouse and the surrounding twenty-five acres. Then I managed to buy the neighboring land and—"

"And before you knew it, you'd finally managed to have your own farm, just like you always talked about."

"Yeah." Except he didn't have her there with him. He often dreamed about Cassie sitting with him on the big front porch of his farmhouse. He renovated the place, always with thoughts of her in mind. Now he was sitting here with her, but they were still worlds apart.

She put down her pad and pencil. "I'm glad for you, Cal. And I'm beginning to understand why you came back here. This place is like home for you."

"Yes." He didn't have to justify that decision. "When I ran into your daddy, I could tell the man was sick. He reeked of whiskey."

"My father, drunk? He never drank before."

"Well, he was drunk that day." He hated telling her that, but she had to understand. "I was shocked that he'd even acknowledged me. But he said he'd been following the articles about me in one of the farm journals. He was impressed with some of my innovations with irrigation and strip-tillage and going green. I try not to let anything go to waste on the land."

Cal stopped, trying to decide how to pick his next words. "He seemed desperate to recapture something he'd lost. He mentioned the good ol' days when Camellia was a thriving plantation. He asked me how I'd feel about coming here for a visit, to offer him some tips. I finally came and stayed a couple of hours. I turned him down when he suggested hiring me."

She watched as two wood ducks glided across the pond. "But you changed your mind. He must have offered you a lot of money."

"No, he didn't." Her father had offered him something more precious than money. "He flat-out told me he couldn't pay me very much. But we worked out the details."

"One of those details being that you'd marry me, of course."

"He threw that in later. He knew better than to dangle that in front of me before I got settled in."

Anger flared hot in her eyes. "But when he did dangle that in front of you, what did you say?"

Cal wouldn't lie on that account. "I said yes, of course."

She tempered the emotions cresting on her face. "I don't like being bartered. But I have to admit, now that I understand the seriousness of the situation, I'm glad you're here."

"Me, too." He'd never thought he'd want to be here again but he loved this land and he knew how to bring it alive. And if he were honest, he'd admit he loved the challenge Marcus had presented—saving this grand old place and maybe having a chance to redeem himself with Cassie, too. Having her here now was both a curse and a blessing. "Your daddy and I have had our differences but I couldn't stand by and watch him lose Camellia."

"I think I'd forgotten how much this place means to me—I'd put it out of my mind."

"I don't blame you for that and I wish I had all the answers."

"But you seem to have a healthy respect for my father. What did it cost you to agree to do this, Cal?"

"I made a deal with the man but I can handle it."

"And that trumps everything. Even your feelings for me?"

Cal got up to pace in front of her, turning to stare down at her. "Don't play that card, Cassie. I don't even know what I'm feeling right now. So much has changed, I might wind up regretting my decision after all."

"But you'll do whatever my father has demanded, in spite of what we had together?"

"No, *because* of what we had together," he said, leaning close. "Marcus isn't holding anything over my head. I decided to see this through because of what you meant to me, because of what we meant to each other. You don't seem to get that."

"Actually I do get it," she replied, her gaze hitting on him, her eyes imploring him. "It's a noble sentiment and I appreciate your efforts. No matter how you feel about me, agreeing to a forced marriage is going way beyond the call of duty."

He wanted to shout it out to her but he couldn't.

"I'd better get on home," Cal finally said. "It doesn't do either of us any good to keep going over this."

"No, I suppose it doesn't." She stood, snapping up

her tote bag. "I tried to talk to my father today, but he wanted to plan our wedding."

Cal whirled at that, seeing the pain in her eyes. "I'm sorry. That's because he wants to go back and change things."

"Don't we all?" Her question echoed over the still water.

"Yes, and maybe that's the real reason I'm here," Cal replied before turning to go.

"Cal?"

He pivoted, waiting.

"Do you know anything about Dr. Anton's death?"

Cal squinted in the glow of the sunset. "No, other than it happened on this pond and your dad was with him."

"They were good friends. My father would have tried to save him. And Dr. Anton was a strong swimmer."

Cal walked back, giving her a serious stare. "And...?"

She glanced at him, some of the fire in her seeming to die down. "Do you know anything else about the day Dr. Anton died?"

"No, other than it was an accident. The boat hit a stump and he was thrown out. Your daddy dove in to help him but it was too late. He hit his head on some rocks."

"Who told you that?"

"Marcus. He was feeling bad one day and I asked him if I should call Dr. Anton. He told me that his friend was dead. And then he told me what happened."

"First my mother, then Dr. Anton." She pushed at her hair again. "I should have been here. But I was afraid of the way he treated me. Now every time I try to get to the truth, you all clam up."

Unable to stop himself, Cal took her tote bag and threw it into the truck's open window. Then he turned back to Cassie, taking her hand in his. "Maybe that's because we're trying to protect you, Cassie."

"Protect me from what?" she asked, the look in her eyes scalding him with the heat of her pain.

"Everything," he said. Then he let go of her hand. "Get in. I'll give you a ride home. That way, we can keep practicing at this truce thing."

CHAPTER ELEVEN

A TRUCE.

Cassie thought back over the past few days, relieved that after telling her they needed to plan the wedding, her father hadn't mentioned his marriage plan again. But he did seem to be slipping away. And after talking to three doctors and calling in yet another specialist, Cassie didn't hold out much hope that her father could be saved.

For the past three days, he'd mostly slept a fitful sleep, his dreams keeping him from a true rest. Maybe he'd forgotten his request that they get married. That would be a blessing.

She and Cal were being civil to each other for her father's sake, but the tension seemed to escalate each time Cal walked into the house. They'd had a quiet ride back to the house the other day, but since then Cal hadn't been around very much. Obviously his idea of a truce was to avoid Cassie all together. It wasn't a bad plan. When she was around him, she wanted to talk to him, hold him, kiss him. Love him.

Did he feel the same way? He's kissed her enough to make her think he stilled cared about her and not just his temporary position on the plantation.

"Cal doesn't come around much," she told Teresa one day after they'd helped Sharon bathe her father.

"Busy time of year," Teresa said by way of an excuse.

"He visits my daddy," she told Teresa while they folded linens in the long, sunny laundry room right off the kitchen. "I think he waits until he knows I'm upstairs or out of the house."

Teresa wasn't a big talker. Her skeptical expression spoke for her. "Cal has a lot on his mind these days. He spent most of this morning working on a broken tiller blade. Jack's been out there with him, trying to figure out what happened."

"Jack?"

"Jack Howard. You might not remember him. He's worked here on and off for the past twelve years. He's a fixture around here. He's been a big help to Cal, considering Cal came in and knocked him down a peg or two."

"I don't remember him, no, but I think I heard Cal mention him a time or two. I'd forgotten how many people it takes to run this place."

"It might look easy, but it takes everything we've got to make it work. Cal's already had to let a couple go to save money."

"You think I'm being foolish, don't you?" Cassie asked, a fluffy white towel held against her stomach. "About Cal?"

"I'm not gonna get in the middle of this," Teresa replied. She pursed her lips then squinted out through the bank of windows that overlooked the backyard. "But I will say...Cal's been real loyal to your father since he came back. And I don't think it's because of any big desire to take over this plantation. Half the time, he talks about his own place. Keeps tabs on the fellows he has renting the land."

"Then what is his motive?" Cassie asked, still skeptical in spite of her feelings. "Nothing is holding him here."

"You can't be serious." Teresa gave her a long direct stare. "Honey, that man is still in love with you. Why else would he even consider coming back here—not to mention going along with that grand marriage plan—after the way your father treated him?"

"And after the way I treated him?"

"You had your reasons. That Marsha Reynolds always was a wild one. She set her sights on Cal the day he showed up in town and she hasn't given up yet."

Cassie thought about that. It still hurt to see Cal with Marsha but she couldn't stop him from being with the other woman. It wasn't her place to criticize. She'd walked away from all of them. And she was determined to not go chasing after him every time he headed toward town. What he did now was his business. She'd have to accept that and be glad for it. They didn't have a future together, no matter what her father might think. No matter how being with Cal made her feel alive again.

"Cal swears he doesn't care about Marsha, except as a friend. That's the oldest line in the book though, isn't it?"

Teresa lifted her head in a nod. "I think he does care, but not in a way that could lead to anything more. He's considerate and a gentleman but he's fought her off more times than I can count."

"Does she come around that often?"

"She used to."

"Before I came home, you mean?"

"Yep, especially when he first came back. I think

she sees the writing on the wall now though. And about time, too."

Cassie placed the stack of towels in a wicker basket. "Marsha and I used to be friends, before Cal and I became an item. Even though she didn't have a lot of opportunities the way I did, we seemed to understand each other. I'd have her over to swim and ride horses on a weekly basis. She always got a kick out of walking around the house, looking at things. But our friendship was beginning to turn sour even before Cal stepped into the picture."

"That's because she never had any of the finer things in life, I reckon."

"No, she didn't. Her daddy was a mean drunk but he left when she was in high school. Her mother worked in that bar day and night. I can't believe Marsha owns it now."

"She seems to enjoy herself," Teresa said, grinning. "And at least she's moved out of that dirty old trailer."

"Where does she live now?"

"A cute little house out on Highway 19. You should go by and visit her."

Cassie frowned at that. "I don't think Marsha would be glad to see me at her door. Too much water under the bridge."

"You might be surprised about that." Teresa fluffed a towel then folded it into a precise square. "If you look around, this town needs some encouragement. You could do a lot while you're here. Beside mope, that is. You have a lot of resources and we need jobs. Marsha has supplied lots of people with work. So cut her some slack."

Teresa took her basket and left Cassie standing in the bright, clean laundry room.

Too surprised to speak out, Cassie stared out the window, marveling at all the undercurrents swirling around in this creaky old house. So she was supposed to save this place and the whole town, as well?

"That's a tall order," she mumbled, deciding she'd mope around a bit more while she tried to decipher Teresa's suggestion.

Without thinking about it, she started walking through the old rooms, her soul absorbing the beauty of her home. Between helping the nurses care for her father, phone calls to doctors and work-related calls to Rae in Atlanta—and trying to avoid Cal—she hadn't stopped to actually look over the house. These old rooms probably needed updating.

The entire front part of the downstairs consisted of the formal living and dining rooms. Each big square room held precious antiques that had been passed down from generation to generation. Cassie couldn't bear the thought of those priceless pieces being sold at auction.

She remembered family dinners during the holidays at the long walnut Chippendale dining table. She thought about how her mother always insisted on a big Christmas tree in the corner of the living room, near the fireplace. She had happy memories here even if this house did make her sad.

And then she had a flash of her parents fighting.

Had she crushed that memory away along with so many others, hoping to never hear those harsh words again?

"You're always gone, Marcus. You stay at the camp, hunting with your buddies, or on the golf course, striking up another land deal. I think John Anton spends more time with you than I do. Why can't you just stay home with me more often?"

"I have responsibilities. You know that, Eugenia. This isn't just a farm. It's a corporation. That hunting camp brings in revenue. Those golf trips bring in more hunters and fishermen and that means more revenue. It's a never-ending job. And you certainly benefit from all of it."

Cassie stared at the fireplace, remembering how she'd stood on the stairway, listening in shock, while her mother cried.

The rush of anguish hit her so hard, she sank down on the pink brocade love seat across from the window. She'd only remembered the worst fight, the one that has come right before her mother's horrible accident. But there had been more. How could she have forgotten that?

She'd always believed her parents had a good, solid marriage. What if she'd been wrong about that? Her therapist had told her she suffered panic attacks because she wasn't facing up to her worst fears. Maybe her worst fear was being back here again. And she had rushed out into the garden the other night just as she used to do when she'd hear her parents fighting.

After Cal came along, she'd counted on finding him out in the garden. He became her rock, her strength. And he was quickly filling that role again.

She got up, her hand touching on the fragile floral drapes pulled back from the floor-to-ceiling windows. Cassie rubbed her fingers over the material, wondering what secrets the aging drapery held inside the intricate fabric. When she looked close, she could see this house had changed. It was showing its age. But worse, it was showing the telltale signs of despair and disgrace that had echoed the tragedy of her mother's death.

We were the ideal family.

We were dysfunctional and messed-up, too.

No wonder she'd needed therapy to get her through college.

In a clear, concise moment, she realized why she'd never been able to take that next step toward finding happiness. There was something buried deep inside her soul that wouldn't allow her to accept love, because she didn't feel worthy of love.

CAL KEPT REMEMBERING his childhood. Before he'd bought his place, he hadn't had a real home since he was a child and even then, he hadn't realized the meaning of home. After his parents divorced, his battered, angry mother went from man to man and place to place. Savannah was the last place she landed. She married her third husband there and finally fell into the high society she'd always craved. But Cal didn't fit in and his stepfather didn't exactly welcome Cal's attitude. After several fights where the stepfather mostly lost and Cal's mother mostly took up for the jerk and not her son, Cal left. Andrea had always been too afraid of not having a man to take care of her, so she didn't stand up to her bullying husband and she didn't take a stand for her son. His mother never looked for him and he never looked back.

Now she was Mrs. Judson Singletary. Andrea Collins Peterson Singletary, to be exact. Husband number three seemed to be a keeper. As long as he held a large share in the town bank, at least. Andrea had gone from a little run-down house out on a swampy side street to a fine Georgian mansion in one of Savannah's oldest neighborhoods.

Cal rarely spoke to his mother now. Too little, too late for them. He'd been searching for a home of his own ever since he'd walked out of the big house that was his mother's pride and joy.

The day he'd walked up the lane to Camellia, after seeing a work notice in the local watering hole, had been a good day. He'd just turned eighteen. He was ready for anything. But something about Camellia Plantation had taken hold in his soul and it had never let go. He'd immediately decided he could live here the rest of his life, even if it meant working the stables. Then he'd fallen in love for the very first time. Life couldn't get any better. The only person he'd ever talked about his mother with had been Cassie. She'd listened and accepted him the way he was, and she'd never judged him. At least she hadn't back then. Now, maybe.

Cal walked through the corn rows now, checking for pests and preparing for a long hot summer of irrigation. On quiet days such as this one, he could almost put those distant memories out of his mind. But the sky was so blue, so radiant and tranquil, he couldn't help but remember summers spent in Savannah.

But here at Camellia, he'd only had that one brief happy summer and then he'd been booted out of his safe, secure place on the vast plantation. And he'd lost Cassie because of his own self-sabotaging mistakes.

Well, now he was back. But he didn't feel safe and secure. Now Cassie's nearness and refusal to accept him had him doubting his own judgment, making him wonder if he had sold out just to get even. He didn't need to be here. He should take some time to get away to his own place. He'd hired a good team to take care of things for as long as needed. He still managed to get up there and check on things once or twice a month.

Now might be a good time to take a quick visit.

He stopped now, his fingers trailing over the silky

green foot-high corn stalks, his skin moist with perspiration. Humidity hung like a thick fog over the air. The hint of rain permeated the sky. The storm that had been hovering all week was finally headed this way. It would hit later tonight probably.

After tangling with that greasy tiller all morning, he needed to regroup. The gentle breeze teased through his hair and cooled down the longings inside his heart. This vast field of green soothed him and calmed him, reminding him that he'd come here with one purpose. He had to keep this old place going. No matter what he felt about Cassie or Marcus or that unbelievable marriage deal, he had to see this through. This time.

He'd left out of fear the last time. Not a fear of Marcus Brennan. Cal didn't care what the old man thought of him. No, back then his fear had been all about Cassie and keeping her happy. Her father had bullied him with threats and revelations and offers of payoffs, but he'd also been bullied by his heart's cowardly beating and her princess status. He couldn't get it out of his mind that he'd been the one who allowed Eugenia Brennan to get on that horse. And he couldn't get it out of his mind *why* he'd let her ride to her death.

In a way, he'd been the real reason everything around here had fallen apart. The princess had lost her crown because of a pauper's love. And a pauper's foolish mistake.

"She's not a princess," he said on a low growl, his voice carrying over the wind. "She's just a woman I can never have."

Maybe he'd returned to Camellia Plantation to prove a point or maybe he'd returned mature and settled and hoping for forgiveness, but it would never be enough for a woman like Cassandra Brennan.

Which left him standing in the middle of vast field of green, wondering why he'd even made the effort.

CASSIE HEARD THE KNOCK echoing through her dreams.

But when she opened her eyes, she realized someone was at her bedroom door.

"Who is it?" she asked, grabbing her robe and pulling it around her.

"It's Sharon, honey. Your father's in a bad way."

Cassie's heart lurched so hard, she had to stop and catch her breath. These past few days had been quiet. Her father had talked to her a little bit, seeming to recognize her. But he hadn't talked about Cal or the marriage deal. A reprieve?

"I'm coming."

She put on her slipper booties and hurried downstairs.

Teresa met her in the hallway. "I've never seen him like this. He's fretting about everything. You want me to get Cal?"

Cassie shook her head. "No. It's okay. I'll go sit with him." If Cal came in, her father might start in on both of them again. And, she didn't need Cal soothing her and comforting her at every turn.

The housekeeper shook her head and went back into the kitchen.

Glancing at the clock, Cassie saw it was half past midnight. She'd only been asleep an hour. Outside, the sky flashed white-hot then shook in an angry fury.

"I'll go in and talk to him," she told Sharon.

Sharon followed her into the dark room.

Cassie took a breath. She dreaded coming into this room but it had become a part of her daily ritual. She checked on her father first thing every morning, helped the nurse with his bath and breakfast and sat with him, then she worked as much as she could, making phone calls and talking to her staff via the internet. They went over designs and discussed problems, making her wish she could have a more hands-on approach with her employees at the factory in Atlanta. Then she stopped to help with lunch and then read to her father for a while.

Those few precious hours had become both the best and worst part of her day.

Sometimes, he'd be fully coherent and talk to her about the farm or the now defunct camp house out on the pond. Sometimes he'd remember taking her fishing or allowing her to ride the crop rows with him. Maybe she could calm him down if she talked about those things with him now. She'd tell him she'd walked through the pastures and field, doing her own appraisal of the crops.

And hoping to run into Cal, if she were honest.

"Hi, Daddy," she said, her tone soothing. "Sharon said you can't sleep. What's the matter?"

"The wedding," Marcus said, his bony hand reaching out toward her. He tried to sit up. "I want to see the wedding."

"What wedding?" Cassie wouldn't dare ask if he might be talking about Cal and her. Maybe his own wedding to her mother?

"Gennie. Same dress. Wear that dress."

"Daddy, what are you talking about?"

He gave her an open-eyed look. "You can wear your mother's wedding dress when you marry Cal."

A little gasp escaped between Cassie's lips. He hadn't forgotten. A vision of her mother all in white caused her to turn sick to her stomach with grief.

"Just rest," she told him, hoping to distract him. "We'll talk about that later."

"No, now," he said, grabbing her arm. "Now, Cassandra. You and Cal have to get married before it's too late."

Cassie sank down in the chair by his bed. "Daddy, why is it so important that I marry Cal?"

Marcus smiled at her. A real smile. "So you can be happy."

Shocked, she saw the sincerity and the almost child-like delight in her father's eyes. "What makes you think Cal and I would be happy?"

"You were that way once before. Young and in love. Remember? That's the best kind of feeling."

She bobbed her head. "I do remember. But you didn't want us to be together. You got so angry at us."

He moved his head in protest. "Angry at…someone else. I took it out on you. Shouldn't have done that."

Cassie wondered if he was talking about her mother. He and Eugenia had that awful argument. Had her mother tried to protect Cassie? Was that why Marcus had become so angry with all of them? Had her father already figured out Cassie and Cal were seeing each other?

"It doesn't matter now," she said, hoping to take his mind off that horrible time. "I'm here now and, Daddy, you have to know I love you."

"I know," he said. "But I need you to do this one last thing, Cassie. Marry Cal. Then I can die knowing I did right by you."

She didn't say anything. What could she say?

"You hear me, girl?"

"I hear you, Daddy."

Cassie stayed silent and still, watching as he drifted

off to sleep again. She had so many questions but she was afraid to ask any of them. She wanted her father to die in peace, but how could she live in peace if he never voiced the words she longed to hear? She'd told him she loved him but he hadn't responded in kind. She wanted to believe he loved her, but he seemed more worried about making sure she was married.

After sitting with him until he'd calmed down and drifted to sleep again, Cassie went back to her room and sat down in the chaise lounge by the French doors, her thoughts caught in a turmoil that kept her wide-awake while the night sky hissed and flashed its own frustration. Her father was carrying some sort of burden on his heart, and in his tired mind, he had to believe that if he righted this one wrong—if he put Cassie back with the boy she'd loved—then he could find a sense of redemption. Maybe, just like Cassie, he wanted to remember happier times.

"He misses you, Mama," she said into the night. "Soon you'll be with him again. Soon, all will be forgiven."

He blamed himself because they'd argued. And he'd blamed Cassie for something all these years ago, too. This was something more than just falling in love with a hired hand.

Something so bad, so horrible, that he couldn't get it out of his mind.

She sat up, her thoughts merging into one obvious revelation. She'd never told her father she would forgive him for shunning her and forcing her to leave her home. She'd only reassured him that she was here now. Out of duty? Or out of love?

Maybe if she told him all truly was forgiven, he'd forget this need to bring her and Cal back together. If

Cassie could show him that she was strong and able to take care of herself, maybe he could finally find some rest.

She thought about what Teresa had said earlier.

What can I do to make things right? she wondered. Then she glanced at her designs and another memory filtered into her tired brain.

When she was young, she'd talked about starting a manufacturing company right here in Camellia. She'd hire workers to make her clothes and she'd open a boutique that could become a regional destination place for shoppers. It would bring people into the area and help the local economy.

But that had been before her life had become shattered and torn by grief and heartbreak.

"I could still do that," she said out loud. Then she got up and grabbed her sketch pad, this time drawing out a building design. "I could still do that," she echoed, her body surging with renewed energy.

This would change her whole perspective and her whole life. She'd have to spend a lot of time here.

And her father wouldn't live to see this idea to fruition.

But he might appreciate it enough to be proud of her. Without forcing her to marry the one man she could never have.

It was a long shot, but it was also a start.

She couldn't marry Cal. It wouldn't be fair to either of them. But she could forgive everyone, starting with Marsha and Cal and then her father and she'd tell him it was okay to let go. Because he wouldn't need to worry any longer. She could take care of everything.

And in the process, maybe she could finally convince herself to let go, too.

She reached for her cell phone. She needed to talk to someone.

She dialed Cal's number.

CHAPTER TWELVE

CASSIE HELD THE PHONE and waited while she moved her sketches off the bed with her other hand, leaving them scattered on the dresser. Morose ideas had poured through her head, but she'd managed to sketch a few decent outfits. But most of the pieces looked too dark and sinister to bring out in a spring collection. Maybe for the next year's fall collection. She'd walk the grounds tomorrow to look for inspiration and find the perfect spot to build her factory.

Right now, she wanted to talk to Cal.

"Hello?"

His voice, so deep and strong, sent little shivers down her spine at about the same time a slender streak of lightning carved a laser across the sky.

"Cal? It's me." She hesitated, her mind screaming for her to hang up. "I need to talk to you."

"Everything okay?"

"Yes. I... My father had another spell. He's okay but he mentioned the wedding again."

"Our wedding?"

Our wedding. She swallowed, her earlier pledge to forgive flashing with the same intensity as the skies outside. "Well, the marriage proposal, yes. I can't sleep. I have all these ideas rolling around inside my head."

"Ideas about marrying me, or *not* marrying me?"

This conversation was not going the way she'd planned.

"Ideas about my future and Camellia—both the town and the plantation. I just can't get settled. I can't sleep."

"Me, either," he said. She heard his sigh, even over the booming thunder off in the distance. "And I figured you were awake. I can see your room from here, remember?"

She went to the window. In spite of the fatigue tugging at her like a heavy cloak, she was too keyed up, too wired, to do anything but talk to Cal. So she tightened her silk robe around her gown and opened the French doors to step out onto the upstairs verandah. "I remember. I can see your light from here."

"Bad storm coming in," he said. "I'm worried about the crops."

"Maybe it'll settle down after the wind goes through."

"I can see you out on the porch."

She looked down, straining. His dark shadow appeared on the steps to the little back porch. "I see you, too. Be careful underneath that oak. I don't want lightning to strike you."

"I didn't know you cared."

Of course she cared. She'd always cared about this place. And him. This was her home, after all. And he was her heart.

Hoping to keep things light, she said, "I have to protect my investment, don't I?"

"Yeah, right. So what kind of ideas do you have? Ways to send me packing?"

"No, actually, Teresa said something that got me thinking. She said this town needs new blood and new ideas."

"And...?"

"And, you remember how my friend's comments set me on the path to design ready-to-wear?"

"Yes."

"Well, Teresa set me on a path to give back to Camellia. I want to build a manufacturing plant here. To produce my clothes."

"Wow. That's sure a big commitment for someone who can't wait to get out of here."

The old hurt feelings came back. "I never said that. It's just been hard, coming back with my father so ill. And other things."

"Like me?"

"Yes, like you. It's been awkward from the start. Throw in a forced marriage and well..."

"Are you sure you're not just grasping at straws to please your daddy?"

He still knew her so very well. "Maybe. But if I tell him about this plan, maybe he'll forget about the marriage thing."

"Oh, I get it. But a distraction might not work. The marriage thing is the one thing that man wants. Why, I'll never understand. Our getting married won't fix anything."

Hurt that he didn't seem as excited about her idea as she was, Cassie shook off the pain. "All the more reason to focus on something positive. I can build the factory on plantation land. It'll bring in jobs, help the local economy."

"I'm not saying it's a bad idea, Cassie. It's just... I can't see you staying here long enough to commit to something like that."

"You think I'll bolt again if something goes wrong?"

"Won't you? You resent me being here. You'd be miserable. We'd both be miserable."

She glanced toward the tiny white cottage out beyond the trees. Had she made him miserable over the last week? He was working hard to find a way to save this place but she had accused him of wanting to destroy her father. Yet he talked as if he'd be more willing to stay here than her. But, as much as it hurt, he did have a point. Time to live up to that forgiveness pledge.

"I think I was wrong, about so many things. One reason I called is to say I'm sorry."

"For what?"

"For everything. You had to leave Camellia in disgrace, same as me. I thought you wanted to be with Marsha so I never bothered to find you, to talk to you. And now, my father is demanding the one thing that we can never have."

"Cassie, I'm coming up there so we can talk."

"No, don't do that."

She turned, started into her room. It was so tempting to let him back into her heart. So tempting. They'd both been hurting. She could listen to that little voice in her head that told her to forgive him, to believe in him, to remember the promise he'd made to her so long ago. But she couldn't forget that promise. Nor the grief of a love that had been shattered by so much chaos.

Turning back to stare out into the night, but staying out of sight, she said, "Remember all of our dreams?"

"Always. I told you we'd be together one day."

She nodded even though he couldn't see her. "We'd have our own farm, with a pretty little house and a dog and a cat. You'd farm the land and I'd create designs."

He inhaled. "And once we got secure and on our feet, we'd have babies. Lots of babies."

Her stomach jumped at that reminder. Putting a hand to her tummy, Cassie wiped at her eyes, the tears she'd held at bay for weeks now coming as fast and hard as the raindrops hitting on the magnolia tree by her window. The emptiness she'd felt all these years became a physical pain there deep inside her empty womb. This explained why she'd never been able to love Ned. "I always wanted children."

They'd never gotten past how she would become a designer if they lived on a farm. Or how many babies they'd want. Or how they'd manage to save enough to even have a child. They'd been too in love to worry about the logistics of such things.

"Yeah, me, too," he said. "We were so in love."

"It blinded us," she whispered. "We were too in love to see what was happening around us, Cal."

Maybe that had been their main problem. Too much love and not enough common sense or rational consideration. Had it been more lust than love?

She stared down on the grounds, the scents of honeysuckle and wisteria reminding her of late nights with Cal. Cassie watched the shadows playing across the open lawn, her gaze following the path toward the cottage. The wind slashed through the live oaks and pine trees. But a chill moved over Cassie, forcing her to stay inside.

What if Cal was right? What if she couldn't handle staying here? She'd run away again and then her pride would keep her from returning. This was a big decision.

And calling him had been a bad idea.

"Cal, I'm going to bed. I have a lot to think about."

Then she saw a shadow moving toward the big house. And heard his voice coming through the phone. "Don't go."

Blinking, she thought she was imagining things. But the shadow kept coming. And then it took the shape of a man.

Cal was walking across the yard. And he was headed straight toward her.

LIGHTNING FLASHED ACROSS the night sky in a brilliant arc, showing Cal the way to the wide planked steps leading up to the second floor. But he didn't need a lighted path. This walk was ingrained in his brain to the point that he could follow it blindfolded. He just never imagined he'd be on this same path again.

"Cassie?"

"I have to go." She hung up and disappeared inside.

He had to see her, to hold her. He's fought these feelings for so long, it was impossible to be so near her without touching her and trying to make her see that she belonged with him. All this talk of new plans and old dreams was driving him crazy. He could at least hold her close, just once. Just this once.

But the rain clouds that had been building up all afternoon had finally decided to let loose. The wet, heavy drops shocked him back to reality. He stopped and put his phone in his pocket, thinking he needed to turn around and go back home. But then, the two-bedroom house he lived in wasn't really *his* home. More like a holding area until he could finish what he'd come here to do.

He wanted to be with Cassie.

Long ago, on nights like this, he would have walked through the dewy garden path and climbed the stairs leading to the second floor. He would have knocked softly on the French doors into her bedroom. And he would have waited impatiently for Cassie to open those doors and let him inside.

She wouldn't do that now.

She'd locked him out of her life forever. And now, even when she'd reached out to him in the night, she still believed the worst of him. She believed he was out to do in her father and maybe her, too. Where had she gotten that notion?

Cal ducked underneath a live oak and tried to think how it must look to her.

The man who'd promised her so much, then betrayed her with another schoolgirl who taunted and teased Cassie and lied to her on top of that, was now back and in charge of the only place she'd ever called home. The father who'd doted on her and then turned bitter and mean the day her beautiful mother died, was now lying in a bed, dying. And trying mightily to take some of his secrets with him while he constantly confused Cassie with the woman he'd loved and lost. Oh, and that old man was insisting that his only daughter needed to marry the man who'd broken her heart.

No wonder Cassie didn't trust any of them. She'd stepped right into a web of lies and deceit. It was all about the Brennan legacy. Marcus didn't want to let go of his power, even in death. He wanted Cassie to pick up where he'd left off and he wanted her to go back and right his wrongs, including breaking up her and Cal.

Now, she was desperately grasping at ways to change her father before it was too late. And Cal couldn't tell her that her father truly was the one who'd broken them up and turned Cal toward Marsha. Because if he did tell her what he knew, she'd turn on all of them forever.

Cal's disgust caused him to stop and stare up toward

her room. He couldn't see her through the mist of rain hitting his face. She wasn't going to come back out.

He knew some of those secrets Marcus Brennan was trying so hard to guard. And if Cal had guessed right then everything in Cassie's life was a lie. She'd crumble like the dry, red Georgia clay if she found out the truth.

And she'd be gone again. Forever.

But she's not as fragile now as she once was, he told himself. He had certainly noticed the changes. She was a woman now, confident and self-assured. She's started over, reinventing herself and making her own path, fueling that path with all her angst and confusion and pain. That had to take some kind of courage. The kind of courage he didn't seem to possess.

He remembered the young girl, though. The rich young woman who only longed for a friend or two.

"They all use me, Cal. They want to come and see the house, swim in the pool, ride horses with me. I either have too many clinging friends or too many people who think I'm a stuck-up snob. Like that Marsha Reynolds. She pretends to be my friend but she tries to bully me and tease me, but I'm a Brennan. I have to suck it up and move on."

But she'd been hurt over and over by lies and deception. Instead of being the mean, selfish rich girl, Cassie had been the gentle, kind teenager who wanted everyone to be part of the crowd. Even Marsha. But Marsha had resented Cassie's wealth and status and couldn't see past hurting Cassie. She'd wanted everything that Cassie had, including the stable boy who'd become Cassie's first love.

No surprise that the lies and deception had also driven Cassie and Cal apart in the end, and that Marsha had been a part of that. Cassie didn't like secrets or lies. Neither did he.

And now *he'd* become a part of both yet again.

"What should I do?" Cal whispered to the wind, his plea for guidance drifting away on a wisp of air.

What could he do? Just hold on to his memories and let them keep him company even while they tortured him with unbridled longing. He'd made so many promises, but he could only keep one.

He wanted to make amends to Cassie for what he'd done all those years ago. Right now, that would be his only goal.

And his only hope.

Another round of lightning flashed, this one angry and jagged, followed by an echoing boom of thunder.

Cal looked up at the corner where Cassie had been standing.

She wasn't there. She wouldn't let him in.

Was she still that scared of being around him, so angry and bitter that she didn't even want to see him? More like, she was remembering a night long ago when another storm was coming and he had run through the rain just to be with her.

And that was a memory neither of them could afford to relive.

CASSIE WATCHED FROM THE shadows of her bedroom as the rain began to pound against the roof and eaves. She could just make out the path through the camellias and roses, so she held still, willing another round of lightning to illuminate the gardens below.

Was he still down there?

As if the heavens heard her plea, the sky went white-hot with a shimmering ribbon of sizzling light. She leaned close to the window and was rewarded with a quick glimpse of a man standing there in the rain.

Cassie's heart did a jagged dance of its own, each boom of her pulse matching the fury in the sky. She almost opened the doors to run out into the yard, to tell Cal she couldn't—wouldn't—believe he was here to betray her or her family. To convince him that if she made a commitment with her heart, she'd never break that commitment. But before she could find the courage to do that, the yard grew bright again and the thunder roared, bringing with it a solid downpour.

And the man who'd been standing in the garden staring up at her room was now gone.

Cassie breathed a sigh of relief and hurried to her bed. She dove in, pulling the covers up over her shivering body, and then quickly turned off the light. But the storm kept her from settling down. That and the memories of her other late-night phone conversations with Cal. That summer, if they couldn't be with each other, they talked on the phone half the night. And all without her parents' knowledge.

"That didn't work out so well," she reminded herself as she shifted on the pillows and closed her eyes. Her father had been furious when he'd caught them together in the stables. More than furious. His rage had spooked the horses and brought Teresa running from the main house.

"I give you a job, take you in like family and this is how you repay me?" Giving Cal a murderous look, he added, "Haven't you caused enough trouble around here without seducing my daughter, too?

"And you, Cassandra! My own daughter dallying with the stable boy, right under my nose? I had such high hopes for you, girl."

Cal had given Cassie a long, pleading look. "Everything will be all right, I promise."

But things had never been all right since. Cal managed to sneak into Cassie's room one more time, to promise her his undying love. The next day, Cassie went into town hoping to meet up with Cal. She'd found him, all right. Cal and Marsha were making out behind the Pig and Plow Bar. Crushed and hurt, she'd confronted them.

"He doesn't love you," Marsha shouted, her freckled skin flushed, her eyes wet with tears. "He loves me. He only used you to stay close to your old man and all that money. But he's leaving now, because your daddy gave him a big check. And I'm going with him. We'll get married. I'm pregnant with his baby."

Cal hadn't even disputed anything Marsha had said.

He'd only said one thing. "Remember what I promised."

But it was too late.

She could only remember the screams, the horror, the disbelief of that awful day when her mother had died. And how Cal had broken her heart when she'd needed him the most.

Cassie hated reliving that sorrow and grief.

SHE'D LEFT, PUTTING THEM all out of her life. And she'd never looked back. Until now.

She tried to forget that Cal was down there in that little cottage. But she had to wonder if he was remembering the same awful memories. All these years, she'd pictured him married to Marsha, being a father to his child. Cal had always said he'd be a good father even though he'd never had a good father figure in his life. He didn't have that family he'd dreamed about.

Maybe he considered Marcus the father he'd never had.

Could she make a new life here, with all that baggage holding her back? How could she get through this?

You're here to make amends with your father, she reminded herself. Nothing more. You can't fall in love with Cal again, but you can forgive him and let him get on with his life.

She'd have to put her feelings for Cal aside, so she could rebuild the once-thriving Camellia Plantation. And maybe make some decisions regarding the future of her home and this town.

Save the old farmstead. Pray for her father's forgiveness and forgive him in return. And finally forgive the man she still loved. Tall orders for a woman who'd used bitterness and grief all these years to shield her heart.

CHAPTER THIRTEEN

"THE EARLY CORN LOOKS GOOD," Cal told Jack a few days later. "Fertilization seems to be kicking in. I think that rain last week really caused a growing spurt."

Jack tugged on his John Deere baseball cap and nodded. "Don't need too much water at this point. Could drown this new growth."

"Can't worry about Mother Nature," Cal replied, used to Jack's ornery observations. "We've got the peanuts under control now we just work on the corn and soybeans."

"Not so sure about this double-row technique," Jack replied. "Have to wait and see, I reckon."

"It's easier to irrigate and pollinate," Cal reminded the older man. "Just give it a chance, Jack."

Jack rolled his eyes. "How many more years can we live on chance, Cal? I'm an old man."

"Well, I'm not getting any younger myself," Cal replied. "I'm telling you this method will increase our yield."

"You're the boss."

"For now," Cal retorted. "Let's get back at it, okay. And remember, Teresa's cooking lunch for all the hands today. I think she's saved you a big old piece of fried chicken."

"She knows I like wings and drumsticks," Jack said

before he'd had time to think about it. Turning beet-red, he added, "I'll tell the other fellows. Appreciate it."

"All right." Cal couldn't hide the big grin on his face. At least somebody around here was making points in the love department. Since their near-encounter during the rainstorm last week, Cal had tried to keep his distance from Cassie. But that plan wasn't working, really. He was very aware that the woman was on the premises. He'd seen her riding a chestnut mare through the pasture yesterday. And he'd seen her white convertible driving back and forth to town several times this week. She must have been serious about building a factory here.

Jack slammed his hat down over his ears, jarring Cal out of his musings, and went to crank his tractor. Then he pointed to the dilapidated old camp house. "That's an eyesore. You gonna tear it down or what?"

Cal nodded, enjoying the way Jack was trying so hard to take the attention away from himself. But Jack was right about the crumbling old house. It was just one more thing on his list. Instead of getting back in his truck, he walked around the cornfield then headed down the path to the big, glistening pond to look at the camp house. It wasn't just an eyesore. It was dangerous.

A tree had fallen through the back side of the big one-room building long ago and now both the tree and the roof were rotten and dry. One spark from lightning could send the whole thing up in flames and start a grass fire. The tiny front porch had missing floorboards and broken, cracked wooden steps and the windows had long ago lost most of their panes.

Cal remembered the place as being like a rustic little cabin, tucked in behind a growth of trees. Inside, bunk beds and a tiny kitchen allowed hunters and fishermen to get in out of the cold and have a bite of food or a cup of coffee. Back when he'd been a glorified gofer, he'd often helped Marcus lead hunting parties through these woods.

Including Dr. John Anton.

Cal looked out at the lake, trying to imagine why two grown men who were both good swimmers had suffered through such a terrible accident. Other than what Marcus and Teresa had told him, he didn't have the details of the day Dr. Anton died, but like Cassie, he had to wonder if there was something more to the story. This pond wasn't too deep. Maybe twelve feet at its deepest. Of course, it didn't take much water to drown. And a few incoherent mumblings from a dying man didn't mean there was a big mystery about this.

"Stop thinking the worst," he told himself while he stepped over a hole on the porch and shoved open the old barn door to the cabin. He hadn't been in this place since…he and Cassie had sat out a rainstorm in here one summer day long ago.

Cal grinned at the memory. He'd had a thing for rainy summer afternoons ever since. Seemed like they always managed to come together during a storm.

But today, the sun gave a valiant shot at making its way through the gaping hole in the old shingled roof. No rain in sight. And no Cassie, either.

They could actually get along as long as they avoided each other. Or more like, stayed away from each other. Because he wanted to be with her and that just made staying away that much harder. And that much more necessary. It was a never-ending cycle of frustration.

Cal touched on the broken dining table in the dark, dank building, his mind still on Cassie. Since the day Marcus had suggested that Cal and Cassie get married, Cal had held a vision of her in his mind. Cassie in a white dress with a smile on her face, a smile meant only for him. Their wedding day, a happy day. A magical day.

But not this way, he thought as he opened drawers and shifted through crisp yellowed papers on a desk tucked into the corner, his longings as aged and curled as these newspapers and documents. There were still so many secrets between them.

"I won't force you, Cassie," he said through the swirl of dust balls floating around his head.

And that was why he'd decided to give her some space, some time to get to know her daddy again and mend those fences before Marcus slipped away. Cal only hoped that Marcus would be able to come clean with her and tell her the whole ugly story.

While he hoped this, he also knew it would destroy her and cause her to turn away from him for good. He had to keep his distance so it wouldn't be so hard to accept when the time came.

He went into the little efficiency kitchen and opened cabinet doors then tugged at a door to a tiny closet. A scarf, probably once white silk but now a creamy moth-eaten yellow, fluttered out from a shelf and onto the floor at his feet. Cal picked it up, stared at it. Then blinked.

The initials EB were etched in a delicate blue stitching on the scarf.

This wasn't something a man would wear.

But who? EB.

Eugenia Brennan?

"Maybe it belonged to Cassie's mother," he said, wadding it up so he could put it in his shirt pocket.

He'd show it to Cassie later. She might want to clean it up and keep it as a memento.

"CASSIE, HONESTLY, ISN'T IT time you came back to Atlanta so we can get things back on track?"

Cassie pulled her cell phone away and stared at the screen. Then she held it back to her ear. "Ned, I can't come back right now. My father is very ill." She held to the phone, wishing she could make him understand. "And we've talked about this over and over. I'm sorry things didn't work out for us, but you need to move on."

"You don't mean that," Ned replied, a long-suffering sigh emitting over the air. "You have to get back here. Do you want your business to suffer?"

"My business is fine. I'm on the phone with Rae every day."

She gritted her teeth. Ned was fishing for reconciliation and after very little sleep last night, she wasn't as sharp as she'd normally be. And she couldn't tell him that her first love was back and she still had feelings for him. That would add insult to injury.

"But you've never been out of town this long. I'm worried about you and Rae won't talk to me."

"I'm fine, and Rae is busy holding things down while I take care of some business."

"Your father's business?"

"Yes. He's been so ill he's let things go around here," she said. "I'm trying to keep ahead of everything and keep up with my own obligations. I'm sorry, Ned. Maybe when I get back we can have dinner but nothing more. I can't deal with anything more right now."

After that, Ned let her go. But he promised to check on her again. He really was being considerate about this.

"Who's Ned?"

Cassie whirled to find Cal standing in the hallway. She'd heard the back door but thought it was Teresa coming back from the garden. And since earlier she'd been sitting here thinking of Cal, not Ned, she asked, "Where did you come from?"

"Mars," he said, humor coloring his retort. And hiding the way his eyes slipped over her like a soft rain.

"Very funny. I thought you were out in the corn patch today."

"I was." He walked toward the refrigerator, opened it and grabbed the big glass pitcher of tea. "Who's Ned?"

Cassie shrugged. "My ex-fiancé."

Cal's frown made her cringe. Slamming down the heavy pitcher of tea, he grunted. "Wow. Funny how you never mentioned him."

She stared at her now-cold cup of coffee. "Just goes with the territory around here, don't you think?" Regretting that remark, she added, "Ned and I dated for a couple of years but it wasn't working."

"So you two broke up?"

"Yes. About two months ago."

"And yet he keeps calling?"

"He knows I'm here and that Daddy is ill. I'd rather he not come to visit right now, however. He thinks we have a chance of getting back together. But we don't."

Cal leaned back against the counter. "Is he harassing you?"

Not wanting him to go all cowboy on her, she shook her head. "No. He was just concerned. I've assured him I'm okay. I don't want him rushing down here. I think that would just make things worse."

"And you don't like people rushing in?"

"No. I've learned how to do things my own way over the years." She pushed at her hair, looking everywhere but at him. "Speaking of that, I'd like to take a ride through the crop fields so you can explain all of these new techniques to me. I saw Jack out at the stables yesterday and he mentioned some problems."

"Jack is mad because your daddy hired me. I'm his boss now and he doesn't like that. He can't get used to having to do things my way."

"But he stayed on after you came."

"Yes. The man is old and he really doesn't have anywhere else to go. Marcus wanted to fire him, but I didn't have the heart to do that." Then he lowered his voice. "Besides, Teresa and he kinda have this thing going on."

She let that information settle then with the lift of one slanted eyebrow said, "So tell me about these mishaps Jack mentioned. I need to know about everything."

And Jack had made sure she'd question him. Again, Cassie had to wonder about the underlying secrets around this place.

"No mishaps this week, thankfully. Corn looks good. Peanuts are maturing and the soybeans aren't far behind. That rain we had last week—" He stopped, looked out the window while she remembered everything about that rainstorm and their phone conversation. "We needed the rain and thankfully, we didn't have any severe damage. As far as problems, I'm not sure what Jack's talking about."

"He told me about the broken tiller shank and grumbled about some new-fangled way of plowing that didn't make sense to him—or me, either, for that matter."

"Is that all? Stuff like that happens on a weekly basis. And Jack complains on a daily basis. Farming is unpredictable."

Just like you, she thought. "I still want to ride the property."

"I'm ready whenever you are. My techniques aren't anything that new and farmers all over the south are using them."

She couldn't help but glance at him. He looked tired and aggravated, but he also looked good. He wore a button-up plaid shirt and jeans. His hair was wild and windblown, his face and arms dark from the sun. When he took a swig of the syrupy tea, Cassie's eye followed the lifting of his head and the way his Adam's apple moved when he swallowed.

Maybe she needed a glass of cold tea instead of this black coffee.

"Daddy had another bad night," she said out of the need to say something. Another night of confusing her with her mother and reminding her to get out the wedding dress.

"Sorry to hear that."

He finished his tea then looked at her, his glance bouncing off her face. But his eyes held her. "Has he mentioned—"

"Marriage?" she asked, not caring what anyone thought anymore. "Yes. He couldn't sleep. He still wants me to wear the same wedding dress that my mother wore. He keeps telling me that over and over." She shrugged, then rubbed a hand over her neck, hoping to soothe the tight, sore muscles. "I'm not even sure that dress is still around. And I don't intend to find out because I don't intend to get married anytime soon."

"At least not to Ned or me, huh?"

His words were teasing but the look in his eyes reflected her tormented longings. Impossible not to think about kissing him or running to him in the rain or wondering what it would be like to be his wife. Impossible, or nearly so.

"I can't think about that kind of decision right now." She lowered her head. "I do think about my parents and how their marriage has shaped my life. I think that's probably why Ned and I didn't work out."

His nod was quick and filled with understanding, but his eyes held that old longing and an immediate disappointment. "Oh, speaking of your mother, I found this in the old camp house." He tugged a wad of material out of the pocket of his shirt. "I think it might have belonged to her."

Cassie took the tattered material, let it flutter open onto the counter and then spread it out into a big square. "A scarf?"

"Looks like one to me." He pointed to the lettering. "Initials."

"EB." Cassie rubbed her fingers over the old silk. "It's almost falling apart."

"Maybe if you soak it."

"Eugenia Brennan." She touched on the lettering again. "She loved scarves. Always wore one, summer or winter."

"Do you remember that one?"

"I don't know. She had so many."

Cassie closed her eyes, memories of her mother dressed in capri pants, a sleeveless summer sweater and a pretty white scarf clouding her mind. "She must have been down at the camp house with my daddy and left it there. Sometimes, she'd go sit on the porch there while he fished. Or she'd cook breakfast for some of the hunting parties." She glanced up at Cal. "And sometimes, she'd go for long walks and wind up down there for hours—all alone. She loved sitting by the water, reading one of her favorite books."

A wisp of a memory fluttered like the white scarf across Cassie's mind then disappeared into a dark fog.

Cal leaned over the counter. "I remember them having dinners down there. They'd fry up quail or dove, roast a duck or two. Sometimes they'd have a big fish fry."

"She enjoyed cooking for my father and his friends."

Cassie pushed the scarf away, more of the muted memory clawing at her consciousness. A teakettle whistling, a woman laughing. A man's chuckle. "I don't remember this scarf."

Cal picked up the scrap of material. "Do you want me to throw it away?"

"No. I'll clean it up and put it away. I need to go through the master bedroom closet, anyway. Teresa told me all of my mother's things are still in there."

Cal tilted his head, his eyes capturing hers. "The old man didn't sleep in that room. Or at least, he wasn't sleeping in it when I came back."

"Where did he sleep?"

"In a guestroom down the hall. Teresa had told me that and then when he got so bad off, I helped her move his things downstairs. Jack and I helped get him down there. He fought us all the way."

Cassie closed her eyes to that image. "I just keep finding out more and more about how horrible things were around here." She lifted her head to stare over at him. "You know, I went to him the morning I was scheduled to leave for the University of Georgia. I told him I wanted to stay here and take care of him. He refused my request. Told me to get out of here and to get on with my life. He said I needed a college education and he had the money to buy me one, so to stop being childish and to go."

She took in a breath and glanced at the old scarf, the pain of her father's harsh words killing her all over again. "The man couldn't even look me in the eye. I didn't want to leave him, Cal. I wish I'd insisted on staying."

"He wanted you to go to college, follow your dreams."

"He wanted me out of his life. Sometimes, I think both of you wanted that."

He came around the counter, his hand on the aged tile near her. So near she could feel the heat of his fingers burning her. "I never wanted that."

She gave him a direct look, her eyes holding his, his nearness making her brain turn all fuzzy. "Then why did you turn to Marsha?"

CAL WAS SO SHOCKED by the question, he didn't say a word. She could never, ever know the truth.

"What's the matter? Afraid to tell me?"

Her blue eyes challenged him, dared him. He'd tell her what he could. "The short answer? I knew you were going to leave that week. And after what happened with your parents, I guess I figured you weren't coming back."

Cassie threw down the pen she'd been holding. "So instead of trusting me, you just went ahead and found someone else?"

Cal decided it was time to throw all of his cards on the table. Or at least give her the story in his head. "Well, since you asked. No, I wasn't trying to find anyone else. I wanted *you,* Cassie. But when I tried to comfort you after your mother's death, you seemed to shut down. Think how you felt when your father changed overnight. Remember how upset you were? Well, that's how it seemed with you and me, too."

She put her hands on the counter and pushed up off her stool. "How can you even compare the way my father treated me to what happened to us? I was in shock, distraught over my mother. I was trying to figure out what to do about my father's attitude and his grief."

Cal wanted to help her understand, but what did it matter now? He wouldn't hurt her with the disgusting details of the things he knew in his heart. "We were all upset. Your daddy caught you and me together and things went downhill from there." He leaned close, his eyes locking with hers, his heart in his hand. "I felt responsible."

She got up to whirl around, her coffee cup in her hand. "What do you mean?"

He'd never told her this. Never told anyone about his guilt. But this part of the past he could share. "Cassie, I let Miss Eugenia get on that horse. I told her not to, but didn't try to stop her. I could have. I could have refused to give her the reins, could have told her Heathcliff needed to be brushed down and fed. But I just stood there and…watched."

Cassie slowly set the teacup in the sink. "You saw my mother die?"

He nodded, closed his eyes for a minute. "Yes. I was the first one to…reach her."

She turned, her back against the kitchen sink. "I saw it out my bedroom window. I saw her coming up the lane in the pasture. Then I ran out onto the porch and down the steps and by the time I got to her, she was already on the ground. I don't remember seeing you there."

"Your daddy sent me to get his rifle. Heathcliff broke his leg in the fall."

She closed her eyes, lowered her head. "He was screaming. He kept holding her. I...I thought he shot the horse because he was so angry." She looked up at Cal. "I don't even remember you handing him the rifle. I just remember the sound of that gunshot. I never knew Heathcliff was hurt, too." She put a fist to her mouth. "How could I have missed that? What else have I missed?" Then she looked up at Cal. "Sometimes, I get these images, these memories. I think I might be blocking something out, Cal. Something really bad."

Cal came around the counter and put his hands on her shoulders. "Do you remember me taking you into my arms and holding you?"

Cassie nodded and before he could move, she laid her head against his shoulder. Cal held his breath then put his arms around her and held her there, his memories hitting hard with each heartbeat, his regrets cutting through him like tangled shards of steel.

"I do remember that. You shielded me, protected me." She looked up at him, a gasp escaping through her lips. "You're still trying to do that, aren't you?"

"Yes," Cal said, a great relief washing over him. "Yes. That's what I'm trying to do. And, Cassie, I'm trying to make up for the past, for my actions on that day and the things I did back then to hurt you. I shouldn't have let your mother get on that horse."

Cassie looked up at him then and he saw a change come over her. Her features softened into a bittersweet smile. "It's not your fault, Cal. You have to know that. It's not your fault."

"It's not yours, either," he retorted. "We both need to let go of all of that and start over."

She stared up into his eyes. "I'd like that."

Cal held her chin in his hand. "Don't turn away from me again, okay? Just don't turn away."

"I won't."

He leaned in and kissed her, the touch of her lips on his as soft as a blossom on the wind. She returned his kiss, her soft sigh reminding him of how much he'd cared for her, how much he still cared for her.

In spite of everything that had been between them, Cal knew things had just taken a new turn.

For the better.

CHAPTER FOURTEEN

AT LEAST THEY'D STOPPED fighting against each other.

Cassie sat on a gentle roan named Ladybug, watching Cal's face while he held the reins on a dark brown gelding and explained everything from crop rotation and soil conservation to double-row corn and pollination. The man lived for the land.

She'd always admired that about Cal. His work ethic had never been in question. Maybe that was why Marcus had asked him to come back and work at Camellia. Her father trusted Cal. Or he had once. But was he too sick now to understand what bringing Cal back here had cost all of them?

"You're mighty quiet over there," Cal said now. "I guess I've been rambling, though."

Two days after their kiss in the kitchen, Cassie suddenly felt completely shy around Cal. But this was more than just renewing an old acquaintance. This was new and raw and fresh and...like falling in love all over again with a new person.

"I'm just absorbing everything," she admitted. Including him. "You've had a lot to deal with here."

He soothed the anxious gelding. "Steady, Cocoa. We'll have a good run later." Then he glanced at Cassie. "Well, this is a big place and there's always work to be done."

Cal had changed. She could see that now. Since she'd

been back, she'd been so wrapped up in her father's illness and what everyone was *not* telling her that she'd neglected to get to know this new and improved Cal. But what about her? Had she truly grown up since she'd left here? Or had she just been pretending?

Time to test that theory.

"I was just thinking about how all of this falls on me now and trying to weigh the pros and cons of building a factory here. I've got my lawyers and business managers working on some projections so they can give me an estimation of the cost, but I really think I can pull it off. As much as I'd love to see my father recover, I know that's not possible. That puts a tremendous responsibility on me."

She stopped to gaze at him. "I owe you a lot. You made a big sacrifice, coming here to help. You made the commitment."

He didn't say anything. But his soft smile showed he appreciated what she'd said.

"And it would mean a definite commitment from me. If I do this, I want to be in it for the long haul. I owe this town and my daddy that much at least."

Cal pulled on Cocoa's reins as they came to the pond. "Well, you've seen the crops and I've explained everything I've done so far. I've kept costs down as much as possible. We're working on a shoestring budget this year but I'd rather do that than take out another big loan with the bank."

"No—no more loans. I have a lot of equity in my holdings in Atlanta. I can sell some stocks if I need to. I can use that for collateral if we need more money. But I'd prefer to hold off until we see the yield this fall. If it looks like we're turning a corner, I'll get to work on the factory plans next year. I can streamline my plans to open two more boutiques in Atlanta and New York and focus on that instead."

He gave her a thoughtful look. "So you think you'll still be around in the fall?"

She'd thought about that, too. "I'll have to travel back and forth. I do have obligations in Atlanta. If I let things go at my flagship boutique then I'll never get another store up and running. I've already committed to building the second one so I want to finish that. The revenue from that and the department-store orders could help with saving this place. I have people in place to run the boutique, but I'll need to be more hands-on with the new construction and especially with the grand openings. But yes, I would be able to come for short visits this fall, to begin the plans for the factory."

He nodded then hopped off Cocoa. "Let's go for a walk."

Cassie dismounted and followed him across the levee built up around the pond, leaving the horses to graze down in a small valley. "It's getting hotter every day."

"Summer has arrived." He glanced over at her. "I have to admit, I didn't think you'd stay a week, let alone almost three weeks."

"I guess I deserved that, but did you really think I'd just up and leave?"

"Well, yes, after you heard about Marcus's grand idea. You know, the proposal that shall not be named."

"I almost did," she admitted. "But then, so did you."

"I didn't get very far."

"No." She swallowed the bitterness in her throat. "I'm sorry for a lot of things, Cal. One being that I jumped to the wrong conclusions about you. I have no right to dictate whether or not you've been with Marsha or whether or not you're still seeing her. And I know enough about my daddy to understand he probably pressured you into agreeing to that marriage thing."

"It wasn't hard to agree to that," he said, his tone low and gravelly, his eyes rich with dark emotions. "But I figured you wouldn't exactly be thrilled."

"And you were?"

"It's hard to explain, but when he first suggested it I just humored him to keep him calm. I thought he'd forget about it. But if I had to be forced into a marriage, you'd be my first pick."

"Thanks, I think." She didn't dare say she felt the same way. "I won't force anything on you. But Daddy's a whole other story. He's still got a lot of stubborn in him."

Cal smiled, the sadness in his eyes belying that smile. "I'm just glad we've managed to get past the shock and get on with trying to hold on to Camellia Plantation. And I'm glad you didn't leave."

Because her throat felt tight and she couldn't breathe, she said, "I can't leave my daddy." She was beginning to see that it would be so hard to leave Cal again. Probably worse this time.

Cal stopped at the end of the old dock. "He seems more settled the past couple of days. Maybe he'll give up on the notion of seeing us married before he dies."

Cassie's heart did a strange little jump. The way he'd said that told her Cal still thought about it, too. But she wasn't going to push the idea. Once she'd dreamed about nothing else. Now, marrying Cal was the last thing on her mind. Or maybe the *only* thing she now tried to keep out of her mind. But it couldn't happen for so many reasons.

She thought about her father's demanding proclamation. "He hasn't brought it up over the past few days.

But he stays confused. And he sleeps a lot more than he did." She wrapped her arms against her stomach. "The doctors say it might be days or it could be weeks. It's hard, watching him like this. I never knew how precious time could be. And I wasted so much time, refusing to come home."

Cal stopped by an old bench and turned to face her. "I know. I'm glad you're here. The old man and me, we didn't always see eye-to-eye, even after he hired me back. But he needs family with him now."

Cassie stared across the pond to where the old camp house stood. "I should get back. We have a routine now. I'm always there for his meals and his medications. But it's getting harder and harder to make him eat and take his pills."

Cal checked his watch. "We won't stay long." He pointed to the camp house.

"So you wanted to talk to me about that?" She glanced at the dilapidated old house. "What's the plan?"

"We need to tear it down."

Cassie let the memories roll over her like the wind. Off in the distance, a storm cloud was picking up steam. More spring showers were on the way. "I guess so. We don't have hunters here the way we used to. Maybe one day we can revisit that, but for now you have your hands full with the crops and the livestock."

Cal stood silent for a minute, one eye on the changing skies. "Okay, then. I'll get some of the men on it. Jack says we can take the wood to one of the recycling plants in Albany."

"That's good." Cassie turned, a strong gust of wind blowing her hair away from her face. "How long will *you* stay, Cal? After, I mean?"

Cal glanced up at the darkening sky again. "I haven't

thought much about that. But I plan on seeing this harvest through. And later this week, I need to take another drive up to my place. I've got a good man working the land for me, but I like to see how things are going from time to time. I went last week and everything looked good." He reached out and pushed her hair off her face. "Hey, how'd you like to ride up there with me? I mean, if you're daddy's doing okay. Maybe Friday. We could eat dinner on the way back here. An early dinner so you won't miss visiting with him."

Cassie smiled, a tingling warmth moving through her. "Are you asking me out on a date?"

"I reckon I am." He tugged her into his arms. "Will you go?"

"Let me see how much work I get done between now and then," she said. "I want to clean out my mother's things. And I need to get some samples going on my new collection. Teresa's already pulled out the old sewing machine I used long ago—just so I can play a bit until I hit on the right combination. I've ordered some fabric. I like to work with the patterns before I send my pieces into production."

"Okay. I'll check back with you on Thursday."

He kissed her on the forehead then pulled back to stare down at her. "I missed kissing you."

Cassie couldn't hide her feelings on that regard. "I missed you. So much."

He pulled her back and settled his lips against hers, his hand holding her neck while his mouth covered hers. "I could get used to this. But I *can't* get used to this. We both know it would never work."

Cassie felt him pull away then teased him to lighten the mood. But she had to wonder why he was holding back. "So our summer romance won't extend into the fall?"

"Are we having a summer romance?"

"No," she replied, wishing she hadn't blurted that out. "But I do like this truce between us. We work better together when we're not bickering. I guess we can't expect anything more, of course."

He looked expectant then hesitant. "I don't think so, no. You'll go back to Atlanta and I'll go back to my place. And never the two shall meet."

His words said one thing while his eyes told her something entirely different. She had her reasons for resisting, but would she ever know what he was fighting?

Not ready to delve into that, she said, "But Camellia Plantation will carry on?"

"Somehow," he said. "You can hire anyone you want to run it and if you do go through with your plans for building a manufacturing company here, you'll have to make more frequent visits. I'll help you find a good foreman."

"Or I could just forget the whole manufacturing idea and sell it. Let it go and get on with building Cassie's Closet boutiques all over the country."

"Are you thinking of doing that?"

She didn't know how to answer that question. But in her heart, she knew she could never sell Camellia. "No. I mean, one of my goals is to build more boutiques. But I'd never sell this place. Only as a last resort."

The relief she saw on his face made her heart jump again. Warning herself to keep her distance in spite of their truce, Cassie wondered for the hundredth time why Cal seemed to care so much for this land.

Then she reminded herself that he'd gone along with

her father's plan that they marry. She'd probably never really know if he did it just to appease a dying man or if he did it so he could gain control of Camellia.

What if he really did it for you? Just you? Only you?

She couldn't wrap her brain around that, no matter how many times he tried to convince her. Or kiss her.

He cared a lot. So much that he'd been willing to marry her without warning her of her father's plan. She needed to remember that whenever he kissed her. And she needed to remember that Cal might still be guarding some secrets of his own.

But she also needed to remember that Cal hadn't pressured her into this farce of a marriage. Maybe because, just like her, he didn't really want to be married.

Or maybe he didn't want to be married to *her*.

And no amount of land or holdings could change a man's mind on such a serious issue as that, if he didn't really want it.

A chill went over Cassie as they stood there. She'd never force Cal into something he didn't want. It wouldn't be right. So why did she all of a sudden feel so disappointed that he hadn't fought a little harder to convince her?

Don't be silly, she told herself. *You don't want this marriage. You're not the marrying kind.*

"Let's get home before this rainstorm hits," she said.

Cal glanced at the sky then pulled up the local radar app on his phone screen. "Good idea. That's a bad system. I need to check the weather radio. We need rain but we don't need a storm. The crops are at a tender stage right now. I don't want to have to replant."

A flash of lightning danced down the horizon to the west, followed by a crash of thunder that shook the trees. Ladybug and Cocoa, untethered, took off for the stables.

Leaving Cassie and Cal with no way home.

The first fat drops of rain hit hard and heavy. Cal pointed toward the camp house and grabbed her hand, dragging her across the pasture.

And then, the hail hit.

HAIL.

Cassie remembered what big, fat drops of icy hail could do to a tender, budding crop. She glanced at Cal after he hauled her up onto the old porch and saw the concerned frown on his face. "What can we do?"

"Pray," he shouted over the golf-ball-size chunks of hail hitting what was left of the old tin roof. "I don't think we're gonna make it back to the house. This is a bad one." He put a hand on her back. "Let's wait it out inside here."

Cassie nodded, her light clothes now giving her a chill. But when she glanced into the dark recesses of the run-down cabin, another kind of chill hit her.

"You okay?" Cal asked, his expression etched in concern.

"Yes. I think so. Just I haven't been in here in a long time. It doesn't look the way I remember."

Memories, dark and gray, hissed and danced in a sizzling clarity that matched the lightning outside. What was it about this creepy old place?

Blocking the darkness, she instead thought about being here with Cal. She'd felt safe here with him.

Cal pulled her in through the door. "It's not much, but it should keep us dry. Let's hope the roof holds up though."

"Nice," Cassie said, the word shouted over the sound

of hail smashing to the ground. She glanced around, saw an old bed frame and the broken dining table, remembered there used to be a big puffy plaid couch on one wall.

"This is not the best place to be," Cal said, straining as he watched the dark skies. He checked his phone again. "Severe thunderstorm warning. We need to take cover immediately."

Cassie smiled at his humor, but her heart was pounding as fast as that falling hail. Or maybe it was the assault of memories pounding. "That weather report doesn't sound promising."

Cal squinted in the dark, the *drip-drip* of rain coming through the hole in the roof echoing around him. "More rain and thunderstorms throughout the night. Possibility of more hail and tornadoes." He tried to scroll down. "Service is getting weak."

"I'd forgotten how volatile the weather can be," Cassie said, shivers racing down her spine. "This one sure came up fast."

"You're cold." Cal went to an old trunk and tore through some blankets then pulled up a blue chenille spread. He shook it out then brought it to Cassie. "I think it's clean."

Cassie pulled the old blanket close, a familiar scent wafting up to her nose. The blanket felt warm but that sweet scent clogged her brain with a hint of some long-lost memory. "That's better. Thanks."

Cal nodded, his gaze on the heavy hail that continued to fall outside. "This is gonna be a mess."

His cell rang. "Yeah? Jack, you okay? Where are you? You're cutting in and out."

He listened then responded. "Just stay there. Make sure everyone is safe and dry. Probably won't get much done the rest of the day. We're in the camp house." He put the phone away. "He's at the main house. They made it that far so they're waiting it out in the stables. He said he was worried since our horses showed up without us."

Cassie saw the worry on his face when he disconnected. "How bad do you think?"

"Bad enough. Jack's worried about another worker who's on the other end of the property, checking fences. He's waiting it out in his truck. Can't call him. He doesn't have a cell phone."

Cassie glanced outside. "The wind's picking up. I hope he'll be okay."

"Me, too." Cal went to stand in the door, the sound of the hail dying down around him. "If it clears on out, the crops could dry out and hang on to survive. But if this settles in, well, it could mean having to replant some of the corn and soybeans. Not to mention the peanuts could rot on the vine."

"That's not good."

He came back into the room. "No. It's a farmer's worst nightmare."

Cassie saw the strain around his eyes, heard the fatigue in his voice. "What about your place?"

Cal pulled out his cell and listened. "Can't get through. I'll try later." He threw the phone on the old table. "My guess is this system hit up there before it reached us. I knew rain was coming but this kind of snuck up on me."

The look he gave her told Cassie that he'd been distracted.

By her.

"I'm sorry. I shouldn't have dragged you away from your work to give me a tour."

"You're the boss."

He was angry now. She tried not to take it personally. But she had a right to see the crops. She needed to learn everything she could about farming if she wanted to keep this place.

"I'm not so sure I'm up to this, Cal," she finally said over the drone of rain hitting tin.

"What do you mean?"

"I mean, I'm not a farmer. Sure I can hire someone, but I've watched you dealing with different problems every day. How can I do my job and keep on top of this, too?"

"Same as me," he said, going to the door again. "You get up and go about your day and try to take what comes."

Cassie stood there watching him. He paced and stared. Paced and stared. Was he thinking about his own place and wishing he'd stayed there? Was he thinking of all he'd sacrificed to help her save Camellia Plantation?

It had never once occurred to her that Cal might resent all he'd had to give up in order to satisfy her dying father. He'd been forced to return here to the place that he'd left in disgrace, forced to deal with Marsha and her bitterness. And now, he'd been forced to deal with Cassie, too.

She moved past all the leaky spots in the ceiling and came to a stop in front of him, hoping to stop his pacing. "I'll learn, Cal," she said. "I'll learn everything I need to know. I won't abandon you and I won't abandon this farm. I promise."

"You can't promise me that," he said, staring down at her with a solid disbelief and a shocked expression. "You know how that goes."

"Yes, I do know. We promised each other so much, but Cal, we were young and caught up in each other. We didn't think things through. And when we had to deal with a crisis, we both shut down." She touched a hand to his arm. "I understand now. About Marsha. She wasn't complicated and moody and needy like me. She was just a girl who wanted to be with you."

His eyes slammed into hers. "Yeah. She was easy."

"And I wasn't."

"No, you were the princess in the tower. I didn't know how to handle you, Cassie. I still don't know how to handle you."

Cassie put her arms around his neck and pulled him close, a sense of peace coming over her in spite of the roar of the wind and the mist of rain hitting them. "I've changed since then. All you have to do now is hold me. Just hold me."

Then she pulled his head down and touched her lips to his, her kiss confirming that she meant everything she'd just said. She wouldn't leave him again. She wouldn't run away again. Somehow, she'd find a way to make this work. She wanted to be with Cal. Maybe for now, maybe for a lifetime. And she'd find a way to make that happen.

Even if it meant coming home to build a manufacturing company.

Even if it meant having to face Marsha once and for all.

Even if it meant proving it to Cal and her father and the world by agreeing to marry him.

And even if it meant having to face all the secrets holding them apart.

CHAPTER FIFTEEN

CAL SENSED THE DIFFERENCE in Cassie. Even with a storm raging outside and a fine mist of wind and water washing over them, he could feel the tension leaving her body as she pulled him close and kissed him.

They'd kissed before since she'd returned. But this— this was different. This time, she'd initiated the kiss, her touch demanding and endearing all at the same time.

He tugged her to him, his mouth hitting on hers with a need that floored him. How long had he been holding this in, waiting for her to make the first move?

A lifetime.

He relished the taste of her, savored the feel of her, wanted to stay as close to her as possible. This was the past all over again, but this was also something new and fresh and sweet and pure, all wrapped up in longing and love and need.

He drew back, his breath rushing. "Cassie."

She looked up at him, her blue eyes wild with a sweetness that grounded him in the storm.

"Cassie."

"Don't, Cal. Just kiss me again."

He did, taking his time, then growing impatient. He became so lost in her essence that he didn't even notice the skies had darkened or that the wind and hail had stopped.

Then his ears felt weighted with pressure and he

heard a distant roar. At first he thought it was just the roar of his pulse. But it grew louder. Even while the outside world stood perfectly still.

Cassie lifted away, a startled look on her flushed face. "What's that?"

"Tornado!" Cal grabbed her, glanced around for a safe place. "C'mon."

He tossed the broken table over on its side and pulled her down, dragging the blanket and the table with them to the wall that held the closet. He flung open the closet door and shouted over the storm, "We won't fit all the way inside but that extra wall might help."

His heart pumping, he pulled Cassie down and into the dark closet, pushing at cobwebs as he threw the blanket over them. Then he rolled over her, shielding her body with his. "It's okay. Hang on. It'll be okay."

Cassie clung to him, her shout echoing inside his ears. "Cal?"

He braced the table against a wall and the open closet door, forming a wedge that surrounded them. Then he wrapped his hands over her head. "Hold on, Cassie. No matter what, you hold on to me."

She did, her arms wrapped across his back as she closed her eyes and prayed they didn't get blown apart. She heard the roar that sounded like engines rushing out of control, felt the pressure change inside her ears.

Then she thought about her father.

And started thrashing.

"Let me up, Cal! I have to get home. My daddy—"

The earth shifted and changed and the old, rotten tree that was crushed against the back of the big room lifted and crumbled and swirled away. Cassie caught sight of it just before Cal curled his body around hers and held her with a vise grip of protection.

The wind hit them with debris. The rain stung against Cassie's skin with a knifelike intensity. Small branches and bits of wood and dust lifted around them, but Cal held himself over her, protecting her.

She screamed but the sound of it was muffled against Cal's soaking wet shirt and the old blanket. She closed her eyes, shock and memories fighting against each other inside her head. A teakettle whistling, a woman's laughter, a man's voice.

What was happening to her?

I need to know. I need to understand.

I need to tell Cal I love him, no matter what.

She'd been to this camp house so many times and now, she remembered bits and pieces of another time, the memories roaring over her with the same force as the tornado.

No, I won't think about that. I can't. I won't.

"Cassie?"

She heard Cal's voice inside her head, in her dreams, in the wind.

Then she heard silence. Complete silence.

"Cassie, honey. It's over. Are you all right?"

Cassie opened her eyes, the pain of clenching her teeth tearing through her temples. "Cal?"

She looked around, saw the sky over her head, felt the soft rain hitting her face. "It's over?"

"Yes." He sat up and helped her into his embrace. "It's all right. We're safe."

She sat there for a minute, her mind whirling, her chest tightening while she savored the strength and warmth of his body against hers. She tried to take in air but she couldn't breathe. "Cal. My daddy. I have to go to him. Teresa and the others. Jack? What about the town?"

"I'll get you home," he said. "But we have to be careful. We don't know what we'll find out there."

He helped her up, checking her as he brushed debris away from her hair and face. "You have a cut right there over your eye." He touched a hand to the stinging spot.

"I'm okay," she said, needing to get away from this place. Her mind held to their kiss then recoiled back into the past, confusion whirling around her like the chaotic wind that had just passed over them. She checked him over, her fingers touching on his hair and his face, her eyes locking with his. "I want to go home."

"Okay. Let me make sure it's clear."

Cal went to the front of the shell. The back of the house where the old tree had fallen so long ago was now completely gone, leaving a wide gaping space over the old floors. Only the kitchen and the closet next to it remained.

Cassie looked down. They'd been in each other's arms near the old tree. Cal had saved her life.

She went to the door, thinking how ironic it was that they'd forgotten to shut it. Maybe that had saved them, too.

Cal stood out in the yard looking around, his hands on his hips. She slushed through the wet ground and took his hand in hers. "We're lucky to be alive."

He gave her hand a squeeze then tugged her close, his eyes dark as night. "Yes, we are."

Trees were down around the pond and big chunks of hail lay melting all over the pasture. The dock was gone, parts of it floating in the water, the rest of it strewn to kingdom come.

"I think I lost my cell phone," he said, turning

toward the cabin. "It was on the table. Let me see if I can find it then we'll start walking."

Cassie followed him back inside to help. Together, they searched the debris-covered floor. She spotted the black phone crushed up against the open closet door. "I see it," she shouted. When she tugged at the phone, a dark object lying next to an old rusted safe inside the tiny closet caught her eye.

Cassie reached inside and found a small brown leather box with an intricate gold lock on it. And the initials EB scrolled across it in gold ink. She handed the phone to Cal then pulled the damp box out of its hiding place. "Look. Another part of my mother's past. It must have been in the safe, but the door came open."

Cal glanced at the box then at the safe. "The safe lock's broken. No telling who did that."

Cassie's dread multiplied tenfold. "I'll have to break the lock on this box if I want to find out what's inside."

"Bring it with us," he said, motioning for her to come with him. He grabbed the phone from her. "This is useless. We need to get to the house."

Cassie tucked the square little box against her side, hurrying to check on her father while she wondered what secrets the storm had finally released.

CAL HELD HER HAND all the way up the muddy lane. They were both soaked, their shoes and pants dirty. Cassie didn't speak, but the look of terror on her face kept her moving toward the big house. And the way she held that box so tightly broke his heart.

What if her home was gone? What if her father had been hurt or worse? And what was in that box? He didn't know whether to pray for answers or ask for every secret on this old place to stay buried.

As they neared a curve in the lane, she tugged her hand free and rushed ahead of him, a squeal of joy rising out of her throat. "It's still there, Cal. The house is still there."

"Thank goodness."

Cal rushed to catch up then looked over to where the cottage should be. The little white house had been shifted right off its foundation and lay crumbled and crushed amongst a stand of clipped pine trees.

"Oh, Cal." Cassie turned to him, her eyes wide. "Your house—"

"I can see." He motioned toward the big house. "Let's go check on your dad first. I'll figure out what to do about that later."

As they trudged up the sloping yard, Cassie's rush of breath told the tale. Several of the camellia bushes were uprooted and broken, but many of them remained intact. A couple of pine trees had been snapped in half and lay across the pool and the back patio, their trunks twisted like taffy candy. Shingles from the hipped roof, scattered across the yard and pool, lay about as if someone had tossed out a deck of cards. The twisted awning from the patio floated like a ship's sail against the poolhouse fence.

The back door opened and Teresa rushed out. "Cassie!"

"Teresa!" Cassie ran to hug the older woman. "Where's Daddy? Is he okay?"

"He's safe, honey. Sharon rolled his bed up to an inside wall and practically threw herself over him. I held him on one side and her on the other. He woke up during the worst of it, but he's okay. He's asking for you and Cal."

Cassie hurried into the house, oblivious to the mud she was tracking inside. Putting the dirty wet box on the hall table, she rushed into her father's room.

"Daddy?"

Sharon grabbed Cassie and hugged her close. "We're so glad you're all right. He's been so worried."

"Cassie-girl," Marcus said, his hand reaching toward her, his eyes wild and roving. "That was some storm. Remember that time your mother got lost in a storm? Couldn't find her for hours. She rode it out in the camp house."

Cal stood at the door of the room, allowing Cassie some time with her father. But he didn't miss the hiss of breath leaving her body as she leaned over and took her daddy's hand.

When she glanced back at him, the look of sheer terror on her face brought him closer. "Cassie, what's wrong?"

She looked back down at Marcus. "I…I don't recall—"

Marcus went right on ranting. "Tell me where you were? How bad is it? We'll need to check the corn and peanuts. Hail damage could mess with the bottom line. I need to round up several of the workers to help clean up."

Cal stepped up to the bed. "I'll get on that, Marcus. Don't worry. I need to call Jack. He was out at the stables."

Teresa heard him and called out. "He's all right, Cal. But one of the hands is still out there in the far field. They're trying to find him."

"I need to go." Cal shot Cassie a glance, worried

about her. She'd gone still and silent, her eyes blank. Maybe a delayed shock? Or something else. "Cassie, are you sure—"

"We're fine. Go." She didn't look up again.

He left, a sick feeling covering him with the same heaviness as the leftover humidity from the storm. Did she regret kissing him back there at the camp house? Did she regret getting caught in the storm with him?

Probably just distress, he thought. She'd just survived a tornado and, of course, she was worried about her father and this house. Nothing more. He didn't want to leave her but he couldn't leave a worker out there alone and possibly hurt.

He'd come back and check on her later. Because after that kiss, he had to know if she felt the same way he did.

SHE FELT ILL. AS IF SHE might be sick. Her stomach roiled and coiled until dizziness made her light-headed. Cassie looked over at Sharon. "Are you sure you're okay? And you've checked his vitals?"

Sharon nodded, giving her a thorough look. She came around the bed to reach out to Cassie. "I'm fine, honey. But you don't look so hot. Let me check your blood pressure."

Cassie pushed her away. "I'm all right. Just worried about everyone here."

Sharon stepped back to the bed. "My heart is still beating like a rock band, but I'm okay. I've checked him and rechecked him. His vitals are strong. Tough old bird."

Marcus opened his eyes. "I'm right here and I'm fine." He held tight to Cassie's hand. "You know, I went out in the storm that day. Found her there all alone. She was crying. She'd lost her favorite scarf." He grabbed Cassie's arm. "I brought her home and put her to bed. She was so distraught. So upset."

Cassie's heart leapt so hard against her chest, she felt faint. "I'm sorry, Daddy. I don't remember much."

"You need to marry Cal before I die."

That statement jarred her out of the despair that had taken over her soul. "You must be all right. You're back on that subject."

He chuckled then coughed. "I want you to be happy. Really happy."

"I don't need to get married to be happy, Daddy."

She just needed him well again and back the way he used to be before her mother died. She needed to go back to that summer when she and Cal were so in love and her mother was still alive and everything was covered in a shimmering golden mist of hope.

She needed…Cal. Oh, mercy, she still loved him so much. It had taken a storm to make her see the light. But she couldn't act on that love until—

Until she could find out the truth.

She needed to find out the truth between her parents. Because she knew in her heart that something had happened in that camp house, something shocking and disturbing and real.

And she was pretty sure she'd been there to witness it firsthand. Whatever it was, she'd blocked it out of her mind until today.

Which is why she intended to break into that box.

CHAPTER SIXTEEN

BONE-TIRED AND ACHING all over, Cal headed toward the main house just as a rich burnished sun began to set over the tree-strewn pasture. Amazing how the weather had changed back to sunny and calm now. But the drenched woods, pasture and lawn all showed the damage of the storm.

And the little house where he'd stayed was gone forever.

He didn't have a place to sleep tonight. But that didn't matter right now. He'd find a hotel room and start all over tomorrow. With *starting all over* being the key.

The back door slammed and Cassie came running down the steps. She'd cleaned herself up and was now wearing jeans and a pretty flower-covered T-shirt.

"Cal, I'm so sorry." She took him in her arms, her shower-fresh hair smelling intoxicating and sweet. "Jack came in to give us a report. He told me about Bert Calhoun. Then we heard the ambulance." She stared up at him, her big blue eyes moving over his face. "I was afraid something had happened to you."

"I'm fine. But I'll sure miss Bert."

"Jack said Bert didn't have time to find shelter."

Cal pulled back, his hands on her waist. "A tree hit his truck. We found him and managed to get him out, but it was too late. Jack and me...we had to go and tell his wife."

Tears welled in her eyes. "It's so horrible. And the worst—I didn't even know the man. He works for my father and I didn't even know him."

"He was a good man—just trying to make a living."

"I want to go visit his wife. We have to do something, make sure she's okay financially. Would that be insulting, to offer to help her with the funeral expenses?"

Touched, Cal gave her a tired smile. "No, I think that would be appreciated. She works at a shop in town, but they don't have a whole lot. We'll go see her when we get a few things taken care of around here."

He gave her a report on the livestock—all accounted for. Horses were safe inside the stable. It had some roof damage. A few trees down in the pasture and near the pond, but then she'd seen that with her own eyes. "No equipment damage, thankfully. We store most of the big machines in the equipment barn each day anyway. Except for the tractor Bert was using. He didn't have time to even think about that."

She kept her hands on his shoulders, her gaze questioning. "What did you hear about your place?"

He breathed a sigh of relief on that. "I finally got through on one of the workers' phones about an hour ago. Just some wind and rain up that way. Seems the southern part of the state got the worst of it." Lifting a hand in the air, he mapped out the storm's path. "A clear swath through the eastern end of the town and the pasture and right over the pond. No telling what kind of damage we'll hear about tomorrow."

"Teresa has a battery-powered radio, but it's got a lot of static. We're hearing a lot of different reports about damage all along the river but we're not sure about anything right now."

He glanced around. "I wanted to make sure y'all were okay before I go search through what's left of the cottage. I need to get some clothes and I'll have to find the safe I kept in the office. It has a thumb drive with all the business and financial information backed up on it."

She exhaled a little breath. "That's good, at least."

"If the safe survived the storm." He stepped back to leave. "Jack said I could stay with him or I might find a hotel."

"You'll stay here," she said, her hand on his chest. "You'll stay with us."

"Cassie, I don't think—"

"Cal, I need you here."

Letting that authoritative declaration wash over him, he could only nod. "Yes, ma'am."

She lifted her gaze, giving him a direct look. "That's not an order. You're family."

He wished that were true. But he was just the hired help who was in love with the rich girl. "I wouldn't feel right."

Even frowning, she still got to him. "Because of me? Because I'll be in the house?"

He tugged her close again. "Yes." He thought about that kiss in the camp house. And all the emotions brewing inside him, just waiting to break free. "Cassie, a lot happened today. We had our own little twister going on before the real storm hit."

"I know." She lowered her gaze. "I know, and we need to figure that out at some point. But I refuse to let you go to a hotel when we have extra rooms." She glanced back toward the door. "I'd feel better if you were nearby. Daddy's been restless since the storm and he isn't making any sense."

Alarms went off in Cal's head. "What's he saying now?"

She shook her head. "Talking about my mother and another storm. And...other things."

He saw the worry and the fear in her eyes, felt the heavy dread falling across his shoulders. "Did you open that box?"

"No. I'm almost afraid to, and besides, I don't have the key." Giving him an imploring look, she said, "I'd appreciate it if you could help me get it open."

Cal looked around at the broken tree limbs and scattered debris. "My toolbox is in the truck. I'll get it when I go for some clothes."

"Thanks." She stepped away. "I'll get up the courage to see what's in there. Later when I'm alone and I can think straight. It might be nothing, or it might be everything."

"You don't need me around when you do open the box."

Giving him a questioning look, she went into that cool, calm mode he knew so well. "If you don't want to stay here..."

"Having second thoughts?" he asked, his eyes holding hers.

She held two knuckles to her chin. "Yes. No. You need to be here on the premises. We'll deal with this together."

What could he say? It would be a lot more convenient for him to be on site. They'd have to hit the ground running tomorrow. But he'd need a good night's sleep tonight. Looking down at her face, her lips, her eyes, he doubted that would happen.

"No, it's okay. I'll stay." He turned, anxious to get to his destroyed residence. "I do need to be available for the workers. I'm going to look the place over, see what I can salvage."

She stood with her hands by her side. "Teresa has sandwiches for dinner since the electricity isn't back on yet. We'll dine by candlelight."

"Good."

He kept walking, the thought of Cassie surrounded by candlelight making him almost trip over his own feet. That should be one dandy meal.

Then he thought about their kiss in that storm, his heart twisting and flipping like a twig in the wind.

At least he had lots to keep him busy. And hopefully keep his mind off her.

Right. Like that was gonna happen.

Two HOURS LATER, they sat in the kitchen listening to a battery-powered radio tuned to a local station, candles of all sizes glowing around them. The news wasn't good, but it could have been worse. The town proper of Camellia had suffered a little damage, mainly from trees falling on roofs and power lines going down. Even though it had no electricity, the Pig and Plow seemed to be the gathering place.

Cal figured that made sense. Everyone would want something to eat and drink after this harrowing experience. Probably mostly drink. "I should call and check on Marsha," he said, bracing for what was sure to be a frown from Cassie.

"Go ahead," she told him, her water glass in her hand. "See if we can do anything, if anyone needs help."

Surprised at her new attitude, he nodded then used the house phone. At least the phone lines were back up.

When Marsha answered, he heard music and chatter in the background. "Just checking on y'all," he said, his eyes on Cassie.

"That was mighty nice of you," Marsha retorted. "I heard about Bert. Hard to believe."

"Yes, it is. Cassie and I are going to ride over to see his wife after we finish eating."

"Cassie and you, huh?"

"Yes. He did work here."

"Yep, he did." She went silent then said, "Thanks for calling, Cal. I got customers lined up. We're grilling up some of the meat out in the barbecue drums since the freezer isn't working."

"Maybe you can save the rest if the power company can get things fixed."

"Yeah, well, if we don't, we'll just eat hamburgers and steaks for the rest of the week. On the house, I reckon."

He hung up, admiring Marsha's spunk, then turned back to the woman he loved.

Cassie in candlelight.

No one else could hold a candle to her. He'd loved her for most of his adult life, but today in that storm that love had surpassed his daydreams and his long-held hopes. What was he doing, resisting her at every turn and then turning to her every time he got a chance? They needed to settle this, one way or another. If he'd lost her today, he wouldn't have gotten over it. And he would have never been able to forgive himself.

"Everything okay?" she asked.

"Yes." Had he been staring at her? "They're cooking up everything on the outside grill so it won't all spoil."

"Good idea. We did the best we could with what was in our freezer. Hopefully, we can keep everything iced until the power comes back on."

Teresa came in from across the hallway and listened to Cassie, then added, "I've got it all in ice chests right now. Took what ice was still left in the refrigerator and packed it all down. I sure don't want all those vegetables I canned from the fall garden to go to waste."

"Maybe we should throw a barbeque for all the hands," Cassie said, her sandwich half-eaten. "They'll need to eat."

Teresa nodded then took her own sandwich and started toward her room. "Your daddy's awake but Sharon's getting him settled down for the night, we hope. I'll be reading by candlelight if y'all need me."

"Thank you," Cassie replied. "I'll go in and see him before I go to bed." She looked over at Cal. "He didn't eat much earlier. The storm sure made him fidgety."

"He's never liked storms."

Surprise colored her eyes. "I didn't know that."

Cal shrugged. "He's said things to me, things he's probably never told anyone. I can't be sure if it's the sickness or his memories."

"Such as?"

Cal wasn't ready to get into that. Not tonight. He had too much else to deal with. "Just memories, Cassie. Or possibly delusions. It's hard to say and I don't want to give you any false impressions regarding your daddy. Besides, I have to get back out there and check on my workers and make sure we've covered everything." Cal needed some time to digest this day. Just like so many days lately, this one had been earth-shattering in more ways than one.

She got up to follow him to the sink. "You're still not being completely honest with me, are you?"

He whirled to stare at her. "I can't be honest when I'm not sure about things. I'm not gonna stand here and repeat the rants of a sick old man, no. It's not fair to him or you. I don't get what you think we're all hiding from you, anyway."

He hated telling her that, hated not being able to pour his heart out to her and explain all the pieces of this puzzle he'd been putting together for the past few months. But he wasn't going to be the one to break her heart again.

She looked as if she might be ready for a confrontation but then she dropped her hands to her side and shook her head. "I'm not blaming you. It's just nothing makes any sense anymore. My daddy is frantic for me to marry you. And it can't be because he has a sentimental heart. It's almost as if he's trying to make up for something that happened back then."

Cal came close then and lifted her chin, his eyes locking with hers. "Maybe he's just a dying man who wants to make amends for the past. We were all a part of what happened that day, in one way or another, and I think he regrets how he treated you and me. That's it. That's all." His hand moved from her chin to her cheek, his fingers brushing over her satiny skin. And because he'd survived to live another day and because he'd decided he wasn't going to let her go this time, he finally asked the one question he'd been dying to ask. "Would it be so bad, being married to me?"

STUNNED, CASSIE COULDN'T speak at first. After finding her next breath, she put her hand over his. "If you had asked me that a few days ago, I would have said yes, it would be awful."

"Wow."

He moved his hand away, but she held on tight. "That was then, Cal. But today, during that storm, with you there beside me, holding me and protecting me..." She stopped, a sigh escaping through her parted lips, her hand clutching his. "I realized something today. I could have lost you. I could have lost you and my home and my father, all in one day."

He tugged her close with his other hand. "You didn't. We're here. We're right here. I'm here."

"But I lost everyone before in just one day. One horrible day, and my world shifted and changed forever. I can't go through that again, but I don't want to let you go, either."

"Cassie..." He brought her hand to his face then kissed her fingers. "I'm not going anywhere. I told you I'd only marry you if you wanted that, too. You just say the word."

She backed away. "But I can't just say the word. It's a big step."

"What about us, then? What about our dreams?"

She pushed a hand through her hair. The humidity had made it curl around her face. "We can't go back to that time. We can't pick right up where we left off, no matter how hard my daddy is trying to make that happen." Dropping her hands to her side, she looked up at him. "We've both changed. I don't know how I feel now. Confused. Unsure. Afraid. I won't force you into anything."

"Or maybe it's the other way around," he said. "Maybe *you* don't want to be forced into anything."

"I don't want to be *rushed* into it. There's a big difference."

"I agree. We can't be together just to ease our guilt. That would never work."

"Exactly." She wished he hadn't said that, but it had been the same thing she'd been thinking since the day her father suggested it. "My father's guilt can't make a marriage."

Cal lifted his chin then gave her a long look. "I wonder if we could have stayed together back then. You always planned on leaving anyway, so I don't see how it could have worked. College girl, stable boy. Not a good match." Then he looked off into the sunset. "And it's still not a good match."

Horrified that he could even say that, she shook her head. "You know I'd planned to come home as often as possible. I would have spent every weekend here, just to be with you. And you were going to come to Athens and visit me, remember?"

She could see the memories in his midnight eyes. And she could also see the pain and doubt. "Here's something else I realized. The same thing that tore us apart all those years ago is still tearing us apart."

He grabbed her arm then and nodded. "You're right. And that thing is this, Cassie. I'm not good enough for you, even now, even today."

Her heart hammered a warning but she couldn't stop now. "Is that another reason why you turned to Marsha? Is it, Cal?"

His expression told the truth, at last. He didn't move. He stood staring into her eyes. "Yes. Yes, Cassie. I wanted you to be able to walk away, to get on with your life."

Anger poured through her system with all the fury of the earlier storm. "Well, guess what? I didn't have very much of a life after that day. You helped my father destroy me. So instead of being honest about your feelings, you decided to hurt me to my core?"

"I'm sorry." He held her there, his eyes searching her face. She could see the shame and the guilt in his guarded expression. Her heart sank. He'd done it on purpose. He'd deliberately tried to hurt her so she'd turn away from him. But why? She wasn't buying that rich girl/poor boy routine. They'd been too in love for that to stop them.

"You're right. I did hurt you. And that's why I came back. To set things right, same as your father. When will you finally see that?"

"Oh, I see everything now." Cassie dropped her head, still in shock. "It all makes sense at last. You couldn't trust me enough to believe I truly loved you, so you had to go and mess things up by turning to the one person who would break us apart. You deliberately sabotaged us, Cal." Then she was in his face, her fist lying against his chest. "You didn't even give me a chance. You didn't give us a chance. You gave up."

"*I* never had a chance," he retorted. He let her go then stalked toward the door. "I have things to take care of. I'll come back later and help you open that box."

"Don't worry about it," she said, her whole body aching. "I'll figure it out, the same way I've figured out everything else around here—on my own. I'll just keep pounding away until I find the answers."

But she had a horrible feeling that she wouldn't like those answers.

CHAPTER SEVENTEEN

UNABLE TO SLEEP, Cassie rummaged through the kitchen drawers until she found a set of pliers. Now, back in her room, she sat cross-legged on her bed with the square little box in front of her.

Still reeling from the storm and Cal's revelation about why he'd hurt her so badly, she was determined to maintain control over something in her life. Beating this little box to a pulp seemed like a good solution.

She had to know what was in there. But her stomach seemed to freeze up each time she looked at this leather-encrusted treasure chest. She didn't remember her mother owning such a box. But it had to be Eugenia's. The initials EB couldn't just be a coincidence.

Reaching for her hot tea, she thought about the whistling teakettle again, a sense of dread coloring the memories that fought to push through her conscious thoughts.

A whistling teakettle.

A woman laughing.

A man's deep voice.

She touched the box, ready to do battle with it and then stopped, the pliers falling out of her hand.

She'd heard the teakettle whistling away one day when she'd been at the camp house!

No, she'd been outside the camp house, standing on the steps.

Walking? She often walked through the pasture on spring days like this one. Or rode Heathcliff and tethered him on the old porch railing at the camp house while she sat and read out on the dock. But in this memory she had been younger, afraid. She'd never gone this far from the house on her own.

What else?

What about this particular day?

A woman's laughter? Her mother maybe?

With her father?

Shaking off the memories, she made a face and picked up the pliers. "Maybe they were having a little afternoon tryst and it embarrassed me."

Nothing wrong with a married couple enjoying their love.

But what about the teakettle?

"Maybe you're imagining things," she said on a low whisper, the pliers pressed against the rusty little lock on the old box.

Or maybe she'd been avoiding the truth.

In the same way she'd avoided the truth about Cal.

Her fingers hurting from the tight grip she had on the pliers, she let go to rest for a minute, her thoughts on Cal and all the feelings moving between them. When he'd come back to the house, carrying a bundle of clothes and a few of his other possessions, she'd shown him to his room and turned to go to her own.

"What about Bert's wife?" he'd asked.

She wasn't in any shape to console. "First thing tomorrow. It's so late now."

"What about the box?"

"I think I need to be by myself for a while. I'll worry about that later."

He'd given her one last long look before going into his room and shutting the door.

Now, he was footsteps away down the hall, and she had to wonder if he was awake, too. Cal, right here in her house, so close. Yet still there was so much holding them apart.

She looked around her own room, memories coming sweetly and softly to touch her heart. Her broken heart.

He'd let her go. Deliberately let her go. And he'd used Marsha to make sure Cassie would break up with him. Why? Why hadn't he come to Cassie and told her everything—his fears, his doubts. She would have reassured him. Apparently, he didn't trust their love enough to fight so he'd done something to make sure she'd break up with him.

"Guess what? It worked."

All these years of doubt and pain and longing, simply because he didn't think he could make the cut with a Brennan. Or he didn't care enough to stay with her. Not good enough for her? He was ten times the human being she'd ever been. He'd come back to this place even after her father had threatened him and sent him packing. She'd sent him packing, too. He'd allowed her to do that, allowed her to believe the worst of him.

But how could he have come to that conclusion when they'd held each other and promised each other a lifetime commitment? How, on the week when she'd needed him most, could he turn away from her and break her heart in such a decisive way?

"Maybe *I'm* not good enough for you, Cal." After all, she hadn't had the strength to fight for him.

Then.

Did she have the strength now?

He'd sacrificed for her, then and now. He'd given

her up. But he'd come back and he kept telling her she was the reason. Did he still truly believe he didn't have a right to her love, or had she missed something all along? Some other reason that he wasn't willing to reveal to her?

Would it be so bad, being married to me?

His whispered words, so full of longing and need, played through her head.

Cassie held to the lock on the box, her eyes closed as she imagined being Cal's wife, imagined walking down the aisle to say her vows to him, imagined having his children and laughing with him.

A woman's laughter.

She heard it over and over now, as if this very box were trying to play a tune to her. Before she could sort through her problems with Cal, she had to sort through this little trinket box.

Determination and curiosity won out over her need to go down the hall and beg him to tell her his innermost thoughts. She stood up and braced her knees against the bed then placed the pliers against the old padlock and pressed with all her might. With a grunt and a little muscle, she managed to get a firm grip and go to work.

A click and then, a release. The thin circle of metal fell into pieces amid the floral design of the bedspread.

Taking a deep breath, Cassie sat down, her hands shaking, and opened the little chest.

Inside, she found a stack of what looked like letters tied together with a white ribbon. They glowed golden in the muted candlelight.

Eugenia.

Letters addressed to her mother.

Love letters? From her father?

Cassie's heart pounded, her pulse crashing against her temples, sweat glistening on her skin. Letters from her father, of course. They'd loved each other so much. So much. Obviously, her mother had hidden the letters in a special place, a place where they went to laugh and love and be together.

Cassie sat holding the bundle of envelopes, the paper as brittle and aged as her recessed memories. Her flashlight shined brightly into these memories.

She'd been what…maybe eight years old? She was upstairs, supposedly resting before dinner. She sneaked out of the house and ran down the outdoor staircase and away before Teresa realized she was gone. She wanted to go to the camp house because she knew her mother was there. She'd heard her mother on the phone, whispering.

"I'll be there. The house is quiet. We're alone. I'll see you at the pond. Yes, the camp house."

Cassie had waited and waited. She wanted to see her mother, surprise Eugenia. But when she reached the little house, she heard laughter. She heard the teakettle boiling away, whistling through the buried passages of her mind. But no one bothered to move the teakettle off the stove. The laughter grew and grew, feminine and dainty and sultry. And the man's voice drew out each word with a deep and strong declaration.

"I love you, Eugenia. Only you."

Cassie threw down the stack of letters, her mind whirling with all sorts of scenarios.

And then, it all came rushing back.

She crept up onto the porch, to an open-screened window. She peeked inside, quickly. One look and a few more whispered words between them, then Cassie turned and ran all the way back home to hide in her room. She never told Teresa she had left her room that day.

She never told anyone about that day and what she saw through that window. Instead, she somehow managed to bury the whole episode deep inside her psyche.

Because the man in the cabin with her mother that day had not been her father.

"OH, NO, NO." She dropped the flashlight and backed away from the bed, her mind spinning so fast, nausea threatened to overtake her. "No, no."

She had to be wrong. Her father would have been there. Shutting her eyes to the memories, Cassie saw herself standing on the porch peering through the big window into the darkness of the cabin.

She'd never actually seen the man's face. But she knew now without a doubt that he had not been her father. Maybe she'd tried to convince herself later that she'd made a mistake. But there was no mistake. No mistake.

She'd only thought—hoped—her parents were together, enjoying a quiet afternoon. Except they hadn't noticed the teakettle screaming away on the stove, the steam from the water rising up to float like a cloud in the late afternoon darkness.

The couple lying across that old bed hadn't even been aware that the kettle was boiling over. Or that a little girl was watching them through the window.

But even now, she didn't want to be sure. She didn't want to think of someone else there with her mother. She couldn't pinpoint why she hadn't seen this before or remembered the words the way they sounded in her head now. What else had he said?

She pushed at the vague memories, refusing to allow

them to the surface. *Enough,* she thought. *I can't take this, not now. Not tonight.*

But she couldn't get the scene at the old camp house out of her mind. She'd stood in almost the same spot and kissed Cal, held Cal, and she'd fallen in love with him all over again.

"It had to be my father that day," she said, staring down at the letters, denial still pushing through her system. "It had to be." She was just a little girl. She could have imagined the whole thing.

A knock at her bedroom door caused Cassie to jump, her hands going to her midsection. "Who is it?"

"Cassie, it's Cal. Teresa just woke me. You need to come downstairs."

She couldn't face Cal now. Not now. She couldn't blurt this out to him, even though she longed to do that. He'd never believe her.

"I'm tired, Cal."

He knocked again and then opened the door, the expression on his face dark and brooding. "I'm sorry but you have to come down. It's your daddy. He's…he's taken a turn for the worse. Karen put in a call to the doctor."

CASSIE FOLLOWED CAL down the winding staircase, her father on her mind now. "Is it bad? Should we call 911?"

Cal took her hand to guide her down the last step. "I don't think calling 911 will help. I think this might be it."

She put a hand to her mouth. "How long before the doctor gets here?"

"He told Karen ten minutes. Marcus gave instructions long ago—no ambulance and a 'do not resuscitate' clause in his medical file."

Of course, she'd be the last to know that, too.

She whirled past Cal and hurried down the hallway and into the big room on the end of the house. She hated this room, hated what it represented. At first, it had been her father's base of power, his domain. Now, it was a sick room, holding him prisoner with its darkness and despair.

"Daddy," she said, the memory of that scene in the camp house overtaking her and with it, all the pain and deceit hitting her solidly inside her gut. "Daddy, I think I understand. I think I know what you've been trying to tell me."

He opened his eyes, his breathing ragged and torn, his chest rattling like old chains hitting against wood. "You look just like her. Hard to look at you. Love you, though. Love you, no matter what."

She cried, hearing those words she'd longed to hear. She cried and pushed away those other distant memories that needed to be released. Not right now. Right now, she only wanted to remember the good. There had to be some good.

"It's all right," she told him, rubbing his arm, smiling through her tears. "I'll be all right, I promise."

"Marry Cal?"

She looked up, felt Cal's hand on her shoulder. And knew what she had to do. "Yes, Daddy. I'll marry Cal. I want to be his wife. I love him, and I promise you I will marry him. You just rest now. It's okay, it's okay."

Marcus looked from her to Cal, his eyes hooded and sagging, the muted light making him look ethereal. "Take care of her."

She heard Cal's rush of breath. "I will, Marcus. I will."

Then her daddy said something that touched Cassie and broke her heart all over again.

"I believe you, son. About everything. Wasn't your fault. Wasn't anybody's fault. I loved her, always. Forgive, just forgive. Love her...my own. My very own."

Cassie let the tears go now, her face moist, the collar of her robe damp. He'd never stopped loving her mother. Or her. And in his own way, he did care about Cal, too. He wanted them both to know that he'd forgiven them for that horrible time, for all that he thought they'd done to disgrace him and betray him by being together. And in return, he needed their forgiveness.

"I forgive you, Daddy," Cassie said, holding his hand, hoping to give him some of her own strength and life.

"That's my girl." Marcus smiled and then closed his eyes, his breath becoming shallow. "You'll always be *my* girl."

The doctor came in, followed by Teresa, and hurried to the bed. He nodded to Cassie then went to work, checking and poking and testing. Then he glanced up and shook his head. "He's going into renal failure. It's just a matter of time now."

"His body is shutting down," Karen said behind Cassie. "He might not wake up again, honey."

"I don't want him to suffer," Cassie said. "No more suffering." She turned to Cal. He pulled her into his arm and held her there.

"He's not in a lot of pain," the doctor said. "We've been giving him a slow drip, but I can give him a shot. You can still talk to him and comfort him. It's okay to reassure him, too."

Cassie turned to look down at her father. "Cal, bring me a chair. I want to sit with him."

Cal did as she asked, setting a chair next to the bed. Then he went and got another one and placed it next to Cassie's.

"I'll stay with you."

She nodded, unable to speak her gratitude or her despair.

And unable to reconcile in her heart that her beautiful, gracious mother had had an affair with another man.

And had destroyed the man lying in this bed, who even now, regretted that he hadn't forgiven her before she died.

CHAPTER EIGHTEEN

CAL STOOD IN THE formal living room, holding a cup of coffee and chafing at the neck because he was wearing a tie. The room was full of people who'd come to pay their respects.

People, as Cassie had whispered during the service two hours ago, who had once respected and admired her father. She hadn't finished her sentence, but he knew what she must have been thinking, sitting in that old church. Those same people had deserted Marcus Brennan, the same way she thought she'd deserted him.

Cal didn't know how to console her. She hadn't mentioned the box she'd found or what was inside that box. But he'd seen it lying open on her bed the other night. Whatever she'd found, it seemed to have made her grief that much harder to bear.

Did that box hold some sort of verification of everything that had brought them to this point? He couldn't ask her because he was afraid she'd tell him she knew everything now. Everything. And even more afraid he'd have to tell her that he'd known a lot of it already and suspected the rest.

Cal would have to bide his time and see what she planned to do—about Camellia Plantation and about him.

He watched now as she talked quietly with neighbors and friends, her pearls intact around her throat, her sleeveless black linen dress tailored and appropriate, her hair shimmering like golden threads of sunshine in the light coming through the big windows. He couldn't take his eyes off of her, because he loved her and because he was waiting for the moment when she finally cracked and that polished veneer shattered to pieces.

He'd be there for that moment. He'd show her she still had him. He'd show her that he loved her.

He'd promised Marcus. And he'd promised her a long, long time ago.

A well-dressed man with dark blond hair approached Cassie and she turned, her mouth open in what looked like a gasp. The man took her hand, but she pulled away. Cal glanced at Rae standing with her mother by the dining table. The assistant shook her head then mouthed "Ned."

Ned. Ned Patterson. Cassie's ex-boyfriend.

Cal didn't do anything, but he watched. Then Cassie fell against the other man, hugging him close. Their embrace brought everyone around to stare.

Jack came up to stand beside Cal, his plaid shirt and crooked tie making him look different. But his frown was still intact. "I hate funerals."

"Me, too," Cal said, putting his coffee cup down on a nearby table, his gaze on Cassie. She seemed to be holding her own now. She stood back and gave Ned a soft, sad smile. What was she telling him? "But they're a part of life, I reckon."

"Yeah, but two in as many weeks. That ain't supposed to happen, son."

Cal shook his head. "I hear that. It was hard enough to have to bury Bert. But Marcus…"

Jack leaned close, the wrinkled hand he held to his

mouth covered with scratches and scars. "I figured that old cuss would live to be a hundred at least."

He'd said it with a sad smile on his face and a bit of moisture in his eyes.

"He was larger than life."

"But life got the best of him. It always does."

Jack turned to greet someone else, leaving Cal to his musings.

They'd sat there with Marcus most of that night and the next day. Cassie had refused to go very far from the hospital bed. She'd slept on the sofa in the other corner of the room, but only for a few minutes here and there.

Then around dawn on the second day of her vigil, she'd gone to sit with her father and she'd talked to him in soothing, loving tones, her hand on his, her voice low and cultured and calm. "It's okay now, Daddy. I understand. I have Cal back and I'm going to be okay. You can rest now. Just rest."

Marcus had died an hour later, as the sun came up outside his sick room window.

And Cassie, beautiful Cassie, had shut down and gone into her prim and proper mode, making arrangements, meeting with ministers, ordering a catered dinner for this time after the service and ignoring her own feeling and the promises she'd made at her father's side.

They had not discussed getting married.

Yet.

That was one promise Cal couldn't ignore.

Had she given that promise only to bring her father some peace? Or did she really mean what she'd said. Did she love Cal? Did she want to marry him?

He'd have to let her work through losing her father then help her figure that out.

She came toward him now, her smile soft, the fatigue pushing through her carefully controlled demeanor showing in the dark spots underneath her sky-blue eyes.

The other man was with her. "Cal, this is Ned Patterson. I wanted Ned to meet you."

"So this is the famous Cal Collins." Ned reached for Cal's hand, but his eyes didn't seem so friendly. "Cassie has been singing your praises. She tells me you've helped her a lot lately. Back together after all these years."

His tone held a hint of suggestion and accusation. And regret.

"That's my job," Cal replied, trying to stay neutral.

The other man gave Cassie a questioning smile. "I'd like to personally thank you for helping Cassie. I wish I could have been here sooner."

Cal nodded. "Yes. Thoughtful of you to come all this way for the funeral."

Ned put a hand on Cassie's shoulder. "Even though we're apart now, Cassie still means a lot to me."

Cal looked at Cassie and saw the warning in her eyes. "Ned has to get back to Atlanta."

But Ned didn't seem in such a hurry to go. "I could stay the night," he said to Cassie.

"No." She gave the other man a stern look. "That's not necessary. I appreciate your coming but you don't need to stay."

Ned leaned close to her. "Cassie..."

She shot Cal a glance then tugged Ned toward the front door. Cal watched as they whispered then resisted the need to hurry toward them when Ned grabbed Cassie's arm.

He didn't have any right to interfere in Cassie's life. They'd grown closer, true. But a deathbed promise could be broken. Especially if Ned convinced Cassie to give him one more chance.

They went out the front door, leaving Cal to worry and wonder. Jealousy made him sweat and wish he could take off his infernal tie. He was about to bolt out the door to find her when Cassie came back inside.

She closed the door then straightened her spine. "He didn't take the breakup very well but he was gracious today. It was good of him to come. If not a bit awkward."

Rae came hurrying over. "I told him not to upset you."

"He's gone now," Cassie said, her head down. "I'm almost glad he came, though. Now I know I made the right decision, breaking up with him." She lifted her gaze, her eyes meeting Cal's. "I belong here now."

Was she trying to reassure him?

"Are you sure?" Cal asked, the need to know eating away at his soul.

"Yes. I have to keep Camellia going, don't I?" She glanced around, her smile serene again. "Ned was right about one thing. The service was nice."

"It was just right," Cal replied, taking her hand in his, hoping to distract her. "Marcus would have loved it. The stories from old friends, the laughter, the memories. A good mix. A good celebration."

"I wanted a celebration."

Rae's big brown eyes widened. "Cassie, why don't you eat something?"

"I'm not hungry, but thanks."

Cal could see it coming, could just make out the shaking inside her body. He felt the tremors in her hand, her fingers clinging to his. "Cassie?"

"Get me out of here, please," she said on a quiet

whisper. "I can't breathe, Cal. Help me get through this."

He put his hand on her shoulder and guided her out into the hallway. "It's okay. Hold on to me."

She did, her smile still intact as people turned to stare, her head held high even while tears streamed down her face. By the time he had her out of the house and deep into the camellia path, she was sobbing.

Cal glanced around to make sure they were secluded then pulled her into his arms and held her close. Kissing her sweet-scented hair, he murmured, "Shhh. It's all right. I'll make sure everything is all right."

He let her have a good cry.

When she lifted her head and wiped frantically at her eyes, his shirt was still warm with her tears.

"I'm a mess," she said, holding a hand to her bent head. "Seeing Ned here got me rattled and only reminded me of all the mistakes I keep making. I can't do this. I can't fall apart. People are depending on me."

"You're allowed. You've been through a lot in the past few weeks."

She nodded and then put her hands on his shoulders. "I need to thank you, for being here, for taking care of this place. I know my daddy appreciated you. He loved you, too, Cal."

Cal wasn't so sure about that, but he wouldn't be cruel to a grieving daughter. "We made our peace."

"That's all he wanted, a little peace. He held things so close inside. That's really what killed him." She shrugged. "I think I inherited that trait."

Cal gritted his teeth against the truth. "I believe that's true about your father. I think he was a lot more caring and sensitive than we gave him credit for."

"He was so much more, too. He was trying to protect me." She lifted her head, her eyes touching on his. Her lips parted to speak and then she shut down again.

Cal *knew* Marcus had protected her, but he couldn't tell her that. There was still a lot he couldn't say to her.

But there was one question he had to ask. "Did you love Ned?"

She stared up at him, surprise lighting her eyes. "Are you jealous?"

"Yes."

She wiped her eyes again. "You saw us in there. He came to pay his respects and say his goodbyes. He took a new job in Dallas. He's going straight there from here."

Relief flooded through Cal. "I hope he stays in Texas then."

"He wanted me to consider coming out there for a visit. I told him I couldn't. He asked me if it's because of you."

"So he knows about us?"

"I told him about what happened before, yes."

"I'm sorry I asked. I just wanted to be sure."

She touched a hand to his face. "I still have a lot of decisions to make, but I can tell you this. I didn't love Ned the way I should have. I'm sorry I couldn't. He's not a bad person, really. But it's over."

Cal held her at the waist, his heart aching for her to tell him she loved him. How could he tell her that he still held a few secrets close? They'd come so far. So far. And he wanted to marry her, take care of her, watch her grow and continue to be the woman she should be. He wanted to be the kind of man who made her proud. But he couldn't do that until everything was out in the open, until the last of the secrets they'd all hidden from her were finally told. That might end things for them forever.

Soon, he thought. *When she's had some time.*

But right now, he couldn't put any more pain on her.

So he held her close and kissed her tears away and prayed that when the time came, he'd be able to tell her the truth at last. And that she'd be able to accept it and love him, no matter what.

CASSIE WOKE UP, her black dress still on. The sun was setting outside. She had a blanket pulled up around her and someone had left the French doors open to allow a warm breeze into the room.

Cal.

He'd talked her into coming up to her room to rest. Then he'd sat on the bed with her and held her in his arms. She must have fallen asleep.

Groggy, her body heavy and fatigued, she sat up and pushed at her hair. All of the guests would be gone by now.

And reality would set in.

She heard a knock on her door. "Cassie, it's Rae."

Rae had been a trouper. After Cassie had called to tell her the news, she'd flown down, bringing her mother with her. They'd rented a car at the Albany airport and vowed to stay as long as Cassie needed them.

"Come in," Cassie said, still a bit disoriented.

The door opened and Rae entered, carrying a tray.

"Hi," Cassie said, getting up to help with the tray. "I'm really not hungry."

"Mama said you'd say that," Rae replied, her dark eyes full of concern. "But Mama said to tell you to eat. You didn't have anything at the reception. And Miss Teresa seconded that."

"I couldn't eat." Even now, she felt sick to her stomach. "I'm sorry."

"Don't apologize." Rae took the cover off the food. The scent of pot roast wafted through the room. "It's your favorite."

Cassie's empty stomach growled. "Okay, maybe a bite."

She went into the bathroom to freshen up, shocked to see her reflection in the mirror. It looked as if she'd aged overnight. "Who's downstairs?"

Rae came to lean in the doorway. "Teresa and that Jack person, Mama and a redheaded woman—"

"Marsha," Cassie said, whirling back into the bedroom.

"*The* Marsha?"

"She was at the funeral."

"How do you feel about that?"

Cassie thought about that. "I'm okay with it. I've been through so much, Marsha isn't high up on my radar anymore."

Rae sat down on a footstool and motioned to the plate of food. "Eat while we talk."

Cassie took her plate over to a chair by the open door, the sight of Cal's destroyed house marring the beautiful spring day. After taking a few bites of the mouthwatering roast and rice, she pushed her plate away. "I found a box of letters, Rae."

Her friend leaned close. "What kind of letters?"

Cassie hadn't told anyone about the letters, not even Cal. They hadn't really had a chance to talk much. "Letters to my mother." She looked up at Rae, her heart thumping a tight little beat. "From another man."

Rae let out gasp. "Oh, my goodness. Do you think your daddy knew?"

Cassie nodded. "Yes. I'm pretty sure that's what he wanted to tell me, but he didn't know how. He did say he always loved her. I think he wanted me to know that he had forgiven her and that he was sorry for what he did, forcing Cal and me apart."

"So your daddy gave you his blessing?"

Cassie pinched off a creamy slice of pound cake then nibbled on it, the buttery sweetness making her think of Sunday dinners. "Yes. He wants me to marry Cal."

Rae lifted her dark eyebrows. "Really, now? And how does Cal feel about this?"

"He seems to like the idea."

"So how do you feel about this?"

Cassie took a drink of sweet tea. "I don't know. I...I think I'm falling in love with him again."

"But you have to be sure?"

"Yes. I made a mistake with Ned and I'm still reeling from that, plus I don't want to go through what I did when Cal broke my heart."

"But if he's willing and able—"

"I don't want him to feel obligated to honor a deathbed wish. That sounds so antiquated and strange, not to mention we're just now getting to know each other again."

"You love him." Rae got up to kneel in front of Cassie. "What are you going to do?"

Cassie didn't have the answer to that question. "I don't know. First, I have to decide what to do about this place. I can't let it go." She smiled for the first time in a long time. "Before Daddy died, I had this brilliant idea of opening up a plant here—to manufacture my designs."

Rae shot up then settled back on the bed. "You mean,

create Cassie's Closet ready-to-wear right here in Camellia?"

"Yes. People are out of work around here and I need to do something to help. I have the land and I can funnel some of the capital I'd planned to use to open up a second store in Atlanta."

"What about the New York boutique?"

"That would have to wait. If I decide to do this."

Rae's smile was soft and sure. "I think you've already decided. And I'm fine with that. But how will you handle being here and keeping up with things in Atlanta?"

"I have a very good person in mind to take over operations in Atlanta," Cassie said, glad to be back to business for a few minutes.

"Yeah, who?"

"You, of course." When Rae started shaking her head, Cassie held up a hand. "You're in the stores more than I am, anyway. You train the staff and keep everyone motivated. I've been so busy lately, the only time I show up is for special events and holidays. You'd.be great. It's about time you tried your hand at designing for Cassie's Closet."

"I know that," Rae said without modesty, "but I'd miss you."

"I'll be able to come in and visit for those same special events and holidays," Cassie said, realizing she probably had already decided. "I'll still have a hands-on approach. We can make it work."

Rae shrugged then grinned. "Would I get a raise?"

"Of course." Cassie got up to hug her. "But this is all in the very early stages. I have to sort out a lot of things before I can move forward. I might not have enough funding to pay for the upkeep on this place, let alone plan a whole new industry."

"When will you know?"

"We'll hear the reading of the will tomorrow," Cassie said, dreading that scenario. "Cal says things were really bad but he's managed to clear out some of the debts by selling off equipment and scaling down the entire operation. He's done a good job."

Rae elbowed her. "He's a fine-looking man. And the way he looks at you—well, as my grandma says, look like he could eat you up with a spoon."

Cassie felt the same way each time she looked at Cal. She just wasn't sure how to move forward from here. They had so much history, so much to work through. "He told me once he'd only marry me if I wanted it. He told me I'd have to say the word."

"Then maybe you'd better do that."

"Not yet," Cassie said. But soon. First, she had to read those letters and clean out her parents' bedroom. Maybe by then, she'd have a clue as to what happened here right under her nose.

And maybe she'd have a clue about the man who'd written those letters.

Downstairs, Marsha Reynolds sat in the kitchen talking to Teresa. Cal walked in, took one look at her and wished he had somewhere else to go.

"We need to talk," Marsha said, not seeming to care that Teresa was in the room.

"About what?" He wasn't in the mood for any of Marsha's games.

"You know what," she said, getting up to follow him out onto the back porch. "Cassie's a smart woman. She'll figure the rest of it out."

Cal let out a sigh. "Just stay out of it, Marsha. I'm planning on telling her everything when the time is right."

Marsha looked out across the yard, then lowered her voice so only he could hear. "I hope so. I'm tired of being looked down on as the bad girl here, Cal. I did what I had to do all those years ago, because I thought you and I might have a chance. But we don't. I know that. I've always known that. Now if you love Cassie, you need to do us all a favor and let her in on what really happened that day her mother died."

"I told you, I'd take care of it!"

"Take care of what?"

He turned to find Cassie standing in the open door.

CHAPTER NINETEEN

CAL STARTED TO SPEAK, but Marsha cut him off.

"I wanted to find you and tell you how sorry I am about your daddy," she said, taking Cassie's hand in hers.

Cassie stared at Marsha, shocked by her words and especially the soft smile on the other woman's face. Would she ever figure out this thing between Marsha and Cal?

"Thank you, Marsha." She pulled her hand away and glanced at Cal. He looked uncomfortable. "Daddy always enjoyed seeing you around the place before—"

"Before you and I had our differences and your world went kind of wacky," Marsha finished. "Cassie, it's hard for me to tell you this but—"

Cal stepped between them. "Marsha, she's tired—"

"I can speak for myself," Cassie replied, wondering why she wasn't surprised. Cal always got jumpy whenever Marsha was around. Had he been fooling Cassie just long enough to find out what she'd say or do? Was he still hoping to marry her and keep Marsha on the side? "What do you want to tell me?"

Marsha glanced at Cal then looked back at Cassie. "I don't hold any grudge against you. I had this big crush on Cal—that's true. But even when he was with me, I knew he still cared a lot about you." She shrugged then turned to go. Glancing at Cassie one last time, she said,

"You might want to remember that, no matter what happens around here."

Cassie watched as Marsha marched down the steps in her high heels and tight brown sundress. "What did she mean by that?"

Cal let out a long breath. "She thinks you'll leave again."

Cassie leaned back against one of the big round columns, confusion warring with her feelings for Cal. "Sometimes I think that might be the best idea."

He stood with his hands in the pockets of his jeans. Cassie had changed into denim capris and a white tunic and she noticed he'd taken off the suit and now wore jeans and a dark T-shirt. And a dark scowl to match.

"So all that talk about opening a factory here, was that just a bluff?"

How could she explain her feelings? "No, that wasn't a bluff. I still want to pursue that idea. But I've got to talk to business managers and lawyers and get a solid plan. It could take years."

"We've got nothing but time around here."

She sensed the tension in each word and each glance. What had happened to that gentle peace she'd experienced when he'd held her there and let her fall asleep in his arms?

Hoping to change his mood, she said, "I see the men have started clearing away the debris."

He turned to look at the spot where his house used to sit. "Yep. They got back to work right after the service today."

"The work never stops around here."

He looked down at his boots. "No. I'll be pretty busy the rest of the week."

A brush-off?

Finally, she'd had enough. "Cal, what's wrong?"

He looked up at her, his eyes as dark and blue as chiseled granite. "We haven't discussed that promise you made to your daddy."

Cassie swallowed, allowed her heart to jump a beat or two. "I know. But there's been a lot going on. Now that the funeral is over and everyone is gone, maybe we can sit down and decide what we need to do."

He nodded then stepped over to her, putting a hand on the white column near her hair, so near she could feel his warm breath on her neck. "How about dinner? Later this week. I need to go to my place anyway. I've neglected it enough and with the storm, I want to see for myself if the crops up there are progressing. You could ride with me, take your sketch pad and when I'm finished up, we can stop in Albany at that little Italian restaurant you used to love."

Cassie closed her eyes for a couple of seconds. "That'd be nice. I've got Rae here so we'll do some work before she goes back to Atlanta tomorrow morning. Then I want to go through the master bedroom and decide what to do with all my parents' things." Holding her head up, she added, "And Teresa and I decided we'd clean out the study. Get the hospital bed back to the medical supply store and maybe hire someone to redo the whole room."

"It would make a good office for you."

"I can't work in there."

He touched a hand to her hair. "I wasn't thinking. Of course not." Then he dragged a finger down her cheek. "How you doing?"

"Okay." She let out a sigh, thinking she liked it better when they were intimate and quiet like this. Everything else—the rush of feelings and need, the decisions that had to be made, could wait for now. "Thanks for staying with me—earlier."

His eyes moved over her face with a hungry intent. "You needed to rest. I didn't mind at all."

"Cal?"

He leaned close, his nose grazing her neck. "Hmm?"

"I haven't forgotten what I told my daddy about us. I'll honor that promise."

His head came up, his brows lifting. "Out of duty, or because you really want to be my wife?"

How could she be sure? She wanted him. That much she knew. But what if she made another mistake? What if he lived to regret getting involved with her?

He stepped back. "I see."

"No, you don't," she said, her hand on his arm. "I have a lot to work through. I haven't read those letters yet."

"Letters? Is that what was in the box?"

"Yes." Shame made her hold her head down. "I think my mother was having an affair."

She looked up in time to see the shock and concern coloring his eyes. And the acceptance.

"Did you already know that?"

He didn't answer.

"Cal?"

She used his same words. "I see."

He put his hands on his hips and looked away. "I suspected, yes."

Pain and anger sliced through her system. "And how long have you suspected this?"

His expression begged for understanding, but his eyes held a look of resignation. "Since the day she died."

CAL WATCHED AS Cassie sank down onto a nearby cushioned patio chair and put her hand against her forehead. "I can't believe you just said that."

There was no taking it back now. He wouldn't lie to her about that. He wouldn't lie to her about anything else she might find out, either. Not if she asked him directly. Which meant, he either had to walk away or spill his guts. This one last thing—this one last secret—might be his undoing.

He sat down in the chair next to hers. "I said I suspected, Cassie. I didn't have proof."

She gave him a frustrated glance. "But you've suspected this for twelve long years?"

"Yes."

She closed her eyes then opened them to stare at him. "Why? What made you come to this conclusion?"

This was the tricky part. He looked out toward the lane leading to the stables. "I heard them arguing in the stables, earlier that day. I can't say for sure, but I think he was trying to get her to admit it."

Cassie moaned low in her throat. "But they were in the house right before she rushed out the door and got on that horse."

"Yes. She ran to the house and he followed her." He shook his head. "I'd saddled up Heathcliff for her. She wanted to go for a ride. But he came out there looking for her and they went outside and stood near the stable doors. I heard them fighting, though."

Cassie closed her eyes. "I remember hearing them coming up the stairs. Then they went into their bedroom."

And screamed at each other, the muffled sounds moving through the house. "I couldn't make out what they were saying."

Cal stood and pulled her up, his hands on her elbows. "Listen to me, okay? I never said anything because I never had a chance. Everything happened pretty fast after that and I couldn't be sure."

"You should have told me. You came to me that one last time before you went to see Marsha."

"I didn't want to hurt you with something that might not be true."

He never wanted to hurt her, so he'd protected her and withheld all the things he'd suspected and then he'd pieced together the rest since coming back here. At a loss as to how to explain that concept to her, he just held her, his hands moving to her shoulders. "Even though Marcus let some of it slip in his ramblings, I still wasn't completely sure until you voiced the same conclusion."

"I need to read those letters," she said, pulling away. Stopping at the door, she gave him one last glance. "Is there anything else you haven't told me? Anything I might find in those letters?"

His cell rang then. He pulled it out of his pocket and saw the name and number. "It's Jack. He'll want work orders for tomorrow. I can call him back."

"No, you go ahead." She gave him a look of dismissal and distrust. "I think I already know the answer to my question."

With that, she turned and pranced back inside.

Cal listened to the clicking of her sandals all the way up the hall. But he had to wonder—what would she find in those letters? He almost went after her to finish his confession. But he couldn't make his feet move. Instead, he turned and headed toward his pickup, intent on going back to work.

CASSIE HEADED TO HER ROOM, confusion and anger giving her an adrenaline rush that she planned to use to get her through reading all those love letters to her mother from a mysterious man. But she stopped in front of the closed door to her parents' bedroom.

Without giving herself time to think about it, she opened the door and went inside. She'd glanced in here a couple of times since coming back, but Teresa kept the room clean and fresh-smelling and tidy, so Cassie hadn't spent much time in here before.

Now, she turned on the light and took in the big long room. A large king-size bed took up the far wall on the front side of the house while a cozy sitting room filled the wall beside the French doors to the upstairs porch. A big bathroom and closet completed the rest of the suite.

The room looked like a picture right out of her past. The muted blues and yellows reminded her of her mother's love of flowers. The lingering scent of lilies floated around her like a ghost. Her mother had always loved Casablanca lilies. Eugenia had special sachets made to put in her closet and lingerie chest.

Cassie walked around the room, picking up knick-knacks and touching on Eugenia's hairbrush and old perfume bottles, her mind fighting to comprehend all the revelations she'd discovered since coming back home.

Finally, she sank down on the old floral comforter on the big bed. "Why, Mother?"

Eugenia had everything a woman could ever want or need, didn't she? She shopped in Atlanta and New York, vacationed all over the world, threw elaborate parties and laughed and...

Drank.

Cassie could picture her mother walking around,

smiling and chatting, and always with a martini glass in her hand.

And her father? He'd never indulged that much from what Cassie remembered. And yet, he'd died an alcoholic, riddled with cancer and a bad heart. A broken heart.

What had driven him to drink? Her mother's death, surely.

And maybe, the knowledge that his beautiful, pampered Eugenia had been with another man. Then, his only daughter leaving him all alone in this big house, with only memories to keep him company?

"Why didn't I fight harder for us, Daddy? Why didn't I insist on the truth? Why did I stay away so long?"

Cassie would have helped him get through his grief. She would have gladly given up college and a career, for her father and for Cal's love. She'd thought she'd lost both.

But now, it seemed they'd both manipulated things to make sure she did go away. To protect her. In her father's case, maybe to protect her from the truth of her mother's betrayal and the deep grief it had caused in him. And Cal? To give her a chance to spread her wings and follow her dreams instead of following him?

It would have been nice if they'd both trusted her enough to let her make those decisions for herself, so she could figure out the truth about the facade they'd all created.

Thinking about her parents together, Cassie had to admit her mother often looked sad, her laughing expressions pinched and forced. Sometimes Eugenia would get a faraway look in her eyes and then she'd leave Cassie with Teresa and head off to the pond.

To see the other man?

"How long did it go on, Mama?"

Cassie waited in the still room, hoping for answers that didn't come. She got up and went to the large closet next to the bathroom and opened the double doors, her eyes taking in the evening gowns and cocktail dresses, the rows of designer shoes and brand-name purses and bags. Her mother had given her a love of fashion. And maybe her father had given her the strength she'd needed to survive. If she'd stayed here in this tomb of a house, she wouldn't be the successful designer she's always dreamed of being. But...she was still alone.

She touched a hand to the silks and wools, the pretty linen dresses and the rich leathers. A clear bag hung at the back. It held a yellowed lace dress. Her mother's wedding dress. Cassie touched a trembling hand to the plastic covering the dress. Another facade. Then she whirled and headed to her own room, determined to find a hint of what had gone on with her mother and this other man. Maybe the letters would show Cassie why her mother had cheated on her father.

TWO HOURS LATER, Cal came upstairs and stood staring down the hallway toward the door of Cassie's room. He could just make out a light burning through the tiny slit at the bottom of the door. His first impulse was to kick that door down and tell her that he loved her and he was sorry for all the lies and the betrayals and the secrets.

But he couldn't do that. He couldn't claim her yet. Somehow, he had to make her see that he loved her and only wanted to protect her. Would she understand if he told her the truth? If he poured out his heart and made her see why he'd done the things he'd tried so hard to keep from her?

He stood by his room, his hand on the door handle, his heart lost in the woman behind that door. What would those letters reveal?

Cal went into the guest room, feeling as out of place in here as he'd always felt around all of Cassie's rich private school friends.

If those letters told her the whole story before he had a chance, he'd lose her again. And this time, it would be forever.

He wouldn't get much sleep, so he showered and pulled on sweatpants and a fresh T-shirt then opened the door to the porch and sat there in the dark, caught between his prayers and his sins, hoping to catch a glimpse of the woman he loved.

CHAPTER TWENTY

CASSIE FINISHED READING the last of the aged letters then folded it back up and put it with the stack lying on her bed. Over twenty, some of them one-page short notes, others longer and more drawn out. Some written after what had apparently been arguments and breakups, others written after time spent together. Letters that always started with "My darling Eugenia" and ended with a heart drawn where a name should have been.

Her mother had been in love with another man.

And that man had been deeply in love with Eugenia.

They never mentioned anyone else, but the letters indicated that Eugenia felt trapped in her marriage. Trapped, lonely, depressed and in a state of utter hopelessness and despair.

She stayed because of her child. The letters mentioned Cassie a lot. How pretty she was, just like her mother. So beautiful. A sweet little girl. Like my own. Just like my own.

Had her mother's lover considered taking Eugenia and Cassie away? And why did that endearment *just like my own* seem so familiar to Cassie?

She wasn't sure how long the affair had been going on since the letters weren't dated or signed. But she was very sure of one thing—Eugenia had a whole other life that her husband and daughter never knew about. Until that fateful day, at least.

How had her father found out?

Now, at least, Cassie could understand her father's strange behavior toward her. He'd sent Cassie away because she reminded him of his wife's betrayal and death—and maybe to protect her from finding out the awful truth about Eugenia. Then he'd suffered in silence for years before dying of a broken heart.

No wonder he couldn't stand the sight of her.

Cassie felt dizzy with disgust, her heart breaking bit by bit for all that had transpired behind the walls of this beautiful old house. How could she have been so blind?

She thought about the incident in the camp house, accepting that the affair had been going on even then. That was over twenty years ago. Maybe it had started long before that. Somehow, she'd managed to block out the truth of what she'd seen that day when she was too young to understand.

Amazingly, she'd never mentioned it to anyone, either. Not even her mother or father, probably because she didn't want to get into trouble or get Teresa fired. She was almost thankful she'd put it out of her mind.

Cassie got up to go to the open door out onto the porch, her mind whirling with regret and shame. All these years, she'd considered her mother a perfect example of a Southern lady. She'd learned from that example, built a whole career on the image of her mother, complete with pearls and pumps. And it had all been a lie.

Had Eugenia ever truly loved Marcus Brennan? Or her only child?

Stepping out onto the porch, Cassie pulled her silk robe together and tied it at the waist. The mild summer night brought the sound of cicadas singing and frogs croaking a reply. The intoxicating scents of magnolias and gardenia wafted out and lifted on the warm breeze. Somewhere off in the distance, an owl hooted a sad calling.

She leaned against the railing, the yard below shifting in shadows as the wind moved through the Spanish moss draped against the live oaks. When she heard a cough coming from the other side of the long porch, she turned, instinctively knowing Cal was there waiting for her.

"Hi," she said, seeing him silhouetted there in the shadows.

"Hi." He got up and slowly walked toward her, his bare feet hitting the ancient planked floor. He wore sweats and a T-shirt. "Couldn't sleep?"

"No." She kept her hands on the banister. "I read the letters."

"And...?"

Did she sense a hesitation in that one worded question?

"And my mother had an affair that apparently went on for a long time." Then she turned to stare at him. "I remembered something that I haven't told you about. I've never told anyone about it because I think I somehow blocked it, but I caught them together once down at the camp house. I was eight and I snuck out of the house looking for my mother. I heard them laughing and talking, and I thought it was my parents there together. My mother loved hot tea, so the teakettle was steaming and it was boiling, whistling away. They didn't even notice. They never knew I was there on the porch. I ran away before I saw the man's face, but I think I must have guessed it wasn't my father."

She turned to stare down at the lighted pool. "It all

came back the day of the storm, the day I found that box of letters."

"Cassie." He reached for her, tugging her close. "I'm so sorry."

"You knew, didn't you? You said you suspected, but you've known all along, haven't you?"

CAL RECKONED HIS TIME was up. He had to tell her everything now, while he had the courage. He'd sat out here, waiting, knowing this had to end, one way or another. Better to hurt her now than later. If she wanted him, if she loved him, she'd forgive him, somehow. If not... He didn't want to think about that.

"Yes," he said, a relief in the one word. "I knew that and so much more."

She went still, as if to allow a kind of numbness to settle over her so the agony wouldn't hurt so much. Then she tossed her hair and waited. "When did you first find out?"

He took her hands in his. "Almost from the time I was hired. At first, I didn't know who the man was, just that she would leave the house a lot during the day when Marcus was out working and you were in school. Teresa knew, too, but she never talked about it until I came back. She had to warn me that Marcus would say things that didn't make any sense."

Cassie nodded. "I remember you saying he rambled a lot. And what did my father know? What did he say?"

"He let things slip—calling for her, telling her he'd forgive her if she'd just come home." There was more, but Cal refused to blurt that out to her. Not today, after she'd just buried her father.

Cassie inhaled a sob, Cal's hands on her anchoring her, holding her. "He never stopped loving her," she said, the whispered declaration holding an edge of grief and regret.

"No, and he never stopped loving you, either. Sometimes, he'd call out for you the same way."

"Why did he want us to get married?"

Cal had to tread carefully but he wanted it out, out of his head, out of his dreams, out in the open. "He thought that if you ever found out the truth, you'd be devastated, in the same way he was. He wanted me here to help you through it."

"Because I'm so very fragile and clueless?"

"No, Cassie, because he loved you. More than you'll ever know. He and I talked a lot, even though I told you we didn't, and he always sounded so proud of you. He kept up with you, but he didn't make a big deal out it. He couldn't say it, but the man did love you."

The blank look on her face changed as the numbness wore off and she came out fighting. Tearing away from him, she held up a hand. "No, no more, Cal. I'm beginning to see that neither of them really loved me. They were too caught up in destroying each other. Self-absorbed, selfish, cruel—that's the parents I really had."

"No, you're wrong." He grabbed her, forcing her to look at him. "You want the truth? I'll tell you everything. Then you can decide what to do—stay or go or burn the place down. I don't care about anything but us, Cassie. That's all I've ever cared about."

Her frown was full of heat. "Really, Cal? You say that when all along you've withheld things, covered for my father and basically just felt sorry for poor little Cassie. I wouldn't be surprised if Marsha was in on the whole thing, too."

He swallowed, looked away.

"Oh, no." Cassie turned, holding her arms tightly against her midsection. "Oh, no. Marsha knows? Marsha? But why, how?"

Cal hated this, hated seeing her like this. But he had to tell her now. There was no one else left. He'd held off, hoping her father would confess all, but now it was up to him.

"Marsha's mother…helped them…meet up. After you left, Marsha and I kept in touch. She told me what little she knew, which wasn't much. Apparently, she'd heard a lot of rumors hanging out at the Pig and Plow, helping her mom."

"Oh, that's rich. That's amazing. The irony is almost comical."

He touched a hand to her arm. "Nothing funny about this mess."

"No, and I'm not laughing." She whirled back around. "You said, *at first* you didn't know who the man was. But you do now, right? So tell me, Cal. Is he still around? Was he at my father's funeral?"

"He's dead."

"Dead? All three of them dead now? But who?" Her hands dropped to her side as realization glistened in her moonlight eyes. "Dead?" She put a hand to her throat. "Dr. Anton? Was it Dr. Anton?"

"Yes."

She went pale. He could see it there in the glow from the moonlight and the security lights shimmering out in the yard. "Was his death an accident or did my father kill his best friend?"

Cal took her by the arm and pulled her onto a wicker settee. "Are you ready for the whole story now?"

CASSIE BENT OVER, holding herself. Her pulse hit against her temple like a hammer hitting a nail. She felt it ripping into her, tearing into her. Dr. Anton, her father's best friend, the man who'd taken care of her whole family for as long as she could remember. Could he have been the man she'd glanced in the camp house that day?

"Yes," she finally said to Cal's question. "Tell me what you know."

He didn't try to hold her or touch her, thankfully.

"The day your mother died, my life changed. One minute I was working here at a job that I loved and I was in love with you. I had all these plans to somehow make you mine, to better myself for you, Cassie. All of those things we'd dreamed about and talked about, that was true. That was real to me."

Oh, how she wanted to believe him. "What happened?"

He let out a long breath. "From what I managed to get out of Marcus after I came back, he found the letters. Or he found a letter. I don't know where or how and I don't think he knew who, but he discovered what was going on and he confronted your mother." He stopped, took another breath. "I wish I didn't have to tell you this. But your mother was down at the stables with me that morning. She'd asked me to saddle up Heathcliff so she could go for a ride. She seemed agitated and upset so I did as she asked."

Cassie looked over at him. "But then my father came down to the stables?"

"Yes. They started arguing, so she told me to hold Heathcliff until she came back."

Cassie closed her eyes, seeing that whole day in a different way. Seeing it with the truth glaring at her.

"So they returned to the house and had that horrible fight."

He nodded. "Yes, and then she came back to the stables and you know the rest."

Cassie knew there had to be more. Much more. "You said you'd tell me everything, Cal."

"Things went downhill from there. Your mother died, Marcus was angry and devastated and he blamed me, Cassie. He blamed me."

Cassie's head came up. "Because you handed her the reins and let her get on that horse?"

"Yes, that and…because your mother told him she was having an affair with *me.*"

"What?" Cassie shot up to pace the porch. "You can't be serious? The affair was going on much longer than just that one summer, Cal. I know you didn't write those letters." Then she stopped. "But are you trying to tell me that she…that you and my mother—"

He stood and stared at her. "Nothing happened between your mother and me. She was in love with the doctor, only no one knew that back then. And she was desperate to protect him from your father. But me, I was expendable."

Cassie thought she'd heard everything, but she realized this was just the tip of the iceberg. "Why didn't you tell me?"

"I didn't want to hurt you. I knew it wasn't true, but I was afraid you'd believe it anyway. And then after she died, it just didn't seem to matter. I told you, I only wanted to be with you."

She went back over everything in her mind. "But I thought he fired you because of us."

"He did."

"So he was already angry at you, and then when he found us together, that was it. That just made it worse."

Cal tented his hands in his lap. "I don't think he believed her—about it being me. He didn't confront me that day because he was so devastated about her death and the whole affair thing. But after the funeral, when he found us together, that's when he let me have it."

Cassie leaned back in her chair. "I remember how he shouted at you and cursed both of us. He never once accused you."

"No, not in front of you. That came later."

"What do you mean, later. You left but you came back to see me that one last time and then…"

"And then, you caught me with Marsha."

Cassie took a shiver of a breath. "Is there more to that story, too?"

CAL MADE A SNAP DECISION after that question. He'd tell her all of it, all the ugly details, but he wouldn't be the one to finish the job. He'd never tell her the one thing that would destroy her and pull them apart. He couldn't do it, no matter how hard it would be to keep one last secret.

Telling himself it didn't matter now that Marcus was dead—now that Eugenia and her lover were both dead—he swallowed and hoped she'd forgive him for his part in this whole sordid mess.

"Cal?"

Keeping her hand tightly in his, he inhaled deeply then let out a breath. "Wow, I didn't realize how hard this would be."

Pulling her hand away, she said, "Don't stop now. Might as well spill the rest of it."

He held on to the chair arms, his fingers using the sturdy wicker for strength. "What you saw between Marsha and me—that was a setup, Cassie. Marsha flirted with me and made it pretty clear that she was interested, no doubt there, but I only wanted you. Always you."

She held up a hand. "You did what you thought you had to do, so I'd break up with you and leave. That part worked at least."

"Yeah, worked too well. I didn't want to do that to you, but your old man gave me an ultimatum. He said I needed to go, get out of town, or he'd tell you what Eugenia had told him. That it was me she'd been with."

"That's crazy. You said he found a letter. Couldn't he tell it wasn't from you?"

"The letter wasn't signed or dated. Apparently, your mother and her friend were very careful with their letters—no names, no mention of anyone or anything except how they felt for each other. He had no way of knowing anything else." Cal let go of the chair and stood. He went to the porch rail then turned to face her. "I'm pretty sure he'd figured it all out by then, but he had to blame somebody so he picked me. I was just as expendable to him as I was to your mother. And he wanted you to hurt the way he was hurting, I believe."

"Why? How could a father do that to a child?"

Cal turned to grip the porch railing, willing himself to stays silent on that account. "He wasn't himself. He'd just found out the worst a man can hear and then, he'd lost his wife, too, and found his daughter with a glorified stable boy. It was pretty bad all the way around."

She got up to come and stand beside him. "So you took the ultimatum seriously, and you staged this get-together with Marsha, making sure I'd see you two together."

He angled around to look at Cassie. "Yes, after he gave me a big fat check to get out of town. More than just my regular salary. It was a lot of money, Cassie."

She gasped. "Marsha said he paid you off, but I didn't believe her."

"She was right except I never took the money. I gave it to her to keep quiet and to help her with some of her mother's bills. She used it to pay off the mortgage on the Pig and Plow. And she never looked back." He shrugged. "None of us did. I left. You left. Marcus went into his downward spiral. It was over."

"Over?" Her question lifted in the air. "Over? For all of you maybe. But not for me, Cal. I can't tell you how many nights I lay awake, wondering what had happened to make my father hate me so much, what had happened to make you walk away without a fight. I compared myself to Marsha over and over, and I always came up short. And I believed you two were together, with a child at first. Even after I found out that wasn't true, you never came for me. How could anyone be so cruel?"

He reached for her, took her into his arms. "I'm here now. Cassie, I'm here now." He kissed her, tugging her close, holding her until she fell against him and kissed him back. Just for a moment, the world receded and they were back there, young and in love and yearning to be together always.

But the truth tugged her out of his arms. "No. No. We're not doing this now. Since I've come home, it's been one lie on top of another, until I honestly don't know what to believe." She stared at him, willing him to be honest. "Did my father kill Dr. Anton?"

CAL NODDED AND TRIED to catch his breath. "I think so. I don't have proof but he said so many things in his ramblings."

"Such as?"

"That he'd waited a long time, waited for the right moment, to get even." Cal closed his eyes, the shock of that deathbed confession still ringing in his ears. "Something about an argument. I think he wanted to get even but then, when the time came it turned into an accident. The doctor fell overboard and hit his head."

"Stop. Stop." She put a hand to her mouth.

He reached for her again. "It's over now, Cassie. We can start fresh."

She stepped away. "It will never be over. This cover-up…this horrible secret…ruined my life."

"No, it didn't," he said, hoping to show her that she'd been the one who made it through. "You got out, Cassie. You got away from this place. You survived and you made it out there on your own. You have to see what an accomplishment that is."

"Oh, I see, all right. I see that the man I loved didn't tell me the truth."

"I wasn't a man then," he said, using his only defense. "I was young and stupid and scared—not of your father, but that I'd lose you anyway. You were like this princess, standing here on this porch. I had nothing to offer you. Nothing. And your daddy made sure I realized that."

"Why didn't you take his money, Cal?"

"You think he could just buy me off? No. I let him think that, but I knew the difference. I knew the truth. No one had to buy me off. I walked away, for your sake."

She tried to turn away but he grabbed her hand and held it in the air, a hot wind whipping around them as they faced each other. Then he pulled her into his arms and kissed her, over and over, his touch pleading with her to give him another chance.

Cassie gave into the kiss and returned it, her soft moan showing Cal what words couldn't say. She still loved him.

"Cassie," he whispered against her lips. "Cassie, it's over now. We can make this work. I love you. I love you. I'm sorry."

She stilled against him. "I love you, too, Cal. But I don't think I can marry you, not after all of this. Not after all the lies." Pulling out of his embrace, she looked down. "I feel like a fool, an idiot, for not seeing any of this."

"We hid it from you," he said, trying to make her see.

"Yes, you did. And it worked. Or maybe I did see and I just buried it along with all my other memories."

"You stayed away. That was the best thing for you."

"No." She started backing up, a hand touching his face. "That was the best thing for everyone else. You said you were trying to protect me. I think you were trying to protect yourself and my father. And my mother, too, for that matter. The best thing for me would have been you, coming to me and telling me, being honest with me, all those years ago. But you didn't. You let me believe—"

"I let you believe that your mother was the wonderful woman everyone thought she was."

She bobbed her head. "Yes, and that did keep me sane. My father might have hated me, but my mother, she loved me. She was my rock."

"Exactly. You would have hated me even more if I'd told you what had happened. Think about it, Cassie."

She remained still, her eyes closed. "I just wish you hadn't felt such a need to protect me. We could have talked, worked through this."

"I didn't think so," he admitted. "I had to let you go. It was for the best."

"But you came back to set things right. That's why you kept saying you came back for me?"

Cal felt relief washing through him. "Yes. When Marcus asked me to come back here, he told me he'd known all along I'd never been with your mother, said he had proof then and even more now. And he begged me to never tell you the truth. He was ashamed of breaking us apart, of offering me a bribe. So I kept his secrets intact, to save you even more pain. To save you from this. Is that so wrong, what I did?"

"What you did? It's what you *didn't* do that's killing me now. You couldn't trust me enough to let me decide, to let me handle this. We could have been together, Cal. But you decided to end things instead, never once trying to find me to set things straight. And for that, I can't forgive and forget. I'm sorry, but I just can't."

Then she turned and hurried back to her own room, effectively slamming the door behind her.

CHAPTER TWENTY-ONE

SHE WAS RIGHT.

Cal knew that in his heart and he'd had the long sleepless night to think about it. He should have felt better after finally telling Cassie all the sordid details of the events that had kept them apart. Instead, this morning as he stood in the kitchen drinking coffee, he only felt empty and tired.

"Rough night?" Teresa asked, placing a piece of toast with mayhaw jelly in front of him.

"The worst." He stared at the crisp toast, his stomach roiling. "I told Cassie everything."

Teresa's dark eyebrows shot up. "Everything?"

Glancing around, he made sure they were alone. "Not that. But everything else."

Teresa shot him one of her shrewd glances. "Might as well get the worst of it out. She'll need to know one day."

Cal took a long swig of his coffee. "Marcus swore he'd tell her but he didn't."

"The man was ill. He probably didn't even realize most of what he said to her."

"I can't be the one," Cal whispered. "I've hurt her too much as it is."

Teresa refreshed his coffee then poured herself another cup. "You held it all in for a long time, Cal. How's that working for you?"

"Not very well. I think I've lost her again."

"Maybe you never had her."

He nodded, bit into the toast then pushed the dish away. "What will *you* do now?"

"I don't know," Teresa admitted. "Jack wants me to stay, but I think it's time to move on. Go see my sister and her kids down in Florida. She could use a hand. I've got a little saved up. Might buy me a little beach cottage."

"Well, you could use a good long rest."

Teresa nodded, her dark eyes misty. "I miss the old coot."

"You stayed longer than any of us."

"He needed me."

And with that, she turned and went into her little room off the kitchen, leaving Cal to have yet another revelation. Teresa had loved Marcus Brennan. But she'd never made any move toward telling the man that. Another highly guarded secret.

This place was worse than one of those reality television shows. He turned to head out and heard Cassie coming up the hallway. She walked into the kitchen but stopped when she saw him.

"Good morning," he said, hoping she'd had time to settle down.

"Hello." She went to the coffeepot and poured some of the dark brew then stood with her back to him and stared out into the yard.

"Look, I threw a lot at you last night. I hope you'll forgive me and understand my reasons."

"I understand a lot of things now."

She was back to the cool-blonde routine. He had it coming.

But he wanted her to smile again. "It's over now,

Cassie. And we're still standing. We could try to start fresh."

She finally turned to look at him. "Start fresh? Here at Camellia, you mean?"

"Wherever you want. I could move to Atlanta."

"You don't want to live in Atlanta. You have your own land, Cal. Why don't you go back to it?"

"Why don't you come and live there with me?"

He saw the flare of awareness in her eyes, saw a deep longing emerge before she put up her guard again. "As you said last night, I managed to get out. I made a life for myself. I came when I was called, but I think it's high time I get back to that life."

She was hurting, but her attitude worried him. Would she leave again and never look back? Or were her harsh words a cover to hide her pain?

"And what about Camellia, Cassie?"

"What about it? After I go to the lawyer's office for the reading of the will, I might decide to auction off this place to the highest bidder after all."

Anger boiled up inside Cal. "After we've worked so hard to save it, after all the promises—"

"Don't talk to me about promises." She brushed past him. "I have to get dressed. Rae and her mother are leaving in an hour and then I have things to take care of."

"Cassie, wait."

She started to leave then turned. "What?"

He put his hands on her waist. "Think about what I said to you long ago. I asked you to trust me and to remember what we'd promised each other. I had to protect you. And that meant I had to watch you leave. Don't leave me again."

She took in a breath that sounded close to a sob and

then she pulled him close, kissing him, holding him, touching her hands to his hair. Finally, breathless, she pulled away. "I always thought I belonged here. But I don't. I'd only destroy you, Cal."

She reached up to push his hair off his forehead, her eyes full of need and longing. Then she turned and walked out of the room. And she didn't look back.

Cal put his cup in the sink and went out the back door. He had damaged crops to assess. They'd probably lose about a fourth of the corn crop and maybe as much in the peanuts. He had men clearing away fallen trees and the mess left from the destroyed cottage. There was a lot to keep him busy.

What did it matter now? He'd tried to do the right thing to help Cassie. But yet again, she was willing to turn her back on everything, every promise, no matter how much they loved each other. He knew she had some fight left in her but maybe she didn't think he was worth that fight.

He wouldn't force the woman. He'd meant what he'd told her early on. If she wanted to marry him, he'd gladly oblige. But he wouldn't settle for some grand gesture brought about by grief and guilt. There was really nothing he could do now, except let her go.

CASSIE PULLED HER CAR into the parking space on the main street in Camellia. The post office and courthouse stood side by side, with big long black iron benches sitting in front. A couple of old-timers sat on the bench directly in front of the courthouse. They waved as Cassie walked by, both giving her an unabashed stare.

Did they know? She wondered. Did everyone in town know what her mother had done?

Did she care anymore?

She was numb, cold, broken and still in shock. She just needed to see the will, to find out what she already knew. She'd have to sell Camellia if she wasn't willing to stay here and fight for it. Rae had questioned her about that.

"But what about building a factory here? What about all your grand ideas?"

"I'm not so sure that's feasible right now. I need to give it some time." After breaking down and telling Rae the whole story, she'd hugged her friend goodbye and told Rae and her mother that she'd be back in Atlanta in a week or so.

She'd come home not knowing what to expect. But with Cal here and by her side, and her father drawing her close before he died, she'd believed she could fight to keep her home intact.

Her heart wasn't in that fight anymore.

Looking around this town, she could see that someone needed to come in and do something for the people who lived here. She'd had such high hopes to be that someone. But how could she stomach being in this place now, knowing what she'd found out about her mother?

Cassie entered the stately old building that at one time had been a private residence. Now it was mostly offices. Her father's lawyer, Richard Eisner, had a huge suite on the second floor. She took the stairs instead of the creaky old elevator and walked into the plush, quiet office, bracing herself for the worst.

"Cassie Brennan," she told the cute dark-haired receptionist. "Here to see Mr. Eisner."

"Of course. He's expecting you." The young girl took her down a hall and opened the door to a big office that had a bird's-eye view of the town.

The lawyer was at his big oak desk but he immediately stood to greet Cassie. "Cassandra, sorry to see you under these circumstances. I'm so sorry for your loss. The service was comforting. Your father would have approved."

"Thank you," she said to the tall, gray-haired man. She'd known Mr. Eisner a long time. Almost as long as she'd known— She stopped, refusing to think about Dr. Anton.

"Let's go over to the conference table," Mr. Eisner suggested, nodding to his assistant. "Would you like something to drink? Some water?"

"I'm fine," Cassie said, suddenly nervous about the whole thing. She sat down, holding her big purse on her lap.

Sensing her discomfort, the lawyer sat down across from her, the small table allowing him to spread out several files.

"I suppose you know that your father's estate has dwindled significantly."

"Yes, I'm aware of that. I've looked over the files."

"Mr. Collins has done a fine job of keeping all the financial records up-to-date."

"Yes, he has." She couldn't fault Cal on that.

"Are you ready?"

She nodded, noticed the trace of sympathy in the older gentleman's eyes. "Yes."

An hour later, Cassie emerged from the building with a file in her hand that contained a letter from her father, for her eyes only, according to Mr. Eisner. Other than a list of cash bequeaths her father wanted her to give to Teresa and the other long-time employees, the will stated that she could sell the plantation and cut her losses. No mention of the marriage. Another of her father's tactics?

Another letter to read, though—maybe it would remind her of her pledge to marry Cal. But what had Marcus Brennan saved for last? Another secret revealed? The apology and forgiveness she'd always craved? Or just a note telling her to either marry Cal or leave?

She reached her car, one hand on the door, when she heard her name. Whirling around, she saw Marsha coming out of the courthouse.

"Hi," Cassie said, waiting as the other woman came toward her.

Marsha, dressed in a tight skirt and clingy knit sweater, pranced up to Cassie, her expression caught between sympathetic and victorious. "How ya doing?"

Cassie didn't know what to say. "I'm okay, considering."

Then she threw her purse and the files in the car and turned back to Marsha. "Can I ask you something?"

"Sure," Marsha said, her expression wary. "What's the matter?"

"Cal told me that the day I saw you two together—"

"It wasn't real," Marsha finished. "None of it was real."

Cassie leaned back against her car. "I wish I'd known. Do you know how long I've resented you?"

Marsha crossed her arms and balanced on one high-heeled sandal. "I think I have an idea. I felt the same toward you." She looked up the street then back at Cassie. "It was always you, Cassie. Always. He went out of his way to protect you and to let you go so you'd never know all the ugly details."

"But he should have told me. You should have told me."

"Me?" Marsha tossed back a clump of red hair. "Would you have believed it, coming from me?"

"No," Cassie admitted. "But I did believe what you told me that day—that you were pregnant."

"I wanted to be," Marsha admitted. "But Cal never took things with me any further than flirting. He loved you and he still loves you. Even after he found out the truth about your daddy. Even more then, I think."

Confused, Cassie went still, hoping to draw Marsha out to see exactly how much she knew. "It's all been hard to accept." She wanted to ask more, but she felt sick to her stomach. And that one last letter was waiting for her to read.

Marsha nodded. "I guess so. But Marcus is gone now and your mama had her reasons for keeping all her secrets. She loved you and I think she loved Mr. Marcus, too. Besides, it would have killed him way back when you were born if he'd known the truth then."

What truth? Had Cal held back yet another thing from her? "Yes, I think so."

Cassie waited, her insides coiling and twisting. Marsha knew something else, something more. What else could have happened? She couldn't ask. Then Marsha would realize she'd revealed too much. It was obvious the other woman was choosing each word carefully. Probably wondering how much Cassie knew. This was becoming a game of cat and mouse.

Marsha tugged her purse onto her shoulder. "Well, anyway I'm glad it's all out in the open now. We can all move on with our lives."

"Yes." Cassie wished that were true for her. But the lies just kept on coming. The only way she'd ever get over this was to go back to her nice, safe life in Atlanta and forget everything that had happened here.

Including falling back in love with Cal.

CAL PACED THE FLOOR in the kitchen. He'd stayed away from the house all day, trying to pour himself into the cleanup efforts and salvaging the crops. The horses were safe in the clean stables. All of the leaks on the barn's roof had been patched and covered until the insurance adjustor could give them an estimate. The livestock, made up of hogs and cows, had all been corralled and checked over yet again. No losses there. And the men were working diligently to get the fields cleaned up. They could claim damage on the crops, but it would be a long and tedious affair.

The rest was up to Mother Nature.

As dusk settled over the yard, he could still hear the sound of chain saws and backhoes. The extra men he'd hired were clearing away the remains of the old cottage.

Funny how he'd lived there, but he had nothing to show for it. Just a duffel bag full of clothes and a few computer files and books.

He had nothing to show for coming here all those months ago, either.

Did you really think she'd marry you? he asked himself, bitterness going down with the longneck beer he was drinking.

This whole thing had turned into a fool's errand.

And he was still the biggest fool of all.

The house was empty and quiet. Teresa had gone into town to help feed the people who'd lost their homes to the storm. She planned to stay at a friend's house tonight.

Deciding he'd go upstairs and shower then maybe

head into town, Cal was halfway to his room when he heard a crash coming from the master bedroom.

CASSIE SAT IN THE middle of the floor, her soul torn and bruised, her mind boiling over with all the bitterness and resentment and confusion she'd held inside since leaving here the first time. All around her, her mother's possessions mocked her and teased her with the sweet facade that had protected her and cloaked her for most of her life.

But the truth—so glaring and so garish—outshined any of her mother's diamonds and pearls.

Cal had been right. She was better off not knowing.

Now, she understood so much more.

Now, she could see it all right there in front of her.

Now she had the whole truth. The whole ugly truth.

The door opened and Cal came bursting into the room.

"Are you all right?"

Cassie wanted to laugh. "No, I'm not all right." She waved a hand in the air. "I came in here searching for my birth certificate. But then, you probably know exactly where it is, right?"

She saw the guilt in his eyes. "Cassie, I'm so sorry."

"Sorry?" She shifted, got up to fall against a brocade stool, the letter she'd crushed still in her hand. Bent over on the stool, she heaved the last of her tears. "Everyone is so very sorry."

He bent down in front of her and she shook the letter in his face. "Did you know this the day my mother died?"

"No," he said, shaking his head. "I only found out from Marcus when I came back. That's why he wanted us to get married. He had this old-fashioned notion that you'd somehow be protected if you were a married woman."

"Protected? Everyone wants to protect me. It's crazy. It's unbelievable. He wanted you to guard me from the truth, that's what he wanted. If I was blissfully happy being married to the man I've always loved, I'd never find out that Marcus Brennan wasn't my real father. Am I right, Cal?"

"He didn't want you to wind up alone, the way he had, Cassie."

She got up to stare down at him, but he stood, too, his hand on her arm. "What did the letter say?"

She glanced down at the fancy stationery, the typed words blurring together. "Other than reminding me to marry you? The letter told me the one thing I never dreamed possible. That Dr. John Anton was my real father. It's stated right here in a matter-of-fact way. So like Marcus Brennan, so cold and dry and clear. Finally."

She dropped the letter to the floor. "And that's the real reason my father—Marcus—couldn't stand the sight of me."

CHAPTER TWENTY-TWO

CAL HAD DREADED THIS moment since the day he'd returned to Camellia Plantation. But he felt a sense of relief sweeping over him now. No more hiding things or being evasive. No more having to step carefully and watch his words. No more keeping the truth from Cassie.

But he hated what this had done to her. She sat back on the big cushioned stool, looking for all the world like a true princess. A broken-hearted princess in a gilded cage.

"I'm sorry," he said again, the echo of that apology ringing out across the room in a hollow whisper.

She stared up at him, her eyes swollen, her hair mussed. "Are you sorry for everything you kept from me, sorry that I've finally found out, or just sorry that I had to beg for every grain of truth?"

"I didn't set out to make you beg." He came and sat down beside her, watching as she stiffened and shifted away. "I didn't want to come back here. You know, this place held a lot of bad memories for me, too. And I certainly didn't want to be the one to tell you about your parents."

Pushing at her hair, she looked over at him. "Being here reminded you of what you did to me, Cal. You always told me you weren't afraid of my father, but you did exactly what he demanded. You covered up for him, back then and still today. I wonder if you would have married me without ever telling me what you knew."

"You're right," Cal said, his hands templed on his knees. He would have married her and loved her and protected her, because the truth was too bizarre to believe. "It's hard to explain but I was lost, drifting, after witnessing your mother's death. I blamed myself for letting her get on that horse. I wanted to comfort you, but then I knew you'd be leaving me soon and I figured if I told you the real story, I'd never see you again anyway. I was a mixed-up kid, Cassie. I loved you so much that I panicked, thought I was being noble. After Marcus accused me of being with your mother, I gave up. I couldn't fight him anymore. He knew it wasn't true, but since he didn't think I was good enough for you, he used that as leverage. He wanted both of us gone and he didn't care how it happened."

"So you were the fall guy?"

Cal looked around the plush bedroom. "Yes. I wanted to spare you all of that anger and angst and your daddy used that against me. You were already devastated about your mother's death. I couldn't add to that by telling you I suspected your mother of having an affair. I honestly didn't know what to do. I couldn't win either way."

She got up to pace around, touching on things, the look on her face full of regret and longing. "So you decided to keep it all inside and let me leave without knowing the truth. And him, instead of being the father he should have been, he turned against me and practically banished me from his life." She shook her head. "I can almost understand your motives, given that you were up against Marcus Brennan. But he was my father. I don't care what a piece of paper says. I would have loved him anyway, no matter what. He couldn't get past the fact that I wasn't his and that I reminded him of the woman who'd broken his heart. How cruel is that? I could never do that to a child of mine."

Cal stood and caught her, pulling her into his arms. "He was full of self-loathing and bitterness. In the end, he regretted what he did after she died. He told me that over and over. That's why he wanted us both back here."

"Yes, he wanted us back, just so he could die with a clean conscience."

"I think so. But also so you could heal, too. So you could finally be happy again."

"By marrying you?"

"By forgiving yourself and him. He wanted me here with you because he felt responsible for our breakup."

She grabbed the letter, holding it up. "So this is supposed to help me heal?"

"It can. It's closure. It's honest. All the secrets are gone now."

"But at what price, Cal? We're still fighting about the same thing. We're standing here, with our hearts open and everything between us finally coming to light, but everything has changed. I'm not the person I thought I was. My whole life was a lie. I believe he pushed us to get married because he knew I wasn't really a Brennan. And having a man in my life would somehow validate me. A strange forced form of protection. A coward's way out."

"He was the coward. I was a coward. But you are not and have never been afraid of him or anyone else. You do have a new beginning, though," Cal said, willing her to see. "We're free now, Cassie. No more demands, no more ultimatums, no more hiding the truth. Marcus can't hurt you again. None of them can hurt you ever again."

"But *you* can," she said. "And that's the part I can't live with."

Giving him one last glance, she took the letter and left the room.

Cal stood still, his heart dropping, his hopes dashed. The wind picked up, shuffling through the old oaks like laughing spirits. He could almost feel the ghosts dancing around him, mocking him with whispered words of triumph.

And he had to wonder. Had Marcus Brennan won this battle after all?

CASSIE PACED THE FLOOR, wondering what she should do. Her first instinct was to pack and leave. But she'd been running from her past for a long time now. No matter her hurt, she had to stay and see this through. She'd get her father's finances in order and put the whole place and everything on it up for auction. It was the only way to erase all the ugliness surrounding her.

She glanced around her room, went to the window and stared down at the oaks and camellias. On the surface, this was a stately old mansion with beautiful landscaping and a vast acreage. But underneath there was a twist of thorny vines that pierced to the core.

She had to break away from those vines.

And that would mean she had to break away from Cal, too.

Being with him would only remind her of all the shame and agony she'd gone through for so long, even more so now that she knew John Anton had been her real father.

And that Marcus Brennan had probably murdered him.

She sat down and made notes on each step she'd need to take to let go of this place. By the time she was finished, she felt somewhat better about leaving Camellia for good.

But after she got in bed and lay there in the dark, Cal's face stayed in her head. She thought about their time together here, the fresh new feelings of loving him all over again coursing throughout her body. What if she'd never seen any of the letters? What if Marcus hadn't left her that one final revelation that told her the whole story?

Would she have married Cal?

Her heart said yes, but her head shouted a warning of no.

She'd had good reason not to trust him completely.

Better to cut her losses and move on, rather than make a big mistake. He'd done a lot to help her father, but no matter his promises to her. He'd still kept secrets from her. Personal secrets about her family and her biological father.

Maybe Cal truly thought he was protecting her. But why hadn't he trusted her enough to be honest so they could deal with this together.

She loved him. But sometimes love just wasn't enough.

OVER THE NEXT FEW DAYS, Cassie talked to lawyers and experts on estate sales and auctions. She kept Cal informed on all of her decisions and he agreed to stay through the fall harvest. After that, the land and the house would go up for auction and it would be over. The money would go to pay off debts and if she was lucky, Cassie would receive any cash that was left. None of that mattered to her, however. She just wanted it over and done with.

"Are you sure about this?" Cal asked her once they'd agreed on how long he'd remain.

They'd reached an uncomfortable truce. Mostly, they only spoke about business. Nothing else.

"Yes," she said. "We finish out the year and then it's over."

"Okay." He got up. "Then I'd better get back to it."

But he turned at the door, his eyes locking with hers. "Will you do me one favor, Cassie?"

"Of course."

"Will you ride with me up to my place? I'd really like you to see it. And this time, I don't want anything to stop you."

She agreed. She wanted to see the place he talked about, the land he'd abandoned to help her and Marcus. In spite of everything, Cal had been steady and strong. He'd done the right thing for all the wrong reasons.

Cassie owed Cal a lot, no matter how their personal relationship might turn out. Deep down inside, she wanted him to be happy. Or maybe she just wanted an excuse to spend time with him away from Camellia and all the tragedy surrounding it.

So now here she sat in his truck, wearing jeans and a white T-shirt. The silence stretched between them as long and winding as U.S. Highway 19. It was the same silence that had held them apart since the night she'd finally found out the truth.

She watched Cal, casting a glance toward him now and then. Why did it hurt so much to look at the man?

Because you still love him, she told herself. Because deep down inside, she knew he'd done everything humanly possible to show her how much he cared.

Even lied to her. Sins of omission?

How could she forgive that?

How could she still love him when her heart hurt so much?

"What are you thinking over there?" he asked, his eyes touching on her before he looked back at the road.

Cassie didn't dare tell him her thoughts. "I'm just sorry that things have to end this way." That was true, at least.

"Yeah, me, too." He turned off the highway and headed down a two-lane road. "Your daddy—Marcus—sure wanted us married."

"He changed his tune," she replied, still uncomfortable calling him her father after what she'd learned. "He thought bringing us back together would right all the wrongs."

Cal slowed the truck then turned down a dirt lane. "He was wrong. I guess some things can't be fixed."

The bitterness of that statement crushed Cassie, but her own regret and anger kept her from retorting.

"We're here," Cal said, nodding toward a sprawling white farmhouse. "Home sweet home."

Seeing the relief in his eyes, Cassie took in the wide porch and the hipped roof of the two-story white clapboard house. It was neat and clean, the yard simple but pretty. Crape myrtles and old roses surrounded the house. "It's beautiful, Cal."

"It's just an old farmhouse."

But it should be a home, Cassie thought. The image of Cal sitting in the swing on the porch, rocking a baby, hit her full force. He'd bought the land to make something of himself.

And he'd sacrificed so much for her.

Why would a man do that?

He loves you, she thought. *He wants a family with you.*

It was that simple. Suddenly realizing that only made her heart hurt even more. She wanted that, too. But did she dare dream it?

"Want to take a look?" Cal asked, opening his door.

"Yes."

He came around the truck but she hopped out before he could help her. "It's a big house. It looks roomy."

"Not as big as Camellia, but a nice size. Three bedrooms and two baths. It's been added on to over the years. Has a nice kitchen and a big living room."

"I want to see all of it."

He smiled at the tone in her voice. "Let's go then."

Cassie could see the pride in his smile, in the way his eyes lit up. "We'll ride the property after I show you the house. It's sure good to be back here."

She turned to him on the porch. "You should have never left."

He gave her a long, open stare, his eyes flaring dark. "I know that now."

He opened the door and guided her into a large living area. "The kitchen's back to the right."

The living room was really a big den, complete with a television and a nice sectional sofa. That opened to a cozy country kitchen with lots of windows. "Did you decorate all by yourself?"

He glanced over at her. "Yep. I've done most things by myself."

They moved through the white kitchen and into a short hallway. "The bedrooms are on this side of the house." He turned to wait for her. "If you want to see—"

"I said I'd love to see the whole house."

Why were her hands shaking? Why did she suddenly feel light-headed?

Cal reached for her hand, the first time they'd touched since the confrontation in her parents' bedroom. Cassie took her hand in hers, awareness tingling throughout her body.

He took her down the hallway and into a long sunny room. A big four-poster bed dominated one wall. A refurbished dresser and matching chest, along with an old rocking chair, completed the look. One lone picture hung over the bed. A mother and a child laughing in a meadow.

"It's so pretty, Cal." She couldn't hide the emotion cresting in her words.

He turned to her then, pulled her close, his hand touching on her hair, his eyes dark and misty. "Cassie... don't leave me. We can make this work."

She held to him, unable to let go. And for the first time in a long time, *she* was honest with *him*. "I'm afraid."

"I know you are, but I'll never lie to you again about anything. I just want to be with you, always."

She closed her eyes, her forehead touching his, images of holding him centered in her mind. But the image of her mother in another man's arms halted her. "I need some time, Cal. I know you had the best of intentions, but I need some time to let everything soak in."

He put his lips to her ear. "We've wasted enough time, don't you think?"

She looked up at him, saw the love and the challenge in his eyes. He pulled her close, kissing her before she could say anything. Her heart pulled and tugged, fighting against the love that overwhelmed her. His touch made her weak with need, but he also gave her the strength she needed to let go.

She loved him. Wanted him. She'd waited a lifetime for this. But before she could give in, she had to clear away all the cobwebs of deceit and betrayal and secrets.

Cassie didn't want this to end. Tears streamed down her face. She thought she felt moisture on Cal's skin. His tears merged with hers as he held her there.

"I have always dreamed of bringing you to this place," he said, his words shaky, husky. "I didn't have to make a promise to Marcus. I want to marry you, Cassie. I want to make a promise to you, only you."

She touched a hand to his face. "I know. I want that, too. But I have to go back to Atlanta so I can think about this. There's so much between us, so much—the new wonderful feelings I have and the old hurts and secrets. My heart...my heart is still torn apart."

"Don't let it happen again," he said, his hands holding her face. "Don't leave me again."

"What if I tell you I'll come back? Will you believe me?"

He stepped back, shock and resignation coloring his face. "That would be better than what you told me the first time you left me."

"Okay, I deserved that, I suppose," she replied. Taking a deep breath, she brushed at her tears. "I can't promise you tomorrow, Cal, until I get past yesterday. But I can't make you wait, either."

"I've already waited," he said, anger edging each word. "I waited after I left Camellia, thinking you'd find me. But you never even tried looking. I waited for Marcus to tell you the things he needed you to know, but he never did. So it was up to me. I waited for you to make good on the promise you made to him when he was dying—that you'd marry me and we'd be together finally. But you still can't do that."

"I'm sorry," she said, tears falling freely now. "You never tried to find me, either. I thought you were with Marsha. I thought you'd had a child with her. If that wasn't enough, now this. I find out you knew all along that my mother was being unfaithful. All those years and you said nothing, Cal. Nothing. This has been too much."

"You're right," he said, shoving a hand through his hair. "And I've had enough. I should have come to you back then and made things right. I should have forced you to see all the wrongs and I should have told you then that I loved you. I thought that by agreeing to come back I could make up for the past, make you love me again. I thought it was a second chance."

He stopped, his gaze bouncing around the room then back to her. "I gave up everything to return to Camellia. I wanted you, Cassie. Only you. I will always want you. I told you I won't force you. So I'm done. The next time, you'll have to be the one to come to me. I don't owe your daddy anything now. And I certainly don't owe you anything else. I'm tired of trying to prove myself. It's all up to you from here on out."

He looked at her, looked at the bed. "The next time I bring you into this room, it will be as my wife. But only if you want that." Turning for the door, he pivoted around. "But don't wait too long to decide. I'm a patient man, but enough is enough."

Cassie couldn't speak. She bobbed her head. "I understand."

He shrugged, dropped his hands. "I need to visit my foreman. You can go with me, or you can stay here."

She didn't answer. She couldn't. Cal took her silence

as his answer. "Stay here and rest. Nobody will bother you here. I'll be back in a couple of hours."

Cassie heard the front door slamming then turned and fell down on the bed.

This time, she'd really messed up.

This time, she'd lost him forever.

CHAPTER TWENTY-THREE

November

CASSIE DROVE HER car up the long lane, taking in the big white house and the winter-bare trees. Remembering the last time she'd been here, she thought back over the summer and fall.

Everything had changed.

Was she too late? she wondered now.

Would Cal be waiting for her?

CAL GLANCED UP from the fire roaring away in the fire-place, wondering who was coming to see him on a cold November day. He went to the window and watched as the white sports car sauntered up the circular driveway.

He recognized the car even if the black top was up.

Cassie.

Turning from the window, he looked around his sparsely decorated house, the echo of his loneliness bouncing off the walls. His heartbeat did the same bounce inside his chest.

She was here, at his house.

He didn't dare hope.

CASSIE HOPED SHE'D find Cal at home.

This had been a long journey. She had a lot to say to him.

But would he listen?

She saw him the day of the estate sale and auction, hovering there in the back of the crowd. She wanted to go to him and tell him everything she felt, but that had been a tough day for her. Having to watch part of her heritage being auctioned to the highest bidder left her drained and empty.

Cal had left before the auction was over.

And she'd missed him so much.

But she knew how to fill the well of loneliness that played through her heart.

She went back to Atlanta and resumed her career, her designs winning awards and her private hurts and pains hidden behind a public facade of success.

She had drinks with Ned when he came to town on business, only to tell him her plans and to tell him she was sorry that things hadn't worked out between them. Sorry, but relieved. Ned told her he'd been to counseling to control his "issues." She prayed that worked for him.

After letting go of that bad relationship for good, Cassie poured herself into getting rid of all the other baggage she'd been carrying around. Then she planned for her future with new ideas and big changes.

But now, she had only one thing in her mind.

She wanted to marry Cal Collins.

CAL OPENED THE DOOR, the cold wind blustering past him with a sharp hiss. He watched as she got out of the car, marveling at how beautiful she was. She wore a white wool coat and tan dress slacks over rich brown boots. Her hair glistened golden in the morning sunshine.

She stepped up onto the porch, her smile tentative,

her eyes bright. "Well, at least Marsha's not here with you." Then she asked, "Is she?"

"Marsha," he said, wondering, hoping. "I haven't talked to her since—"

"Since the day of the auction," Cassie interrupted. "But you left early that day."

He nodded. "Yep. Just couldn't stay around and watch the whole place go." He didn't add that he couldn't stay around to watch her go, either.

He saw the glimmer of pain moving like that cold wind through her eyes, but she didn't say a word.

He stood silent while all sorts of questions shouted inside his mind.

Cassie hugged herself, huddling against the wind. "May I come inside?"

"Yes. Of course."

They were being so civil.

Cal tried to find his brain again. He stepped back and waved her inside. "I just built a big fire."

Once she was in the door, he breathed a sigh of relief. So far, so good. "Let me take your coat."

She tugged it off, her gaze flickering around the big room. "It's so cozy in here."

"It's a cold day out there."

He placed her coat and buttery soft leather purse on a kitchen stool then motioned back toward the big den. "Have a seat. You want some coffee?"

"I'm fine." She gave him a shy smile then sat down on an ottoman in front of the fire.

He waited a beat then cleared his throat. "So why are you here, Cassie?"

She rubbed her hands as if to warm them. "I guess you are surprised to see me."

"More than surprised. Last time we talked on the

phone, you were cutting my last paycheck. And a rather nice bonus."

She gave him a direct stare. "You delivered on your promise. You stayed at Camellia through the harvest."

Yes, he'd done his duty and paid his dues.

And after telling her goodbye over the phone, he'd retreated here and shut the rest of the world away. He didn't want to know. But he wondered every day.

"I've been back here for weeks now. I've been busy getting everything ready for winter. How'd the auction go, anyway?"

"About that," she began then stopped. "I have a lot to tell you."

CASSIE COULD SEE THE confusion on Cal's face. She wanted to get up and grab him and kiss him over and over to show him that she'd made it through. But he didn't look so sure. What if he didn't want her here? What if he was finally done with her?

She swallowed her fear and stood. "Cal, I need to tell you something."

He ran a hand down his jaw, his sweater tugging at his muscular arms. "I want to say something first."

Willing the panic to leave her insides, Cassie took a deep breath. "Okay. Go ahead."

He was going to tell her to leave. She just knew it. She'd pushed him away one time too many. Now it was over and all her grand plans would be crushed.

He leaned against a counter and stared at the fire. "I tried, Cassie. I really tried…"

"Cal, listen…"

He held up a hand. "I couldn't do it. I couldn't make it happen."

He was killing her with each word. "Make what happen?"

He just kept going. "Even if I could have sold this place for the asking price, I still couldn't raise enough capital to make a bid. I'm sorry, but I really wanted to save the old place."

Cassie's breath hitched in her throat. "What are you talking about?"

"Camellia," he said, his eyebrows lifting. "I wanted to buy it. I came to the auction hoping to do just that."

Amazed, she couldn't move. "Why would you even think of buying Camellia?"

He looked at her then, the tension leaving his face, his eyes going soft. "I've tried to tell you over and over. For you. Always for you, Cassie."

CASSIE DIDN'T KNOW what to say. "You'd do that for me?"

He bobbed his head. "I wanted to do that for you. I watched you that day, saw the struggle on your face. I tried everything I could to raise the money, but in the end it was just too rich for my blood. I'm sorry."

Tears pricked at her eyes. "Cal, I don't care about Camellia. I loved the place, don't get me wrong. But I've been gone from there a long time. I don't want to live there ever again."

He looked confused and a tad angry. "It's your home. And you're letting it go."

She reached out to touch his arm. "It let me go, Cal. A long time ago. It was never really mine and Marcus Brennan sent me away. Why would I want to live in a house that held so many secrets and ghosts?"

"But I thought… I thought you'd change your mind. Not go through with the auction. I guess I thought you were bluffing."

She smiled then, dashing at tears. "Well, it's a good thing you couldn't raise the money. Because I came here to tell you, I didn't let the house go to auction. I only auctioned off some of the furnishings and part of the surrounding land. And a few pieces of equipment, too."

The surprise on his face would have been funny if Cassie's heart wasn't hurting so badly.

He sank back on a bar stool. "But if you don't want to live there, why did you save the house?"

Cassie came to stand in front of him. "Because I'm going to work there. I kept enough land to build my ready-to-wear factory. The house will become my main office building. I'll have to have it rezoned, but that shouldn't be a problem since we're miles from any subdivisions. I'm moving Cassie's Closet to Camellia Plantation."

CAL STOOD UP AND grabbed her hand. "You're really doing it?"

"I told you I liked the idea."

"But what about all that happened there?"

She looked up and into his eyes. "I intend to erase all of that by creating jobs and pretty things. I want to wipe the slate clean and start fresh, the way you suggested. I'm bringing that old plantation house into the future. And I'm coming with it."

"And all your plans to open another boutique in Atlanta?"

"Still on the table. But first, I want to get settled into my new office. We have a lot of work ahead, but I've already met with the architect and the interior designers and several contractors. I'll show you the factory design."

"And the house?"

"Will stay the same. I'll redo the inside into offices, of course. But for the most part, it won't change that much on the surface. I'll use the upstairs for my office and workshop room and the downstairs will be a salon for intimate showings and working with models and clients. I can hold parties there to promote all the stores. A personal touch."

He stepped closer, a smile beginning to form on his face. "And where will you live?"

She looked around the den. "I don't know yet, but you seem to have a lot of room here."

His gaze moved down her face. "I do."

Fear held her back. But she refused to give in. She needed honesty. Complete honesty. And she needed to be honest with him.

"You always said I'd have to be the one to come to you."

"I did say that. Are you sure?"

She couldn't tell him how many times she'd rehearsed this meeting. "I'm very sure. I've had months to think about everything. And you didn't do anything wrong. You tried to do everything right. I get it now. You did it for me. Because you love me. Because you've always put my feelings ahead of yours. If I didn't already know that before, I sure see it now." She took his hand in hers. "You were willing to give up this place— for me. I'm so glad you didn't. You've never once lied about that, Cal. It's always been you and me."

His smile lit up the room. "It sure took you long enough to figure that out."

"I know. And I'm so sorry."

Tugging her close he said, "Don't be sorry. Just—"

She didn't give him time to say anything else. Instead, she pulled him into her arms, her body swaying toward his, her mouth meeting his in a sweet reunion.

Finally, she pulled away and touched a hand to his face. "They can't hurt us anymore."

"*I* won't hurt you anymore, either," Cal replied, love shining inside his eyes. "Never."

Cassie put a finger to his lips. "No, I think that should be the other way around. I won't do anything to doubt you or hurt you, ever."

He nuzzled her ear then locked his gaze on her. "So, are you saying you'll marry me?"

She nodded. "I'm asking, if you still want me."

"You'll have a long drive to work every day."

"I don't mind. And I don't have to go into the office every day. I can work from here some, go up to Atlanta a lot and come home to you. Always. I'll be okay as long as I have you."

Wrapping his arms around her waist, he kissed her again. "You'll have me," he said, his gaze reassuring her.

"So, will you marry me, Cal?"

"Yes, ma'am."

He pulled her back into his arms and kissed her again.

Cassie returned his kiss, the heat of it warming her to her toes. She would never doubt him again. She wouldn't leave him again, either.

Nothing had changed.

Except her heart.

The next spring...

CAL CARRIED HIS BLUSHING bride over the threshold, grinning from ear to ear. "You looked so beautiful today."

Cassie smiled up at him, her wedding dress trailing down around her, touching on his wedding trousers. "You look pretty good yourself."

Cal grinned. "It was a nice wedding."

She lifted her lips to his. "The best. Short and sweet and intimate."

"With a lot of special people there."

They'd gotten married in the backyard, here where they would live. Cassie wanted to start her life over right here in her new home.

He thought about Teresa and Jack, Rae and Louise, even Marsha. They'd all been there, cheering Cassie and Cal. Louise, Teresa and Marsha had baked the cake and put together the reception. An old-fashioned barbecue and picnic out underneath the tall pines and old oaks.

A perfect day. Now, everyone had left.

And the bride and groom were alone at last.

He kicked the front door shut and kissed her. "Welcome home, Mrs. Collins."

"Thank you, Mr. Collins. Aren't you going to put me down?"

Cal kissed her again. "Oh, no. Not until I get you into that big bed. I've been waiting to do that for a long, long time."

"Oh, Cal." She laid her head against his lapel and held tight while he carried her through the house.

And he didn't stop until they were in the master bedroom.

Then he closed the door to the past and turned to his wife.

And the promise of a new day.

* * * * *

HEART & HOME

Heartwarming romances where love can
happen right when you least expect it.

COMING NEXT MONTH
AVAILABLE JANUARY 10, 2012

#1752 A HERO IN THE MAKING
North Star, Montana
Kay Stockham

#1753 HIS BROTHER'S KEEPER
Dawn Atkins

#1754 WHERE IT BEGAN
Together Again
Kathleen Pickering

#1755 UNDERCOVER COOK
Too Many Cooks?
Jeannie Watt

#1756 SOMETHING TO PROVE
Cathryn Parry

#1757 A SOLDIER'S SECRET
Suddenly a Parent
Linda Style

You can find more information on upcoming Harlequin® titles,
free excerpts and more at www.HarlequinInsideRomance.com.

SPECIAL EDITION

Life, Love and Family

Karen Templeton
introduces

The FORTUNES *of* TEXAS: Whirlwind Romance

When a tornado destroys Red Rock, Texas,
Christina Hastings finds herself trapped in the
rubble with telecommunications heir
Scott Fortune. He's handsome, smart and
everything Christina has learned to guard herself
against. As they await rescue, an unlikely attraction
forms between the two and Scott soon finds
himself wanting to know about this mysterious
beauty. But can he catch Christina before she runs
away from her true feelings?

FORTUNE'S CINDERELLA

Available December 27th wherever books are sold!

*Brittany Grayson survived a horrible ordeal at the hands
of a serial killer known as The Professional...
who's after her now?*

*Harlequin® Romantic Suspense presents a new installment
in Carla Cassidy's reader-favorite miniseries,*
LAWMEN OF BLACK ROCK.

Enjoy a sneak peek of
TOOL BELT DEFENDER.

*Available January 2012
from Harlequin® Romantic Suspense.*

"**B**rittany?" His voice was deep and pleasant and made
her realize she'd been staring at him openmouthed through
the screen door.

"Yes, I'm Brittany and you must be..." Her mind suddenly went blank.

"Alex. Alex Crawford, Chad's friend. You called him
about a deck?"

As she unlocked the screen, she realized she wasn't
quite ready yet to allow a stranger inside, especially a male
stranger.

"Yes, I did. It's nice to meet you, Alex. Let's walk around
back and I'll show you what I have in mind," she said. She
frowned as she realized there was no car in her driveway.
"Did you walk here?" she asked.

His eyes were a warm blue that stood out against his
tanned face and was complemented by his slightly shaggy
dark hair. "I live three doors up." He pointed up the street to
the Walker home that had been on the market for a while.

"How long have you lived there?"

"I moved in about six weeks ago," he replied as they

walked around the side of the house.

That explained why she didn't know the Walkers had moved out and Mr. Hard Body had moved in. Six weeks ago she'd still been living at her brother Benjamin's house trying to heal from the trauma she'd lived through.

As they reached the backyard she motioned toward the broken brick patio just outside the back door. "What I'd like is a wooden deck big enough to hold a barbecue pit and an umbrella table and, of course, lots of people."

He nodded and pulled a tape measure from his tool belt. "An outdoor entertainment area," he said.

"Exactly," she replied and watched as he began to walk the site. The last thing Brittany had wanted to think about over the past eight months of her life was men. But looking at Alex Crawford definitely gave her a slight flutter of pure feminine pleasure.

*Will Brittany be able to heal in the arms of Alex,
her hotter-than-sin handyman...or will a second
psychopath silence her forever? Find out in*
TOOL BELT DEFENDER
*Available January 2012
from Harlequin® Romantic Suspense
wherever books are sold.*